"What I'm feel[...] romantic. It's p[...] and you're too young for those kinds of games," Jesse told her.

"Stop treating me like a child!"

"It won't happen again," Jesse insisted.

Caroline watched him leave, a slow smile moving across her mouth. If he really thought they could just forget that kiss, pretend it hadn't happened, then he was in for an especially difficult time. Poor darling. He thought he was dealing with a precocious child who didn't—couldn't—know what or who she wanted. But he would see.

He would see that she was a woman with as much to offer him as she needed from him. He would see that no one could love him better than she could, be better for him than she could. He would see that he needed her, too....

Dear Reader,

Hold on to your hats, because this month Special Edition has a lineup of romances that you won't soon forget!

We start off with an extraordinary story by #1 *New York Times* bestselling author Nora Roberts. *The Perfect Neighbor* is the eleventh installment of her popular THE MACGREGORS series and spotlights a brooding loner who becomes captivated by his vivacious neighbor.

And the fun is just beginning! *Dream Bride* by Susan Mallery launches her enchanting duet, BRIDES OF BRADLEY HOUSE, about a family legend which has two sisters dreaming about the men they are destined to marry. The first book in the series is also this month's THAT SPECIAL WOMAN! title. Look for the second story, *Dream Groom,* this May.

Next, Christine Rimmer returns with a tale about a single mom who develops a dangerous attraction to a former heartbreaker in *Husband in Training.*

Also don't miss the continuing saga of Sherryl Woods's popular AND BABY MAKES THREE: THE NEXT GENERATION. The latest book in the series, *The Cowboy and his Wayward Bride,* features a hardheaded rancher who will do just about anything to claim the feisty mother of his infant daughter! And Arlene James has written a stirring love story about a sweet young virgin who has every intention of tempting the ornery, much-older rancher down the wedding aisle in *Marrying an Older Man.*

Finally this month, *A Hero at Heart* by Ann Howard White features an emotional reunion romance between an honorable hero and the gentle beauty he's returned for.

I hope you enjoy this book, and each and every novel to come!

Sincerely,

Karen Taylor Richman
Senior Editor

Please address questions and book requests to:
Silhouette Reader Service
U.S.: 3010 Walden Ave., P.O. Box 1325, Buffalo, NY 14269
Canadian: P.O. Box 609, Fort Erie, Ont. L2A 5X3

ARLENE JAMES

MARRYING AN OLDER MAN

Silhouette®

SPECIAL EDITION®

Published by Silhouette Books

America's Publisher of Contemporary Romance

SILHOUETTE BOOKS

ISBN 0-373-24235-2

MARRYING AN OLDER MAN

Printed in U.S.A.

Books by Arlene James

Silhouette Special Edition

A Rumor of Love #664
Husband in the Making #776
With Baby in Mind #869
Child of Her Heart #964
The Knight, the Waitress and the Toddler #1131
Every Cowgirl's Dream #1195
Marrying an Older Man #1235

Silhouette Books

Fortune's Children

Single With Children

Silhouette Romance

City Girl #141
No Easy Conquest #235
Two of a Kind #253
A Meeting of Hearts #327
An Obvious Virtue #384
Now or Never #404
Reason Enough #421
The Right Moves #446
Strange Bedfellows #471
The Private Garden #495
The Boy Next Door #518
Under a Desert Sky #559
A Delicate Balance #578
The Discerning Heart #614
Dream of a Lifetime #661
Finally Home #687
A Perfect Gentleman #705
Family Man #728
A Man of His Word #770
Tough Guy #806
Gold Digger #830
Palace City Prince #866
The Perfect Wedding #962
An Old-Fashioned Love #968
A Wife Worth Waiting For #974
Mail-Order Brood #1024
The Rogue Who Came To Stay #1061
Most Wanted Dad #1144
Desperately Seeking Daddy #1186
Falling for a Father of Four #1295
A Bride To Honor #1330
Mr. Right Next Door #1352

* This Side of Heaven

ARLENE JAMES

grew up in Oklahoma and has lived all over the South. In 1976 she married "the most romantic man in the world." The author enjoys traveling with her husband, but writing has always been her chief pastime.

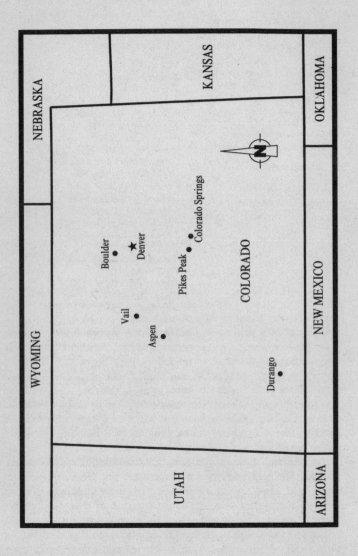

Chapter One

"Happy birthday, baby!" Irene called, her burgundy-colored hair flowing in the wind as she hung out the window, her rolling yacht of a car backing out into the street.

The old hulk had once been a luxury automobile, but thirty years had reduced it to desperation status. Neither comfortable nor mechanically sound, it tended to rock down the road in a slightly sideways orientation, not unlike Irene herself, if it moved at all. Irene didn't seem to know or care that her transportation was questionable at best. She was on her way to sunny California at last! Caroline didn't doubt that she'd get there, one way or another. She just didn't want to think about what "another way" might entail for her devil-may-care mother.

Smiling and waving, she gave Irene an enthusiastic send-off, not that she was glad to see her mother go. Heavens, no. But she'd held Irene here at the foot of the snowy Colorado Rockies for four long years now, the longest stretch of time they'd ever spent in one place, and today was her twenty-first birthday. Irene had not abandoned an underage, ill-equipped child who still clung to the tail of her mother's skirt—or miniskirt, in Irene's case.

Indeed, any who knew them would have said that sober, serious Caroline and flighty, irresponsible Irene had traded roles, if not bodies, years ago, and frankly, Caroline was as tired of riding herd on her vibrant, often-foolish mother as Irene was tired of her doing so. No, even if the circumstances weren't ideal, it was, nevertheless, time that they each got on with their respective lives. But Caroline would miss that zany sense of humor, the bad-as-I-want-to-be fashion taste, the color-of-the-month hair, the indomitable delight in every moment of life.

Blinking away tears, Caroline backed into the house and closed the door, chilled by the sharp edge of the wind. November 11 had dawned clear and cold, but a strong wind was driving clouds against the peaked tops of the surrounding mountains. Durango would see snow again soon, unless she missed her guess, and after four enthralled years, she seldom did. It was the snow that Irene had come to abhor, and this year the white stuff was so abundant that the ski resorts had opened weeks ahead of schedule, and the snowplows were working overtime already to keep the roads clear. Caroline loved the stuff. The house never seemed so cozy as it did when the snow was piled up outside. True, it got old at times, and she recognized the danger in it, but it was part of home.

Her landlady, Nancy Shaver, was sitting on the shabby sofa bed that had been, until this very morning, Caroline's bedroom. She sipped carefully from a mug of hot coffee spiked with whiskey, having toasted Caroline's birthday and Irene's long-coveted independence. "That mother of yours," she said, grinning and shaking her head, "I am sure going to miss her."

Caroline smiled and eased down onto one arm of the rickety chair beneath the front window. "Me, too. But it'll be okay. I'm old enough to fend for myself, and she's going to be happy in California, I know. As for you, you'll be married to Bud soon."

Nancy's brown eyes sparkled at the mention of the middle-aged trucker she was set to wed. "His divorce will be final December third," she confided, as if she hadn't announced the same every day for two months now. "But Buddy won't get in until the sixth, and he's only got two days then, so we're waiting until the fourteenth so we can have a real honeymoon. Five days in

Vegas!'' Her happy sigh turned to a belligerent frown, and she added, ''If that witch woman doesn't throw a kink into the works again. It'd be just like her to try it, too. I swear, I don't know how Bud stood her all those years. Well, actually, I do. He just stayed on the road all the time. But you know what? He's not leaving me sitting home without him. I'm going on the road with him! Maybe I'll even get my commercial license, so we can be, like, a team, you know?''

Caroline nodded, even though she didn't understand how the thought of wandering around the country in a ''big rig'' all the time could appeal to Nancy, no more than she understood the appeal of the man with whom Nancy was evidently in love. Stocky, balding and inconveniently married, Bud was the last sort of man Caroline would be interested in herself, but Nancy had always puzzled Caroline in that way. A while ago Nancy had been seeing a handsome widower named Jesse Wagner, a cowboy. He'd come and gone as he pleased, occasionally spending the night. After that had ended Nancy began seeing every man who'd shown the least interest in her. Then one night she'd brought home Bud, and that, as they say, was that. Caroline was still bemused by the whole thing, but it really wasn't any of her business, not that she could have missed the goings-on, living in the same house, so to speak. It just seemed incredible to Caroline that any woman would not prefer Jesse Wagner to...well, to any other man. God knew he'd been secretly taking center stage in her dreams since she'd first glimpsed him through the window curtains. She just couldn't imagine a more attractive candidate for whatever a girl might have in mind.

Gradually, she became aware that Nancy had a real case of the fidgets, one finger going around and around and around the rim of her coffee cup. Obviously she had something more on her mind. Caroline cocked her head thoughtfully. ''Something bothering you, Nance?''

The older woman grimaced and hunched forward over her coffee cup. ''This isn't a good time. It'll wait.''

''Don't be silly. If you need to talk to me, talk.'' Caroline chuckled. ''You aren't going to raise my rent, are you?''

"No, honey, it's not that. It's...well, since I'm going on the road with Bud, we've, um, decided to put the duplex up for sale."

Caroline blinked at the news.

"You're going to give up the house?"

"We want to buy our own rig," Nancy explained apologetically. "You can make good money driving for yourself, but the divorce is costing Buddy big money. Selling the house will give us a good down payment and a little cushion, too. You understand how it is."

But Caroline didn't understand. Never having had her own home, it seemed inconceivable to Caroline that Nancy could so blithely give up hers, but then home was about more than a simple structure. Some deep, innate instinct told her that it took something more, something that had always been missing in her life, perhaps even in herself.

Whatever it was, it was sure missing in Irene. Her mother was a real gypsy, roaming from one place to another with the slightest encouragement. No doubt Irene had known that Nancy intended to sell the duplex. She and Nancy were thick as thieves, after all. Then again, maybe she was being unfair. Caroline slid down into the seat of the chair and leaned forward, hands clasped together atop her knees. "I suppose you spoke to Mama about this?"

Nancy nodded sorrowfully. "She felt it'd be best to leave it alone for a while, until you got used to being on your own."

And you gave me all of five minutes, Caroline mused. Well, better now than later. She licked her lips. "Are you saying I should move out?"

"Oh, no!" Nancy shook her bleached head. "Not right away. Why the house could take months to sell, and you never know, the new owner might want to keep things just like they are. You might not have to move at all, though Bud says it's possible that a buyer would want to convert this old house back to a single-family dwelling. But we don't know that, do we? No, I just thought you should be prepared for some changes, is all."

Caroline sighed. When had her life not been full of changes? Just once, for a little while, she would like to be bored to tears by the very sameness of her existence. But maybe no one's life was really like that, no one she knew, anyway. "I'm sure it'll all work out," she said, because, somehow, it always did. Who knew? A new owner might very well keep the duplex as it was. Better yet, a new owner might actually paint the place or fix the leaky faucet in the bathtub or put carpet down over the cracked and curling linoleum. After all, anything was possible.

Now that the bad news had been delivered, Nancy relaxed back onto the lumpy sofa and sipped her spiked coffee as if she hadn't just added monumentally to Caroline's worries. "So what are you going to do now, sugar? Your mama said you might get a loan to finish college."

Caroline shook her head. Accounting was a good field, but it had never inspired any great enthusiasm in her. Nothing did, really, except... She shook her head again. Dreaming was one thing, pipe dreams were something else altogether. Some people just weren't meant for some things, things like real families with two parents happy to see each other at the end of a day, children too secure and comfortable to worry about anything more than homework and team sports. She turned off the thought and said, "Actually, I'm looking for another job."

"What's wrong with the one you've got?"

"For one thing, it's part-time, and for another, I just need something more fulfilling than keeping books. I want something more—oh, I don't know—domestic, I guess."

Nancy's eyes went round, and she sloshed coffee onto her black pants. Wiping it absently with the tips of her fingers, she confided, "You know, it's a funny thing you should say that. I have a good friend who's looking for someone to help his mother with housework and cooking."

Caroline perked up. "Really? Would it be full-time?"

"Yes, I think so. No, I'm sure of it. I remember him saying that because of her arthritis, she's just not up to doing everything that needs doing on a ranch, like feeding the hands every day."

"It's on a ranch?" Caroline said, practically bouncing up and down in her seat. My, that sounded grand. She'd always wondered what it would be like to actually own a hunk of ground, to know that one piece of the world was yours.

"That's right," Nancy said, her gaze skittering away. "You know what? I probably shouldn't have said anything. My friend, he likes to keep his business quiet, you know, and, um, he's planning to advertise in the paper, so—''

"Well, if he's planning to advertise, then he wants it known, right?'' Caroline pointed out.

Nancy ignored the question and fluffed her hair, still not meeting Caroline's gaze, and in that instant, Caroline's heart literally stopped. Not *him! Oh, God, let it be him,* she whispered silently. She swallowed convulsively.

"You are going to tell me who he is, aren't you, Nancy?'' she asked softly.

"I really shouldn't,'' Nancy muttered, finding something in the corner of the room unaccountably interesting.

Caroline's heart pounded so hard that it felt as if someone had thumped her in the chest. She took a deep, silent, calming breath. "You know I'm a good cook and housekeeper,'' she prodded gently, "and I am the soul of discretion. You know that.''

Nancy smiled at that, one corner of her mouth turning up wryly. "That's true.'' She quickly spirited her gaze away again, however, sweeping it around the small room, one end of which was a tiny kitchen. Caroline knew what she saw. The place was shabby but spotless and organized within an inch of its existence, and that was her doing and hers alone. Irene was satisfied if she could find the bed under her clothes at night, but Caroline craved order and personalization. A nester, Irene always said of her. Caroline waited, a litany playing on a looped reel inside her head. *Please God. Please God. Please God.*

Finally Nancy turned back to her with a little shrug. "What the heck. I'd be doing him a good turn. He couldn't get better help than you.''

Cautious relief filled Caroline. "Thank you.''

Nancy waved away the thanks with a languid sweep of her many-ringed fingers. "It's Jesse Wagner.''

Caroline reeled. Excitement sang through her veins. *Thank You, God! Thank You, thank You! It must be fated that they should meet at last.*

"You've probably seen him around,'' Nancy confessed. "You know, that tall, good-looking cowboy that used to come by all the time.''

Caroline strove mightily to maintain her composure. Clearing her throat, she said as casually as she could manage, "Yeah, I think I've seen him. The one who drives that red and black truck?"

"That's the one," Nancy confirmed. "He has a ranch just south of town. Lives there with his parents. His mama, she's got arthritis real bad, apparently. Anyway, Jesse said she'd finally agreed that she had to have some help, and so he's going to put this ad in the paper. Or he was. Maybe he won't have to now."

"You think he'll hire me, then?"

"I don't see why not. He'd be a fool not to, and one thing Jess Wagner is not is a fool, let me tell you."

"He seems thoughtful of his mother," Caroline said carefully.

"Oh, yes. Always has been. That's why we never publicly..." Nancy's face actually colored as she followed the thought to its natural conclusion. "Well, of course we wouldn't. What I mean is, he's the discreet kind, you know? A real old-fashioned sort of gentleman, if you follow me. He has his needs like every other man, but he likes to handle them privately. You understand."

Caroline understood all right. Even if she hadn't been privy to Nancy's business over the past four years, she'd have her mother to thank for a wealth of such knowledge as Nancy alluded to. Far too many men who couldn't lay the slightest claim to old-fashioned gentlemanliness had wandered in and out of Irene Moncton's life. That was precisely the reason Caroline had kept herself clear of involvements. So far.

But Jesse Wagner was a discreet gentleman who considered his mother's feelings ahead of his own. She felt warmed by the information and hopeful in a way she couldn't explain even to herself. She crossed her long, slender legs. "Tell me more about this old-fashioned sort of gentleman—just so I can have the inside track on the job."

Nancy lifted a heavily penciled eyebrow. "Well, he's all man, for one thing, and he seems to have pretty deep pockets, too. At least, he's generous." She sat forward suddenly. "Listen, kid, I'd say I'd give him a call and put in a good word for you, but he wouldn't like that. See, he told me right from the beginning that he never wanted his family to know about our—'' she paused for several heartbeats then concluded ''—friendship.''

Caroline was glad to know that he'd dealt honestly with Nancy from the start. ''I understand,'' she said, encouraging Nancy to go on with an indulgent nod of her sleek blond head.

Nancy obliged, settling back and drawing her feet up beneath her. ''You must think I'm pretty soft in the head, going for an arrangement like that, but the truth is, I get sick and tired of all the lies and games. With Jesse you know where you stand, and that's worth something, believe me. Besides, he definitely gives as good as he gets. Oh, I know that I was nothing more than a convenience for him on one hand, but on the other, he's been a good friend.''

''I'm glad,'' Caroline said, and she was, knowing too well how many ways a man could take advantage of a woman without once giving anything in return. The only time Irene ever got down in the dumps and weepy was over some man who'd done her wrong. Of course, in all fairness, Irene had broken her share of hearts, and a few of them had belonged to men whom Caroline had genuinely liked. She had never understood why her mother chose as she did. It was as if the good ones bored her silly.

''I can't tell you how many times Jesse's come to my rescue,'' Nancy was saying. ''I broke my ankle once, and when he found out about it, he paid my hospital bills, because he knew I didn't have any insurance. And he's had my car fixed.'' She pointed at Caroline, certain she would remember this next example. ''That time the heater went out, about two years ago...'' Caroline nodded. ''It was Jesse who arranged to have it repaired for us.'' Nancy sighed and shook her head. ''He's one of a kind, that man, but he's not for me, and well I know it, too. And that's why I never let myself settle on him, you know? Besides, he's still in love with that wife of his—and her dead a decade or more.'' Nancy sent Caroline a sage, knowing look. ''Now that's real love for you. Real love and a real man.''

Caroline didn't doubt it, but was he really still ''in love'' with his late wife after all these years? It didn't seem possible to her. Oh, of course he should love her memory and hold close to his heart all that they'd meant to each other, but it seemed to her that being "in love" meant something else altogether. One could love from a distance without ever having one's feelings reciprocated, but being "in love" meant being concerned, if not consumed, minute by minute with the need to hear and touch and experience firsthand the object of one's affections. At least it seemed so to her. Put like that, the bald truth was that she'd loved Jess Wagner for a long while now but from a secondhand kind of distance. She couldn't help wondering if she might not tumble headlong in love with him given enough proximity. And, if so, might not he do the same with her? Well, she wouldn't know unless she got that job, would she? And why shouldn't she have that job? She was perfect for it, and it was perfect for her. Now if she could just convince him of that.

He wouldn't know her, of course. At least, if he'd ever noticed her peeking through the curtains at him, he'd certainly never given any sign of it, and if he had, she doubted he'd have even bothered to ask about her. Certainly he wouldn't have made note of her name if Nancy had ever bothered to mention it. No, she was a stranger to him for certain. Well, she'd just have to arrange an introduction.

What was the worst thing that could happen, after all? He'd simply tell her that he wasn't going to hire her, and that would be that. Somehow, though, she didn't believe that was going to happen. Somehow she knew in her heart that this was meant to be. It just felt right. He felt right. In fact, he was exactly what she wanted in a man. He was mature and responsible, generous, thoughtful, and he had a constant heart, an obvious feeling for family and a respect for women that was too often missing in males of her acquaintance. And he was gorgeous, with that wavy chestnut hair, square jaw, strong features and straight white teeth. She wondered what color his eyes were. She'd never seen him up close enough to tell, but it didn't matter, not with the breadth of his shoulders and the way he filled out a pair of jeans. She shivered just thinking about him. He had to be well over six feet tall, a big man with big hands and feet, a real man's man, but he would know how to treat a woman. Oh, yes, he would.

She realized suddenly that she was smiling and that Nancy was looking at her with an intense puzzlement. Self-consciously she smoothed down hair as straight and fine as corn silk and said, "Well, this is a stroke of good luck, I'm sure. Perhaps if I apply for the job before he has time to get it in the paper, I'll have a better chance. What do you think?"

Nancy shrugged and lifted her coffee cup. "Just be sure you tell him privately how you came to know of it."

Caroline nodded. Yes, indeed, very privately. She picked up the now cold cup of coffee she'd left earlier on the battered side table and saluted Nancy with it, silently wishing herself a happy birthday or at least a successful one, for this very morning she meant to apply for a job.

Jesse hunched his shoulders against a razor-sharp wind. This was nothing, of course, compared to what it would be in a few weeks' time, but today it seemed to cut through his heavy flannel jacket, flannel shirt and undershirt to whip his skin with shivers. Time to get out the insulated long johns. Seemed like he was breaking them out earlier every year. Before long hc'd be dragging them out at the end of summer, just like his father. He was standing on the edge of thirty-eight, but some days it felt more like sixty-eight, like when the wind whipped down out of the Rockies and cut him to bits. Clamping a hand down over the crown of his serviceable old brown felt hat, he ducked his chin below the turned-up edge of his collar and moved briskly toward the house.

He hadn't taken ten steps before he realized what he should have seen the moment he left the barn. Company was parked in the rutted, snow-curbed drive just outside the welded pipe fence enclosing the tight, two-story house where he lived with his parents. He didn't recognize the car, and yet something about it struck a chord with him. It looked like nothing so much as a big, battered tin cup on roller skates, and if it had ever been painted, the color had long ago worn to a dull, dirty gray. As he strode closer, the driver's side door creaked open and what looked like every high school quarterback's dream come true got out and waved a hand at him.

She had pale gold, waist-length hair, long, long legs encased in black leggings that disappeared beneath a cheap, fake rabbit fur coat topped by the face of an angel. "Handsome, you lucky dog," Jesse muttered, for who else could she be here to see but the young cowboy he'd taken on at the beginning of the summer? He stepped up and nodded, not offering his hand because she looked about sixteen. "Can I help you?"

To his surprise, she stepped forward and reached out her own long, slender hand to him. "I'm Caroline Moncton, Mr. Wagner. It's a pleasure to meet you."

He took her pale, cold hand in his own gloved one and shook it. She had a good strong grip for a girl, and mottled blue-and-green eyes, lavishly lashed, that were downright dangerous. He took his hand back and tucked it away. "Handsome's down at the barn. You're welcome to go down and—"

"I beg your pardon?"

He chuckled, figuring he knew what the problem was. "I meant Jerry, Jerry Harris. We call him Handsome Harris around here because of all the g— Well, he seems to have some sort of appeal we haven't figured out yet."

She cocked her head and scooped straight silk out of her eyes. "I didn't come here to see anyone called Handsome Harris," she said. "I came to see you."

"Me?" Now that was a surprise. Who the devil was Caroline Moncton? "I'm afraid I can't imagine what you'd have to see me about."

"The fact is, I want a job."

His mouth dropped open. Shades of Kara Detmeyer Wagner! According to his brother and what Jess had seen himself, his new sister-in-law was as able a cowboy as any man who'd ever sat astride a horse, but at least she looked the part, dressing in jeans and boots, hat and work shirts. Rye swore she was more at ease in chaps and rough-out gloves than skirts and flounces, but he'd hinted—unnecessarily—that what was underneath was all woman. This gal was all girl from the outside in. He couldn't believe she was interested in cowboying. He huddled down into his coat.

"Honey, I don't know what notion you've got rattling around inside that pretty little head of yours, but ranching's rough work, besides which I don't have an open spot, not that I'd take you on if I did. I mean, I'm all for women's lib or feminism, whatever you want to call it, but there are just some things the average five-foot, four-inch female can't manage, and wrestling balky steers is one of them.''

She stared at him without discernible expression for several seconds, and then she bowed her head, giving him the distinct impression that she was hiding a smile. When she looked up again, however, no such thing was in evidence. ''Number one,'' she said, throwing up a hand to tick the numbers off her fingers, ''I'm five-five, not five-four. Number two, I'm not interested in wrestling balky steers or any other kind. Number three, don't call me honey unless you mean it. And number four, nothing rattles around inside my head, thank you. I have a brain in there, quite a good one, if I do say so myself. Now, shall we start all over, or would you like to go on from here?''

He didn't quite know which option to take. He was, in fact, having trouble keeping up. His brain didn't seem to want to move past point one. A quip about an inch only making a difference in certain bed sports came to mind, but he rejected it instantly. She was just a kid, for pity's sake, a bright, determined one, by all indications, but a kid, nonetheless. It just wouldn't do to go crossing tongues with some little high school cutie. He laughed at the very thought. Cute was a deal short of the truth. This little gal was a beauty, all the more reason to mind his manners. He cleared his throat and stuck out his hand. ''How do you do? Jesse Wagner.''

Her smile was electrifying, and he hadn't imagined the solid grip. ''Caroline Moncton,'' she said, ''and I heard that you need a housekeeper and a cook, someone to help out your mother because her arthritis has gotten bad. I'm here to apply for the position.''

He stood staring at her for a long moment before he realized that he still held her hand in his. Then he coughed, reclaiming his own hand to cover his mouth, and tried to think how to let her down easy. She was about the last thing he'd envisioned when contemplating someone to help out his mother, but he was smart enough not to say so. No doubt he'd get his ears pinned again. No, he'd have to play this one by the book. ''Well, uh, what experience do you have?''

"Oh, about ten years of keeping house and making meals. I'm a good cook. Everyone says so. And I have my own system for keeping up the housework."

She was serious, very. Suddenly he remembered her saying, *Don't call me honey unless you mean it.* She was serious about that, too, but he couldn't quite wrap his mind around the implications. Instead, he forced himself to think about the issue at hand. "Your own system? You want to explain that?"

She went on to carefully, concisely explain how she intended to keep his house in order. The funny thing was that it sure sounded workable to him, but then what did he know about it? The only thing he'd ever done that could remotely be considered housework was dropping his dirty clothes in the hamper and rustling up the occasional snack. He'd learned to make a halfway decent breakfast lately, but that was only because it took his mom so long to get limbered up and in working order of a morning. But that was painting it too bright. What passed for working order for his poor mother these days was being able to get around and tolerate the pain at the same time. She sure needed help. In fact, he had an ad coming out in next Sunday's paper.... Wait a minute, that ad hadn't even been published yet! He narrowed his eyes, knowing full well that when he did so the blue leeched out to leave them a cold, steel gray. Something fishy was going on here, and little Miss Moncton was holding the pole.

"Where did you say you heard about this job?"

She grimaced at that, waving a hand helplessly. "I, um, didn't, and I'm not sure you really want me to."

"I wouldn't have asked if I didn't want to know," he pointed out sharply.

She shrugged and glanced over her shoulder at the steeply roofed ranch house. "All right," she said in a you-asked-for-it voice. "Nancy Shaver told me."

Jess felt the bottom drop out of his stomach. "N-Nancy?" His mind whirled suddenly. "Uh-huh. I may have mentioned it to Nancy. Just how do you know her, anyway?"

Caroline Moncton licked her lips, full, bow-shaped lips that he now realized were devoid of artificial color. That dusky, rosy red was natural, for heaven's sake. She looked down at her toes and said, "Well, you might say I live in the same house. She's my landlady."

He let that sink in. "You mean you live in the other side of the duplex."

"That's right."

He had one more all-important question. "How long?"

Her head came up, her wide, blue-and-green eyes meeting his unflinchingly. "Just over four years now."

She knew. There wasn't any doubt about it. He felt his face heating, the tips of his ears glowing white-hot in the cold breeze. This innocent and wholesome-looking child knew all about the most private part of his life. He saw the certain knowledge there in her angel's face. Embarrassment churned in his stomach and burned up his throat. "I see."

She actually reached out a hand toward him, brushing his sleeve with her fingertips. Oddly, it felt like a gesture of comfort. "I wouldn't want you to think that Nancy betrayed a confidence. It wasn't like that at all. She never so much as mentioned your name before, but I need a job and you need help, and Nancy realized that this is just the sort of thing I'm best at. The way I see it, she did us both a favor."

He lifted a hand to the back of his neck, trying to catch all the implications of this news. One thing was sure, Nancy didn't owe him a thing, not even silence, but he'd maintained the connection for so long precisely because she'd kept it so completely to herself. He knew that she wouldn't have mentioned him now if she did not honestly believe that she was doing him a favor. For the first time, he had to take Miss Moncton seriously, and that irritated him. He couldn't say why exactly, but it did. Suddenly a new thought occurred. "You wouldn't be trying to force my hand here, would you?"

She stared at him, her jaw slowly lowering as understanding turned to outrage. "No!"

"How do I know—"

"I could have spread it around a long time ago, if I'd wanted to!" she snapped. "It didn't exactly take a genius to figure out why you were slipping in and out at odd hours of the day and night!"

"And how'd you find out my name?"

"My mother came up with it! I don't imagine it was much of a chore. Everyone around here knows the Wagners."

He gulped. So it wasn't quite the state secret he'd imagined it to be. Still, to be confronted with his most closely held secret by this kid... "How old are you, anyway?" he barked. She smiled as if to say that she was old enough to know everything there was to know about men and women and all that pulled them together.

"I'm twenty-one," she told him proudly.

"Huh. You look like about sixteen."

Disappointment, then anger and, finally, resignation moved over her face. Then suddenly she reached inside the rolling wreck and snagged the long strap of a small purse, which she flipped open. Extracting a small wallet, she broke open the snap and thrust it at him. He recoiled physically.

"My driver's license." She thrust it under his nose, demanding that he look. "Perhaps I should have brought along a birth certificate, as well!"

Something about her sense of outrage tickled him. Oh, to be young enough again to be insulted about being young! Patiently, indulgently, he studied the driver's license, finding the date of birth. Well, well. He looked up and shrugged. "Happy birthday." Mollified, she drew the wallet back, fastened it and returned it to her purse.

"Thank you."

She was regally gracious in victory, so much so that he couldn't help grinning at her. "When I turned twenty-one," he told her, "I went right out and bought a case of beer. It only took about a six-pack to get me roaring drunk, but it was the principle of the thing."

She rolled her eyes. "That's the difference between men and women," she said. "Women mature so much more quickly."

He laughed outright at that. "You think so? Always figured it was an individual thing."

She shouldered her little purse and pushed her hair out of her face again. "About that job, I really can handle it, and I need full-time work to pay the rent."

Deep down he knew that Nancy wouldn't have sent her if that wasn't the case. And she would sure dress up the place. Too much, maybe. He glanced at the house, and she followed the path of his gaze. "My mother has the final say," he told her. "If she's willing, I suppose we could give you a try."

The smile that she turned on him nearly knocked him off his feet. Heavens, she was heartbreak walking. Every male over the age of ten who laid eyes on her was bound to want her, and like every truly beautiful woman ever born, she wouldn't give ninety-nine point nine percent of them the time of day. Thank God he wasn't young enough to seriously consider entering the fray. Sneaking up on forty did have its advantages, after all. She looked back at the house, tilting her head as she studied it.

"It's a wonderful place," she said, and then, "I don't suppose you'd consider room and board along with a salary?"

Surprised, he cracked, "You really are worried about paying the rent! Has the price gone up?"

She shook her head. "But my mother moved out today, so I'm on my own now. Besides, Nancy's planning to sell it now that she's getting married. Didn't you know?"

"No reason I should."

She nodded at that and carefully said, "Listen, I want you to know that I'll never say a thing about you and Nancy, whether you hire me or not. I never have, not to anyone." She grimaced and added, "But I don't know about my mother. I mean, she mentioned it to me a couple times, but whether she'd say anything to someone else, I just don't know. I'd like to think not, she and Nancy being such good friends and all, but..." She let the thought hang, bowing her head as if she were ashamed. He didn't like seeing it, for some reason.

"You're not responsible for what your mother might or might not say or do," he told her. "I'll take you at your word that you won't discuss my personal business with anyone, but especially with my mother."

Her head snapped up, and she smiled. "Absolutely. As God is my witness, not a word, whether you hire me or not."

He nodded, satisfied for some reason that he couldn't quite explain even to himself. Briskly, he said, "As far as the room and board goes, young lady, let's just take it one step at a time for now. First, we talk to Mother.''

She didn't hide her relief, asking hopefully, ''Is this a good time?''

''Good as any,'' he decided, and the grateful excitement that lit her green-and-blue-spoked eyes made him want to hug her. It was the first real inkling that he might be in trouble, but he ignored it. She was a kid, after all. Just a kid. A very pretty kid.

Chapter Two

Caroline shivered inside her coat as she followed Jesse along the walk. Someone had shoveled the snow, piling it up on either side of the brick-lined path. Soon those crumpled-looking mounds would be knee-high and then waist-high, and, if the winter was particularly hard, perhaps even shoulder-high. Caroline was willing to bet that no matter how deep the snow fell, that walk would be shoveled. To her mind, it showed a pride in ownership, as well as thoughtfulness. She could imagine him out here scooping and tossing, scooping and tossing. She would be waiting with a hot drink and a smile when he came back inside from that particular chore next time—if his mother approved of her. She felt certain that he would hire her if his mother said that she would do. She could only hope, and as she attempted not to worry about what she could not control, she put that concern out of mind. Instead, she thought of how he had reacted when she'd mentioned Nancy's impending marriage.

The fact was, he hadn't reacted, not with so much as a shrug or a twitch of a brow. She wondered why that was, and before she could discipline the urge to ask, she had blurted out the question. "Don't you mind that Nancy's getting married?"

He stopped dead in his tracks and turned to face her. "Why on earth would I?" His tone implied that she was incredibly foolish.

"I don't know. I just thought—"

He cut her off. "Why should I mind that Nancy's happy? She deserves it. I wish her well." His glare held for a moment, but then it softened somewhat, and he reluctantly asked, "She is happy, isn't she?"

Caroline nodded emphatically. "Absolutely. Very happy."

He nodded, too. "All right. Good."

He started to turn away, but Caroline stopped him with an uplifted hand. "Do you mind if I ask one more question?"

He rounded on her. "Yes, actually, I do!"

Caroline shrank back. "I just wanted to know how she told you."

His look was incredulous, but he answered. "She didn't tell me. You told me."

Now she was incredulous. "You didn't know until then?"

He shook his head. "It wasn't a surprise, though. I knew she was seeing someone after me and that it was getting serious. End of story."

Caroline's elation soared. "I see." He regarded her a moment longer, then turned away, shaking his head.

Caroline was pleased on several levels. For one, she didn't want him to be hurt in any way, and obviously he wasn't. For another, she was selfish enough to be glad that he didn't care so much for Nancy that he could be hurt, for that could only mean that his heart was not involved in the affair. Also, he seemed to respect Nancy, to realize that she deserved to be loved—just not by him. He hadn't disappointed her so far, except with that bit about her looking too young. She'd have to do something about that—if his mother decided to keep her around.

Suddenly everything hinged on Mrs. Wagner's approval. Caroline took a deep breath, fighting back panic. She could do this. She could do this. She had to do this.

Jesse led her around the corner of the house to a side door. It was quite a place, large but somehow cozy. The prim white siding shone cleanly against the vibrant green of the roof, shutters and trim. The deep front porch was stacked with cordwood to feed the pair of red rock chimneys that climbed above the steep roof, and she saw the spot where a swing would hang come summertime. The peak of the roof sheltered a dormer window, its shutters open to the setting sun.

A wave of warmth hit her as he opened the door and held it for her. She stepped up onto a flagstone floor and looked around. They were in a narrow, wood-paneled hall lined with pegs at a height just above her head, a small closet at the far end. Jesse wiped his feet on the mat, stepped inside and closed the door. Without a word he shrugged out of his coat and hung it up, then peeled off a scarf and his gloves and removed his hat before reaching for her coat, which she'd slipped off herself. He eyed her chambray shirt critically.

"Don't you know how to dress for the weather?"

She tried not to shiver as the warmth caressed her chilled skin. "Of course I do."

He went on to instruct her as if she hadn't spoken. "You need gloves, a scarf and a hat."

"I've been meaning to purchase those items," she said lightly.

"You can't have lived here four years without them," he went on doggedly.

Caroline spared him a dismissive glance. "No, of course not." She shrugged. "I used to have them, but they were borrowed by someone else and lost."

He frowned. "You shouldn't be loaning your things to such irresponsible—"

Exasperated, she snapped, "It was my mother, all right? Would you tell your mother she couldn't borrow something of yours?"

He thought that over and mumbled, "My mother wouldn't lose my things."

"Well, my mother loses everything," Caroline told him, cheerfully blunt, "hers, mine, everything. Now that she's on her way to California, though, I don't suppose I'll have to worry about it anymore."

"You mean she's moving to California?"

"She is."

"What about your father?"

"Never knew him," Caroline said matter-of-factly.

He lifted a brow at that. "Then you're pretty much on your own."

She gave him her most fetching smile. "Definitely on my own."

He frowned but nodded. "All right. We can take that into consideration. Now if you'll wait here for just a moment, I'll go find Mother."

"Fine."

He turned his back, and her smile wilted. She leaned against the wall and folded her arms, breathing deeply. Suddenly he looked back over one shoulder, raking her with a critical look. "You ought to layer your clothes," he said gruffly. "It traps body heat." Then he hung his hat on the last peg and walked away, turning the corner at the end of the short hall.

Caroline let out her breath and rocked up onto the balls of her feet, mimicking softly, "You ought to layer your clothes. It traps body heat." Why was he so concerned about how she dressed? She hoped he wasn't the controlling sort who had to order everybody's life to his satisfaction. She hoped she had a chance to find out.

Shaking her head, she took another look around her. There were four coats hanging in the hallway, including her own. All the others looked like men's coats. Perhaps Mrs. Wagner hung her own coat in the closet, neatly, carefully. Or perhaps she elected to wear a man's coat. Caroline was betting on the former. The neatness of the short hallway told her that someone was meticulous, and she could only assume that it was Jesse Wagner's mother. Would such a woman be less meticulous about her personal things? She didn't think so.

Much more quickly than she expected, Jesse was back, saying, "Come on. She's in the kitchen."

He led her around the corner and down another hallway flanking a large living room, a small den and a formal dining room. All were paneled in golden wood and warmly lit, the floors covered in wall-to-wall carpeting the russet color of terra-cotta tile. Somewhere in the house, a clock chimed the quarter hour.

Jesse halted adjacent to the dining room and lifted an arm, indicating that she should proceed him through the open doorway opposite. Caroline stepped into a brightly lit, cheerful kitchen done in soft yellows and cool blues. It was toasty warm and smelled of peaches and cinnamon. A small woman with a luxurious head of gray hair bound in a bun at the nape of her neck turned from the counter and dried her gnarled hands on her apron.

"Hello."

"Mom, this is Caroline Moncton. Miss Moncton, my mother, Sarah."

"How pretty you are," Sarah Wagner said, reaching out with both hands.

Liking her immediately, Caroline lifted both hands and felt her fingertips being gently squeezed. "Thank you. What a lovely compliment. It's a pleasure to meet you."

"Let's have a seat," Sarah said, turning toward the oval table that sat before the window. Jesse slid past Caroline and quickly pulled out his mother's chair. Thanking him, Sarah placed one hand on the table and very slowly sank down into the seat. Meanwhile, Jesse repeated the gesture for Caroline, who also murmured her thanks and took her seat.

A grimace of pain passed over Sarah Wagner's surprisingly smooth face as she settled herself fully into her chair, but the next moment she smiled, displaying small fans of shallow wrinkles at the outside corners of her eyes. Caroline couldn't help thinking that she would look much younger if she colored her hair. A good cut wouldn't hurt, either. Her eyebrows were a sandy brown but too slight. Just a little pencil would add definition and call attention to her shining, silver-blue eyes.

"Would you like a cup of coffee, Miss Moncton? It's fresh."

"Please call me Caroline, but don't trouble yourself about the coffee."

"No trouble." Sarah turned a smile over one shoulder. "Son, would you pour Caroline a cup of coffee, please?" She turned back to Caroline. "Cream and sugar?"

"No, thank you. I prefer it black."

Sarah nodded with approval. "You're older than you seem at first glance."

"I'm twenty-one," Caroline said.

"Today," Jesse added significantly, reaching past her to place a flowered mug on the table in front of her.

Sarah beamed, blue eyes twinkling. "Well, we have to have cake, too, then, don't we?" She winked, and Caroline smiled, thinking of Jesse dishing up gooey slices of cake for her and his mother.

"Absolutely," she said, and Sarah hunched her shoulders as if giggling before smoothly turning a complacent look over one shoulder.

"Son, there's a fresh pound cake under that cover on the buffet in the dining room. Would you mind cutting two slices?"

Jesse sounded as if he was strangling when he said, "Not at all."

"Use the good china," Sarah directed as he crossed the hall. "It is a celebration."

When he was safely out of hearing, she turned a conspiratorial smile on Caroline and whispered, "He's a dear boy but a little awkward to have underfoot from time to time." She patted Caroline's hand where it rested near her coffee mug and said, "Now tell me all about yourself."

"There's not much to tell," Caroline said. "My father was a sailor my mother met in South Carolina. They married and then divorced before I was even born. I've never met him. She never married again, so there are no siblings."

"So it's just been the two of you all these years," Sarah divined correctly.

"Yes. My mother's parents died when I was small. She has a sister, in Oregon, I think, but they aren't close. Mom's something of a tumbleweed, never stays in one place too long if she can help it. She only stayed here because I refused to go with her when she wanted to move on."

"Have you been here long?"

"Four years," Caroline said, "and as far as I'm concerned, here is where I'll stay. Mom, on the other hand, left for California this morning."

"Oh, my!" Sarah said, dismayed. "So you're all alone now."

"I'm a big girl," Caroline pointed out with a smile. "I'll be fine—as soon as I find full-time work."

Jesse entered the room then, warily carrying two plates of butchered cake. It looked like it had been carved out with a spoon. Sarah swallowed a chuckle and traded looks with Caroline when he plunked both plates down in the center of the table.

"None for yourself?" she inquired sweetly as he sucked crumbs off his thumb.

"Too close to lunch for me," he grumbled, moving back toward the counter.

Sarah waited patiently before gently prodding, "Forks, dear?"

Caroline listened to the drawer slide out, the flatware clinking as he pawed through it, and the whump as he shoved the drawer shut again. Two forks appeared in the center of the table. Sarah carefully picked up one, and just that small movement seemed to pain her. Caroline glanced up sympathetically, and Sarah acknowledged her concern with a smile, then launched into conversation once more.

Before long, Caroline had told her all about college, her boredom with keeping books and her impatience with her immature contemporaries. "All they think about is entertainment," Caroline said lightly, "while I'm thinking about paying the rent."

Sarah laid down her fork and covered Caroline's wrist with her cupped hand. "Don't worry yourself about that any longer. I think we'll manage just fine together, you and I."

Caroline beamed, while behind her, Jesse cleared his throat. "You haven't even heard about her system yet," he pointed out to his mother.

"Oh, that doesn't matter," Caroline said quickly. "This is your mother's house, naturally she'll want things done her way."

"Not at all," Sarah said firmly. "I have a very open mind, I assure you." She started to rise, and Jesse rushed to help her. Caroline literally heard her joints creak. Standing once more, Sarah took a deep breath and briskly said, "We'll discuss this system of yours while we're preparing lunch."

"Now?" Caroline said. "You want me to start *now?*"

"Unless you prefer another arrangement."

"No!" Caroline bounded out of her chair, too delighted to contain her laughter. "Thank you, Mrs. Wagner! You won't regret this, I promise!"

"Now, now," the older woman chided gently, "no formality. Call me Sarah, I insist."

Impulsively Caroline hugged her. She glanced up, catching a look of troubled speculation on Jesse's face. Immediately Caroline backed off. "Did you have something else in mind? Perhaps you'd like to interview a few more candidates?"

Jesse shrugged as if it was of no concern to him whatsoever. "Mother knows what's she's doing. I was just thinking about this room-and-board thing." He immediately turned to his mother, explaining, "Miss, uh, Caroline asked earlier if there might be a possibility of room and board as part of the salary."

"Oh," Sarah began. "Well, we could always—"

"Maybe later," Jesse said, looking at Caroline. "If and when it's necessary." Again, he explained to his mother, "Caroline's concerned because her landlady is thinking about selling the duplex they're sharing."

"Yes," Caroline said, "the thing is, it's an older home that was converted into a duplex, and the landlady feels that a new owner may want it as a single-family dwelling again, but it hasn't even gone on the market yet, so there's no immediate concern."

"Well, let's wait and see then," Sarah said encouragingly. "But I don't want you to worry now. I'm sure that when the moment comes, there will be no problem."

"Thank you," Caroline said, smiling warmly at the other woman. "Now let's get that lunch on. Can I borrow an apron?"

She pretended not to notice when Jesse left the room and then returned a moment later with the newspaper, yet she remained acutely aware of him as he sat calmly at one end of the table, slowly turning through the pages. She found it difficult to believe that he had nothing more pressing to do than sit there reading with lunch less than an hour away. Didn't he trust her enough to leave her alone with his mother? Apparently she would have to assure him again that she would make no mention of his former relationship with Nancy. She was really too busy to worry about it, though.

Sarah had stewed a chicken the day before, and Caroline's first job was to debone it and cut the meat into bite-sized chunks for soup while Sarah painstakingly cleaned vegetables. She was having a very difficult time with a paring knife. After a while, Jess folded his paper and suggested that he could try his hand at the vegetables. Sarah smiled to herself.

"Thank you, dear, but we're doing fine. You really don't have to hover."

Jesse grumbled something unintelligible, got up, stretched and said he had a couple things to do in the office. When he had gone, Sarah sent Caroline a speaking look.

"He tries to help, but there are hardly any vegetables left when he's through with them."

Caroline chuckled. "Well, at least he's willing to help. That's more than a great many men."

"Oh, my, yes," Sarah said, adding in a more strident tone, "his father isn't nearly so understanding."

Caroline said nothing to that, but as she had finished with the chicken, she washed her hands and took over the paring knife, freeing Sarah to mix together a batch of biscuits. From the corner of her eye, Caroline watched Sarah put together the dry ingredients and prepare to sift them. She hesitated only a moment before suggesting that half a teaspoon of cream of tartar would give the biscuits a crisp crust just made for dunking in soup.

"Now that makes perfect sense," Sarah said, reaching into the cabinet. "I wonder why I didn't think of it before."

Beaming, Caroline began putting together the soup. It was simmering fragrantly when Jesse wandered in again.

"Everything okay in here?"

She lifted both eyebrows at him, wondering if he expected her to injure his mother in some way, perhaps splash her with scalding water, mistake her for a vegetable? He seemed to realize belatedly how the question had sounded. Coloring slightly, he looked straight at her and said, "Mother can't reach the dishes on the top shelves."

"I can," Caroline said. "I'm over five feet, you know. In fact, I'm—"

"Five-five, yeah, I got that," he said, clearly amused. To his mother he said, "Looks like I'll not be needed around here anymore." With that, he flipped a kind of salute, turned, and strolled easily from the room.

Laughing, Sarah put her hands to her hips. "What on earth has gotten into him?"

Caroline shrugged. "Maybe he just needs a little time to get used to having another woman around the house."

Sarah measured her with a speculative look. "You could be right about that."

Caroline merely smiled and looked around her. "Now, what else did you have in mind?"

"You can cut the biscuits and get down the noodles for the soup," Sarah said, all business again, "while I get the salad makings from the refrigerator. Then we'll pop that peach cobbler in the freezer into the oven. These boys love peach cobbler."

"Sounds like 'these boys' eat pretty well," Caroline said.

"I get no complaints," Sarah said, "but it will sure be easier with you here."

"That's the idea."

Quickly, companionably, the two women put together the meal, but inevitably what Sarah started, Caroline finished. Finally, Sarah sat down at the table in disgust, holding her hands out before her. "I'm the next thing to a cripple."

Caroline dried her hands and slipped onto the edge of the seat closest to Sarah. A glance told her everything she needed to know. "You're in pain, aren't you?"

Tears gathered in Sarah's eyes as she nodded. Caroline got to her feet again. "Aspirin?"

Sarah swallowed and nodded again. "On my bedside table, upstairs, first door on your right."

"I'll be right back."

Caroline ran lightly down the hall and up the stairs, turning to her right on the landing. A door opened off either side of the stairwell, and a narrower set of stairs at the back of the landing led, supposedly, to the attic. The door to the bedroom that Caroline sought stood open, so she hurried inside and took a look around. A four-poster bed stood dead center of the far wall, taking up a good deal of space, but the many windows with their light, filmy covers gave the room an open, airy feel, just as the massive fireplace in one corner warmed it. A triple dresser stood next to the door, a mirror above it. An antique pants press and small slipper chair occupied a corner, along with a rusty old trunk left open to reveal a stack of colorful quilts. Two mirrored doors opened off of one wall. Caroline glimpsed the sheen of tile beneath one of them. Undoubtedly it opened into a private bath. The other was probably a closet. She turned her attention back to the bed, more specifically, the matching tables flanking it, and spied the aspirin bottle on the far side between the Victorian-style lamp and a pair of reading glasses atop a hardback book.

Bottle in hand, she swung out onto the enclosed landing and came face-to-face with Jesse, who stood in the door across the way. Caroline showed him the aspirin bottle in her hand. He sighed and leaned a shoulder against the door frame.

"She's in pain much more often than she'll admit."

"I've seen the signs."

He nodded. "I've tried to help, but I'm pretty limited in the kitchen. About all I can do is fetch and carry, and that's not really what she needs."

So that's why he was hanging around, in case his mother needed him. Caroline smiled, feeling deeply satisfied. "Don't worry about that anymore. I can do just about anything that needs doing, and if not, I know who to call on."

He looked down at his toes. "I appreciate that."

"I'll take care of her," she promised. "From now on, I'm her hands."

"I just hope she'll let you do more than she'll let me do."

"She will. You'll see."

He nodded. She waited a moment longer, expecting him to say something more, something, perhaps, about how she should keep her silence concerning Nancy. Instead he said, "If she's needing that aspirin, you'd better get it to her."

"Right." She swung around the newel post and quickly descended the stairs. When she got back to the kitchen, Sarah was taking dishes down from the cabinet one at a time. "I'll do that," Caroline said. "You take your aspirin." She twisted off the cap and placed the bottle on the cabinet, then got down a glass and filled it with water. She and Sarah traded places. "How many settings?"

"Six, including you."

Caroline looked over her shoulder in shock. "Oh, I don't have to eat with everyone else. I can always—"

"Don't be silly," Sarah said, having swallowed her aspirin. "The hands eat two meals a day with the family. You will, too. Now set those dishes right here on this table, and I'll get the flatware. We take breakfast and lunch in the kitchen, dinner in the dining room. The men will want coffee, and they'll be bringing in thermoses, too, so we'll pour what's left in the pot into a keeper and put that on the table while we brew another pot."

"Sounds like you need two coffeemakers," Caroline said.

"We used to have two, but one gave out. I've been meaning to buy another."

"I can take care of that for you, if you want."

"Would you? What a wonderful help you are!"

"No problem."

"I'll get the trivet. We'll sit the soup pot right on the table when the men get here. Stays hotter that way. The biscuits we'll just have to wrap in hot towels."

"Do you have a Crock-Pot?"

Sarah blinked at her. "Yes, actually, I do."

"Makes a great bread warmer."

"Now why didn't I think of that? You're so smart."

Caroline laughed. "If this place was as drafty as my place is, you'd hit on it sooner or later."

Sarah opened her mouth to comment, but the windowpanes rattled gently as someone opened an outer door, and then heavy footsteps and male voices could be heard coming down the hall. Jesse pounded down the stairs and into the kitchen, taking a place near the window. "Here we go!" Sarah said laughingly. Caroline hurried to get it onto the table.

"Smells great!" Jesse said, pulling his chair up to the table. The other men came in one by one, after visiting the rest room to wash up. Haney Wagner, Jesse's father and Sarah's husband, was the first. An older, leaner version of his son, he made it obvious where Jesse came by that thick, wavy hair. Surprisingly, he showed only a little silver at the temples. The elements had taken a toll on his face, but he was one of those men whose crinkles and pronounced bone structure only added character. Hale and hardy, he looked younger than his wife by several years.

"Hello," Haney said simply, glancing at Caroline as he rolled down his sleeves and headed for the table. A man of few words, obviously.

Sarah made the introductions, then repeated them for the other two men as they came in. Tiger Stevens was a tall, slim blonde about thirty years of age. He wore no rings and no wristwatch. His light amber eyes flashed over Caroline with interest, but he said little as he took his place. Handsome Harris was not so circumspect. He was, frankly, a very good-looking young man, as his nickname indicated, with dark brown hair and eyes. A year or two older than Caroline and of average height, he had a weight-lifter's build and a flirt's quick smile.

"My, my," he said, looking Caroline over blatantly, "somebody's been holding out on me." He flashed that smile at her. "Thought I'd met every pretty girl in town."

Caroline curbed the urge to roll her eyes and instead ignored him. She lifted the lid from the soup pot and dunked the ladle. Haney Wagner slid his bowl next to the pot, and she filled it. Handsome lifted his next, but she reached instead for Jesse's.

"Mother, you come sit down now," Jesse said, while Tiger chuckled at Handsome's chagrin.

"Yes, sit down," Caroline echoed. "I'll get the bread. That crock's too heavy for you."

"Now don't fuss over me," Sarah protested, taking her chair. Caroline filled her bowl and then saw to Tiger.

"Guess we know the pecking order," Tiger said to Handsome as he pulled his bowl toward him.

"That's all right. I'm a patient man," Handsome said loudly.

Caroline pretended to just then notice him. "Oh, are you ready for soup, Mr. Harris?" She filled his bowl and turned away.

Seeing her empty place beside Sarah, Harris said, "Aren't you going to sit down?"

Caroline ignored him. Sarah said, "Jesse pass the salad," the hint of a chuckle in her tone.

Wearing an oven mitt, Caroline carried the crock to the table and reached inside. She placed the first golden brown biscuit on Jesse's plate and the next on Haney's. She passed out two more, stripped off the mitt and sat down. Tiger snickered as Handsome gaped. "Oh," Caroline said. She lifted the lid so he could reach inside himself. Handsome grinned as he did so.

"Life has sure got interesting around here," he said.

Caroline looked up and asked, "Jesse, did you have anything else in mind for me this afternoon?"

Tiger laughed. Handsome gusted a heavy sigh. Jesse concentrated on his plate, but Caroline was pretty sure he was smiling. "Mom's the one you should be asking that question."

"I thought we'd look around the house," Sarah said, "get you familiar with things. If there's time before we have to start dinner, we could dust the living room."

"Sounds fine," Caroline said. "By the way, what time should I come in tomorrow morning?"

Sarah looked at Jesse. "What do you think, son?"

Jesse shrugged. "Nine to six makes a full day."

"What about breakfast?" Caroline asked.

"Haney and I just take coffee," Sarah said. "Tiger and Handsome eat before they come in, and Jesse makes his own. He's always up first."

Caroline made a note of that.

Handsome said, "Say, maybe you'd like a ride in to work?"

Caroline looked straight at Jesse and said, "What time would you like dinner?"

Handsome dropped his spoon with a clunk, and Tiger stifled a chuckle with his napkin.

It took Jesse a moment to get his smile under control, but finally he said, "I eat when it's put on the table."

Without preliminary, Sarah answered Caroline's question. "About five. The men are plenty hungry by then, and it leaves the bulk of the evening free for them. Of course, not everyone always shows up for dinner," she added innocently. "Handsome, will you be eating in tonight?"

"Yes, ma'am! If Miss Caroline's servin', I'm eatin'."

Caroline smiled at Jesse. "Will you be eating in tonight, Jesse?"

He shrugged. "I always eat in."

"We all do," Tiger volunteered, "except for Handsome. He has a real busy social life." Handsome kicked him under the table. "Ow!"

Haney burst out laughing. Jesse shook his head, no longer even trying to tame his grin . "You'll have to forgive Handsome," he said to Caroline. "He can't resist a pretty girl."

"Especially one as pretty as you," Handsome added quickly.

Caroline inclined her head and said, "Why, thank you, Jesse."

Handsome's chair screeched as he reeled back, thoroughly spurned. All three of the other men laughed heartily. Even Sarah chuckled. Both Jesse and Haney had managed to empty their bowls already. Caroline snatched up the ladle and filled Jesse's bowl first, then Haney's. She passed out more biscuits and asked Jesse if she could get him anything else. Handsome gaped, Jesse chuckled, and Tiger sniggered.

Haney said mildly, "Handsome's not used to sharing the attention."

"Sharing," Handsome said cryptically. "So far I'm mute and invisible!"

Tiger gave off one loud whoop of laughter, then managed to swallow the rest. Everyone else covered their mouths or averted their faces. Caroline pretended not to have the least idea what was going on. Concentrating on her lunch, she forked up bites of salad and shared a grin with Jesse, who kept shaking his head.

Thanks to Sarah, conversation around the table began to focus on other subjects. Handsome, to his credit, did not sulk. His smile was much too quick, his self-esteem much too healthy, but he did tone down the flirtation to hopeful glances and fulsome compliments on the food. Caroline continued to ignore him. Jesse continued to chuckle at Handsome's expense and treated Caroline's regard as nothing more than a tactic to thwart Handsome. But Caroline was in deadly earnest. She liked this man, liked him immensely.

She enumerated his sterling qualities silently. One, he had a constant heart. Otherwise, he wouldn't have grieved his late wife so long. Two, he cared about his friends' happiness. At least, he cared about Nancy's, as he should. But not too much. Three, he was fair and trusting. Despite wanting to keep his private involvements just that, he had taken her at her word and allowed her to speak to his mother, then made no objection when Sarah hired her. Four, he was very thoughtful of his mother and obviously valued her good opinion. Five, he liked to laugh and did so easily with the men in his employ. Six, he was even more potently good-looking up close than at a distance. And seven, if he was a little gruff with her at times, well, it could be his way of protecting himself against the attraction. She felt sure there was an attraction. If not, she meant to try her hand at developing one.

She smiled to herself as she calmly ate her soup and listened to the chatter around the table. It felt good to be part of a group. It was almost like a family. For a moment, she imagined that she was Sarah and Jesse was Haney. The other three around the table were their sons, grown but still close. Mentally, she added daughters-in-law and grandchildren, until the house was bursting with the sounds of teasing and laughter, conversation and even the occasional wail. Oh, how she wanted that, or something very like it, a family of her own extended to several generations. And this was just the place to have it, a real home with a history all its own.

Suddenly the desire, the need, for that dream to come true gripped her so tightly that she could barely breathe. It struck her, in the midst of it all, that she was just what she had so often felt. Alone. Completely alone. From now on, there would not be even a note from her mother saying that she was going to be late. From now on, it was just her, all by herself. She felt a spurt of panic, but then Jesse said something that made everyone laugh, and just the sound of his voice soothed her.

She reminded herself that she had come here for two reasons, a job and to get to know Jesse Wagner. So far, so good. She had the job. Now all she had to do was keep it long enough to fix Jesse Wagner's interest, and she was willing to give it as much time as needed, months, if necessary.

Oh, yes, her interest in Jesse Wagner was very sincere. And if he didn't know that now, he soon would, for she was a determined woman with a mind of her own—and absolutely nothing to lose.

Chapter Three

Jesse set his hat on his head and tapped it into place. As he reached for the buttons on his coat, the door swung open at his back and Tiger stepped down onto the pathway beside him.

"Wind's died down."

"Hallelujah," Jesse said drolly. "Thought I was going to bleed to death, it was so sharp this morning."

Tiger chuckled. "You carp about the cold every year, but I haven't noticed that it slows you down any."

Jesse shot him a narrow look. "No? You just haven't been watching."

"Oh, yes, I have."

Jesse stepped off toward the barn, and Tiger fell in beside him. They walked several steps before Jesse heard himself wondering aloud, "You suppose Handsome's going to spend all afternoon trying to get Caroline to notice him?"

Tiger laughed. "Wouldn't do him no good. That little gal's made her preference real plain."

"Aw, she's just leading him a merry chase," Jesse said dismissively, and he was certain that something clinched, forming a knot beneath his lower rib. He wouldn't admit to a soul, not by word, deed or expression, what Miss Caroline Moncton's pointed regard was doing to him. It'd been a long time since a female's every glance and motion had danced over his nerve endings like electricity between poles. Just the sound of her voice had stoked fires in him that hadn't burned in years. But even if she was serious—and it wasn't likely—he would do nothing about it. He had learned the hard way, long ago, that he was not meant for yoking up. He was one of those old bachelor types not fit for making part of a couple.

Tiger was shaking his head and making negative sounds. "I don't know, Boss. She sure seems mighty fixed on you."

Despite the lurching of his heart, Jesse refused to consider it. "Naw, she's just letting young Handsome know he's met his match and buttering up the boss in the process. You watch, she'll be hanging all over him by week's end."

He wondered if maybe he shouldn't be somewhere else around then. For the first time, he wished Nancy wasn't getting married, but the next instant he backed off that. It was beyond selfish for him to resent having his comfy little arrangement brought to an end, especially as Nance had been so very generous over the years. He'd explained right at the beginning, of course, that he couldn't give her anything but some private fun and the simplest sort of friendship, and he'd been beyond relieved when she'd taken him at his word. It had lasted far longer than he'd intended or expected. If he didn't know quite how to go about making another such arrangement, well, that was probably just another result of the passing years. He was no longer comfortable frequenting the kinds of places where he'd met Nancy Shaver.

Tiger said, "She sure is a looker, that Caroline."

Jesse set his back teeth. She was that. "If you like them barely out of the cradle."

"Oh, I don't figure she's that young," Tiger said. "I did at first, but the way she puts that young buck in his place, she's bound to be past jailbait, anyway."

"She's all of twenty-one," Jesse informed him drily.

"See there," Tiger said with some enthusiasm. "She ain't too young even for you."

"Hell's bells, Tiger!" Jesse exclaimed, coming to a full stop. "That just makes her sixteen, almost seventeen years younger than me! You don't think that's a bit of a gap?"

"Not too much," Tiger muttered, shoving his hands into his coat pockets and hunching his shoulders.

"Huh."

Jesse started walking again. He really didn't want to talk about this anymore, but Tiger wasn't taking the hint. He caught up and matched his strides to Jesse's longer ones, asking, "How d'you know she's twenty-one?"

Jesse's mouth twisted wryly. "She showed me her driver's license, and as a matter of fact, she's only just twenty-one. Her birthday was the eleventh."

"Well, if that don't beat all," Tiger mused, grinning. "Hired on her birthday. Must be some kind of an omen there."

It was an omen, all right, Jess told himself as he quickened his strides, leaving Tiger behind again. It was a sure sign that he was every bit as old as he felt, and that's all it was for him. Usually he didn't mind too much the swift passage of the years, but he found that he was still enough of a bastard not to want to have to watch Handsome make time with that pretty little Caroline.

As a matter of fact, he was darn tired of watching from the sidelines while the world paired up. It was just the sort of thing that had secretly pained him for a long time. It was bad enough that his little brother Ryeland had gotten over his own disastrous first marriage and recently found love again, not that Jess begrudged him his happiness. He'd always suspected that Rye belonged with someone. He'd even encouraged Rye, in his own way, to give love a chance. But Rye was in New Mexico with his new bride, and it was easy to be happy for him at a distance. Now the world's obsession with organizing itself into couples had come right onto the home place where there was no escaping it.

Jess had no doubt that Nancy had meant it as a favor for both himself and young Caroline, but still he wished mightily that she'd kept her lip as tightly buttoned in this case as she had in the past. But there he went again, getting all caught up in himself when his mother so obviously needed the help. Old habits died hard and sometimes not at all, which was exactly why he was on his own—and always would be.

The back door opened, and Sarah recognized Jesse's footsteps in the hall. Her gaze went immediately to Caroline. She had already abandoned the corn bread batter she was putting together and was reaching behind her for the strings of her apron. Tugging them free, she whipped off the utilitarian garment as she moved toward the door. Sarah smiled down at the sink before which she stood. Caroline was obviously doing her best to attract Jesse's attention. She had been throwing herself into Jesse's path at every opportunity for days now. Plunging her hands into the warm dishwater, Sarah listened unabashedly.

"Hello, Jesse," she heard Caroline say warmly.

A heartbeat passed before Jesse boomed in a too-hearty voice, "Well, hello, Miss Caroline," in exactly the same tone he'd use with a precocious six-year-old. Sarah winced.

"Can I get you anything?" Caroline asked hopefully. "A cup of coffee? We have some in the keeper, but I'll be glad to make a fresh pot, if you like."

"Hmm?" Jesse sounded distracted. "Oh. No, thanks. I'll help myself to something later."

Sarah frowned. What was wrong with that son of hers? Didn't he know when a pretty young woman was interested in him? Or had he been alone so long that he'd forgotten the way of things? She shook her head, an old worry nagging at her.

Kay had died so long ago that Sarah sometimes had trouble remembering her late daughter-in-law's face. Yet Jesse continued to hold on to the pain of her loss. It bothered Sarah because it didn't seem right somehow. Before Kay's death, she had worried that the marriage hadn't seemed strong or intense enough. Truthfully, she hadn't been certain that Jesse and Kay were even in love. Having grown up together, they seemed more like friends or buddies than lovers and spouses. But then Kay had died, and Jesse had been stricken in some way that Sarah couldn't even understand. She'd supposed at the time that he'd loved Kay far more than she'd realized. Over the years, however, she'd wondered if it wasn't guilt because of the way Kay had died. It had been an accident, of course, a freakish combination of natural disaster and modern technology, but survivors sometimes blamed themselves, and Jesse did seem compelled to take responsibility for the world at large.

Recently her younger son's happiness in his new marriage had made Sarah realize that she didn't want her older son to continue his solitary existence. Despite the state of her own marriage, she wanted Jesse to know the kind of partnership she and Haney had once had—before age and arthritis had robbed her of the vitality that her husband still possessed. Sarah pushed that thought away as she focused on the sound of Caroline's voice.

"I starched your jeans, just the way you like them," she was saying.

"Did you?" Jesse replied mildly. "That's nice."

Exasperated, Sarah wondered if it was time to have a talk with her thickheaded son. Didn't he realize how hard Caroline worked to please him? She'd put a knife-edge crease on his precious blue jeans. Any food he liked, she saw to it that he had it. He'd gotten his bed changed twice this week because of a passing comment on the pleasure of sleeping on crisp sheets. Sarah expected that Caroline would be ironing them next! And it all went right by Jesse without making the slightest impression. Drying her hands, she turned toward the doorway just as a crestfallen Caroline wandered back into the room. Her resolve suddenly fixed, Sarah lifted her chin.

"Caroline, I completely forgot that I sprinkled powdered cleaner in my shower this morning and it was wet. If one of us doesn't take care of it, that stuff will be set like cement."

"Vinegar will dissolve it. I'll take care of it."

"Thank you, dear." Jesse clumped past the doorway just then, perusing a stack of mail. "Son," Sarah called, "can I have a word with you?"

He stuck his head around the edge of the door frame. "I've got some correspondence to take care of, Mom."

"This won't take long," she insisted.

He shot a wary look at Caroline. Sarah nodded, sending Caroline on her way. Her head down, Caroline slipped past Jess and along the hall, her footsteps light and quick. Only then did Jesse step into the kitchen. Sarah lifted an eyebrow. "You know, don't you, that she's doing everything in her power to make you notice her." It wasn't a question; he'd given himself away in just those few moments. He shrugged.

"Maybe she has a little crush. You know how kids are."

"Yes," Sarah said, "I know how kids are, but Caroline hardly qualifies."

"Oh, come on, Mom. She's practically a teenager."

"I suspect she was practically a teenager at ten. From what she's told me, I think Caroline was one of those youngsters who had to grow up fast. Probably because her mother never has."

Jesse was going through the mail again. "Umm-hmm, probably."

Sarah sighed. "Jesse, haven't you noticed anything special about Caroline at all?"

He nodded without looking up. "Sure."

"And?" Sarah pressed.

He lifted his head then. "She seems to be working out pretty well."

Sarah rolled her eyes. "She's a godsend!"

"Good."

"Is that all, Jesse? Is that really all you have to say about her?"

He shrugged again and turned away, mumbling, "It's kind of nice to have a kid around the place."

Sarah shook her head in disgust and let him go. A kid. He looked at Caroline and all he saw was a kid. She was darned sure that Tiger and especially Handsome, for all the good it did him, saw the lush, lovely young woman that was Caroline Moncton. Well, she shouldn't be surprised, she supposed. Like father, like son.

The one time she'd mentioned to Haney the possibility of Caroline nursing a genuine interest in their son he'd grunted and muttered something about what fools kids could be. It was as if he'd forgotten that he had once quite willingly made a fool of himself over her. But he had loved her then. Before she had gotten too old and too ill to interest him anymore.

Bitterly, Sarah turned back to the sink. The warm water often made her hands feel better, and the ache was suddenly so intense that she felt close to tears.

Caroline looped Sarah's red wool scarf around her throat, tugged the edge up over her ears and stepped down onto the walk, the thermos bottle snug beneath one arm. Clumsy in a pair of Haney's old galoshes, she turned and firmly shoved the door closed. The house was so well insulated and the windows and doors so tightly fitted that it was a little bit like uncorking a bottle when one went in and out. To Caroline that was more proof of how high a priority Jesse placed on his home. Her own airy duplex apartment seemed insubstantial by comparison. God knew that every errant breeze found its way inside to chill her at night. She imagined that Jesse slept warm and peacefully in his neat, second-story room, and it only seemed right, since he had to spend much of every day working in the blustery, freezing weather.

Fresh snowfall had been shoveled off the walk, and she shuffled easily down it in the big boots, wondering how Jesse stood the constant cold. She was a bit worried about him. He hadn't come in for his coffee break this morning in order to nurse a sick horse, and even though Tiger and Handsome had told her that the barn was relatively warm, she felt that he needed the fortification of a hot cup of coffee.

It was just like Jesse to give up his coffee break in order to nurse a sick horse. He sure loved those horses, and in her short time at the ranch she had learned that Jesse's horses brought in as much and sometimes more income than the cattle. She'd felt a spurt of pride when she'd heard that, but she wasn't surprised, not at all. Jesse Wagner was a man who could do things, important things. He could certainly take care of his home, his family, his horses, his vehicles, his ranch and everyone on it. There wasn't much, frankly, that he couldn't and didn't do, at least as far as she could tell, and it wasn't fair that he should have to miss his midmorning coffee.

She reached the end of the walk and stepped carefully onto the ground, keeping to the path that the men had forged through the freshly fallen snow. She had to raise her feet high and curl her toes back with every step to keep the overlarge boots from slipping, but she did so with studied deliberation. Jesse wouldn't like it if she wasn't careful. He expected everyone to be as careful and responsible as he was. When she'd realized that was why he'd scolded her for not having the proper outerwear to endure the weather, she'd gone right out and bought the finest insulated gloves that she could afford. She intended to purchase a warm muffler next, and then a good hat. She hoped he would be pleased. He might not notice the other little things that she had done to please him, but her lack of adequate outerwear had been of some concern to him from the beginning. Surely he would notice.

She was winded by the time she reached the open area around the big metal barn at the bottom of the hill, but at least the snow had been packed down by vehicle and animal traffic so that the going was definitely easier. Every so often, a big, fat flake wafted past the end of her nose, reminding her that more were on their way. She hoped that Jesse's horse would be better before the next big storm broke. Her footsteps crunched across the packed, icy snow, and once or twice she broke through the crust and slipped a bit, but all in all, the trip was an uneventful one.

The bar was set on the big sliding door in the end of the barn, so she went to the small side door and tried the handle. The padlock hung loose, but the heavy metal door felt frozen in place. Gripping the thermos more tightly, she put her shoulder into it and forced it back a few inches, working her way through. This end of the barn was dark and cavernous and filled with vehicles and other heavy equipment, but a light shone about midway down the row of stalls below the loft to her left. She hurried that way, shivering in the heavy shadows, but as she drew closer to the light and farther beneath the loft, the air grew warmer and more fragrant. Her footsteps slowed as she began to take notice of the many animals housed in two rows of stalls flanking a muddy cement center aisle strewn lightly with hay. A horse occasionally neighed or blustered. A cow mooed complainingly. Hooves clunked against stall walls. Teeth crunched and ground bits of feed. Eventually she heard a low voice.

"All right now, let's get this off and see how we're doing. Whoa now. Hold on. Hold on."

She stopped and peered into the stall. The rump of a big, golden brown horse shifted to one side, allowing her a glimpse of Jesse, bending at the waist and lifting a front hoof. He was unwinding what appeared to be a dark, heavy, bulky bandage.

"Almost there. Almost. Ah." He straightened and set aside the fat bandage, draping it over the stall wall. It promptly slid down again, but he caught it before it hit the ground.

"Want me to hold that?"

He jerked around at the sound of Caroline's voice, the horse awkwardly shifting. "What're you doing here?"

She set the thermos on a thick post. "Thought you could use some coffee."

His gaze flickered over her and away. "New gloves?"

She smiled brightly. "Yes. Do you like them?"

He shrugged. "What matters is that they keep your hands warm."

"They do."

He made no answer to that. Instead, he slid her a narrow look and said reprovingly, "Isn't that my mother's scarf?"

Some of the pleasure of having him notice the gloves evaporated. Her smile faltered. "Yes, yes, it is. But I intend to buy my own very soon."

"See that you do."

She looked down at her feet, hoping he wouldn't ask about the faded galoshes, and said, "What's wrong with your horse?"

"He has an infection in the fetlock," Jesse explained. "There doesn't seem to be any cut, though, so I'm hoping it's an abscess caused by a bruise. I'm trying to draw it to a head so I can lance it." He flopped the bandage over the wall again. It slid off again. He tossed it over his shoulder, but when he bent forward, it flopped on the ground. He made a disgusted sound, scooped it up and straightened once more.

"Is there some reason I shouldn't hold that?" she asked lightly.

Reluctance seemed to slow his movements as he turned toward her and extended the puffy strip of plastic and leather. "It's hot."

She took it carefully into her hands, surprised at its weight. "Oh, I see. It's some sort of chemical hot pack."

Jesse turned away and bent to lift the horse's hoof again. The horse snuffled and shifted aside. It seemed unwilling to place any weight on the leg Jesse was determinedly examining.

"What if it isn't an abscess caused by a bruise?"

He studied the fetlock, saying, "Then I'll have to call a vet and get a stronger antibiotic than anything I have on hand."

"But you don't want to do that," she surmised correctly.

He let down the hoof and straightened. "I don't like to use antibiotics unless I have to. Horses are just like humans. They develop resistances and reactions to medications. "He slapped the horse lightly on the rump. "We'll let it rest a few minutes, old son, then apply the heat again."

He let himself out of the stall, sweeping the thermos into one hand. He draped an elbow over the closed gate and leaned against it, pushing back his hat. He seemed intent on avoiding her eyes. She gulped when his gaze dropped to her feet. Something twitched in his cheek, and she heard the humor lacing his voice when he said, "Where on earth did you get those boots?"

She curled her toes back, feeling unaccountably lightened. "They're an old pair of your father's."

He chuckled as he twisted off the top of the thermos and then the stopper. "Somehow I can't see my father wearing yellow galoshes. You sure those are his?"

"Your mother said they were."

"I've never seen him in them."

"She said she bought them for him years ago."

"Ah. That explains it then. He's let her think he was wearing them while they bounced around in the back of his old truck until they looked properly used. He's probably congratulating himself because he hasn't been found out. You won't tell her, will you?" He snapped her a look that was part humor, part warning.

"No, of course not. That would be mean, when he's so obviously tried to spare her feelings."

Apparently satisfied, Jesse poured steaming coffee into the cup top of the thermos and replaced the stopper in the bottle. Setting aside the bottle, he sipped the hot brew from the top. "This is good, but you didn't have to bring it down."

"I don't mind," Caroline said.

He sipped more coffee. The silence grew strained. He turned

and propped his forearms on the edge of the gate, watching the horse. "Well, thanks for the coffee. You can get on back to the house now."

She leaned against a post. "I'm in no hurry. I'd kind of like to rest a few minutes before I head back up the hill."

He nodded and continued to watch the horse. She had the distinct feeling that he was avoiding eye contact. She tried to think of something to say, some topic of conversation so compelling that it would overcome any resistance on his part. Then suddenly she realized that this was the perfect opportunity to discuss something that had been worrying her. She carefully draped the hot pack over the top of the square post against which she leaned and anchored it with her hands, saying, "Actually, Jesse, I want to talk to you about something."

"Oh?" He didn't turn to face her, didn't indicate any real interest in any way.

Caroline gathered her thoughts before proceeding carefully. "I've had some time to get to know your mother. Sarah's a wonderful woman. She's made me feel so welcome and appreciated."

"That's nice."

"Very nice," she confirmed, hurrying on. "I'm sure I don't have to tell you how much of a problem her condition is, but I'm pretty sure that she's in a lot more pain than she lets on." He finally turned to face her. Caroline rushed to explain, "I've caught her several times—accidentally, of course—with tears in her eyes. She'll never comment about what's wrong, but I can tell that she's hurting."

Jesse clapped a hand over the back of his neck and rubbed it distractedly. "I should've been paying more attention."

"It's not your fault!" Caroline exclaimed. "She doesn't want anyone to know. It's only because my work keeps me in the house that I've noticed."

"Why wouldn't she want anyone to know?"

Caroline shrugged. "Maybe she just doesn't want to worry you."

He nodded, frowning. "Yeah, that sounds like Mom."

"Maybe she doesn't think anything can be done."

Jesse's brow furrowed. "She's seeing a doctor."

"Regularly?"

"Well, whenever she needs to."

"But is he a specialist?" Caroline asked.

Jesse looked at her in surprise. "Do they have arthritis specialists?"

"They must," Caroline said. "They have specialists for everything else."

Jesse rubbed his chin. "Hmm, I bet you're right. Wonder where we could find one?"

"Maybe your family practitioner could recommend one," Caroline suggested. "Or maybe someone else. I'll ask around if you like, see if anyone I know has had any experience with this kind of thing."

He was nodding. "I'll mention it to my brother and some friends."

"What about your dad?"

Jesse inclined his head thoughtfully. "He tried a while back to interest her in some clinic, but she resisted, and he let it drop. Maybe I should ask him about it."

Caroline nodded. "Maybe you should."

"Poor Mom," Jesse said with a sigh.

Caroline resisted the urge to reach out to him. He seemed so troubled now, and it really wasn't his fault. "Your mother has a kind of nobility about her that I really admire," she told him softly. "She obviously loves you so much that she'd rather suffer in silence than worry you."

He smiled. "That's true."

"She obviously realizes what a very good son you are."

"Oh, it's not that," he said. "You know how it is with parents. Always putting their offspring first."

Caroline lifted her brows and said with some humor, "Spoken like the very secure product of a stable, mature, two-parent family."

He jerked his head around, spearing her with a probing look. "You sound like your experience in the area has been pretty dismal."

She shrugged again and propped her chin atop her folded hands, which were toasty warm now because of the heat radiating from the hot pack through her gloves. "Just different. I mean, my mother and I love each other, but she's not what you'd call the selfless type. In fact, I'm not sure she understands the concept."

"Sounds like it might have been pretty tough for you," he commented gently.

"Let's just say that I intend a different experience for my own kids."

"How so?"

She smiled. "Well, for one thing, they'll know their father, singular on the father, and they won't have to wonder where I am or what I'm doing when I'm not with them or if I'll be coming home that night. They'll have everything they need—but not everything they want. There's a difference, you know."

He smiled at that, his smoky blue eyes sparkling. "So my parents explained to me many a time."

"See, that's what I mean. A really good parent puts what's best for the child first, even when the child might not understand at the time."

"Sounds like you're going to be a good mother."

"Well, thank you. What a lovely thing to say." Caroline was thrilled. She wanted to laugh and throw her arms around him. Instead she said wistfully, "I just know you'll be a good father, the very best."

The warmth and good humor slid from his face, and it was as if an invisible wall went up. When he spoke again, it was with the same polite, interested tone, but it came from a disturbing distance—and he completely ignored the compliment. "You must have had some pretty good influence from somewhere."

"Experience is a powerful teacher."

"What about other family? I know your grandparents are deceased and your aunt's up north somewhere. Any uncles? Cousins?"

She shrugged. "Not so far as I know. Really, there's just my mom."

"Who's off in sunny California."

"I'm sure she is by now."

He looked her over contemplatively. "You haven't heard from her?"

"Oh, it would never occur to my mom to call to let me know she's all right. But don't worry, I'll hear from her if there's a problem."

He frowned. "Boy, you really are on your own, aren't you?"

She nodded. "For now."

He studied her a moment longer before tossing back the last of the coffee in the cup. He screwed it back into place and set the thermos atop the corner post at his elbow, saying, "Well, I have work to do, and I'm sure Mom's waiting for you back at the house."

She knew when she'd been dismissed. "Sure. Just bring the thermos back to the house with you when you come in later."

"Will do," he said reaching for the hot pack. She backed away, pressing her warm hands to her face. He carried the hot pack into the stall, concentrating on the horse again. She stepped up and shut the stall gate behind him.

"See you later."

"Mmm."

Reluctantly, she moved away. She'd taken two steps when he said, "Oh, Caroline?"

She turned back hopefully. "Yes?"

He cast a look over his shoulder. "Thanks for telling me about Mother."

She smiled and nodded. He looked away, bending to wrap the hot pack around the horse's fetlock. She started down the corridor once more.

"And be careful!" Jesse called, his deep voice skittering along her nerve endings.

Caroline smiled to herself as she shuffled away. He just couldn't help it. Jesse cared for everyone and everything around him. He would be a good father. Her smile faded at the memory of his reaction to that statement she'd made earlier. What was it about the idea that troubled him so? Perhaps even frightened him? Or was it something else, something...deeper? She shook her head. It didn't make any sense. Jesse was everything any child could ask for in a parent. She must be wrong about what had happened back there. Something else had been going on, and in time she was sure she'd come to understand. What mattered right now was that Jesse see her for who she was, that he get to know the real her. What happened after that, only time would tell.

Jesse waited until Caroline's shuffling footsteps receded before he straightened and turned to watch her make her way down the long corridor between the stalls. She ought to look ridiculous in those enormous, faded yellow galoshes, like a kid playing dress up, but somehow she managed to maintain a certain fragile dignity in her borrowed gear, not to mention a rampant sexuality that made him distinctly uncomfortable. She was barely out of her teens, for pity's sake, an innocent. He had no business noticing the sway of her hips beneath that ridiculous, fake rabbit coat or the long, slender length of her legs.

She might be an innocent, but she was no airhead. Her sensible suggestions concerning his mother's condition illustrated that. In fact, he was grateful for her concern. It disturbed him greatly to hear that his mother was often reduced to tears by the pain of her arthritis, and he was newly determined to do something about it. He'd been concerned himself for some time now, but discussions with Haney had induced him to let it go. In Haney's opinion, arthritis was a natural condition of advancing age, one that Sarah would want to endure with as little fanfare as possible. But how could he stand by and allow his mother to suffer to the point of tears? Surely something more could be done than merely taking frequent doses of aspirin. Jesse made a mental note to call his brother for his input that very evening, and then he would properly thank Caroline. He hadn't meant to seem ungrateful before; it was just so difficult to know how to deal with her.

Unfortunately she was not the complete child he wanted to believe her to be. What little he knew of her mother caused him to wonder if she ever had been. Apparently her mother's lack of maturity had forced Caroline to grown up much too quickly, and Jesse considered that a great pity. Every child deserved a carefree, secure childhood. God knew that he and his brother had enjoyed that halcyon period early in their lives. He sure wouldn't have wanted to endure what had come afterward without those golden days to remember. Those were still his best memories, playing good guy and outlaw with his brother, taking turns rescuing Kay from pretended dangers.

He wished to God above that he truly had been able to rescue Kay from that jolt of electricity that had taken her life, and he knew that the best way to have done it would have been not to marry her in the first place. If he hadn't married her, they wouldn't have been in that mountain hideaway trying to rekindle a fire that had never blazed to begin with. The storm that had knocked down the utility poles in the restaurant would have been nothing more than an inconvenience, and she wouldn't have stepped in that puddle where the live wire lay. The jolt wouldn't have knocked them both off their feet and knocked the life from her. He still occasionally had nightmares about it, especially about the way her hand had clutched his even in death. It had been as though her hand had welded to his. Even now he wasn't completely free of it, and he never would be.

Poor sweet, naive Caroline thought, assumed, that he would make a good father. Once he had thought so, too, but a good father first had to be a good husband, and Jesse knew from bitter experience that the role of husband was one he was not cut out to play.

Chapter Four

"Are you sure you want to do this, dear?"

Caroline laid down the pencil and reached across the kitchen table, covering Sarah's gnarled hand with her own. "Absolutely."

"This goes above and beyond the call of duty, you know."

"I don't see it that way."

"Don't see what what way?" Jesse asked, suddenly appearing in the doorway, his empty coffee cup in hand.

Caroline beamed. She couldn't help it. He was such a delightful sight, so tall and solid and powerfully male. He didn't seem to be avoiding her anymore, at least not as assiduously as before. He leaned a shoulder against the door frame and casually stared back at her while his mother explained.

"Caroline's going to cook Thanksgiving dinner for us. I'm going to call Rye and Kara and Champ and see if they can come. Oh, and Shoes Kanaka. It's been too long since we spent time with him. Tiger will be here, too, of course." She turned her attention back to Caroline. "Handsome has family here, but Tiger's always with us. His folks are way down in south Texas."

Jesse was still looking at Caroline. "Uh-huh. Sounds great. Still doesn't answer my question, though."

Caroline smiled patiently. "Your mother thinks cooking Thanksgiving dinner for you is, to use her words, 'above and beyond the call of duty.' I disagree." She glanced at Sarah. "I'm grateful, actually. I've never roasted a full turkey before. I'll need guidance."

Sarah chuckled affectionately. "I've yet to see anything you couldn't and didn't do to perfection."

"That's because you just see what I want you to see," Caroline told her truthfully.

Sarah shook her head. "I see more than you think." Her eyes glinted knowingly.

Jesse pushed away from the door frame and walked across the kitchen to pour coffee into his cup. He leaned back against the counter, crossing his legs at the ankle. Caroline didn't have to look at him to know that he was listening and watching. She tried to wrap her mind around the question of whether or not Sarah was implying that she knew Caroline was interested in Jesse, but she couldn't think beyond Jesse himself. After a moment Sarah bent her head over the piece of paper on the table between them.

"Let's see. We have turkey and dressing and giblet gravy. That broccoli thing you were talking about for me. Sounds so good! And Haney's deviled eggs. That man loves deviled eggs. And Tiger will want candied beets. I'll write down the recipe for you. We ought to have some kind of potatoes, don't you think? Creamed, probably. We should do a lemon meringue pie for Shoes. He dearly loves lemon meringue pie."

It was obvious to Caroline that Sarah was trying to put together a menu with something special for everyone, and she kept waiting for Jesse's favorite to come up, but her patience was pretty quickly exhausted with him standing there, his presence permeating everything in the room. She pivoted in her chair to look at him. "What about you, Jesse? What do you want for Thanksgiving dinner?"

He shrugged. "All sounds good to me."

"But isn't there something special you want included?"

He set aside his coffee cup and folded his arms. "Mustard greens," he said.

Caroline's eyebrows went up. Mustard greens? She didn't know anyone who actually liked mustard greens.

Sarah laughed. "Mustard greens swimming in a clear jalapeño sauce, hot enough to melt the bowl," she said.

"For Thanksgiving?" Caroline asked.

Jesse rubbed a hand over his chin. "You asked."

Caroline picked up the pencil and wrote down mustard greens in jalapeño sauce. With corn bread. She trusted that Sarah had that recipe, too.

"What about you?" Jesse asked.

She sent him a surprised look. "What about me?"

"What favorite of yours are you going to include on the menu?"

She blinked at him. She honestly hadn't thought beyond cooking the meal itself. "Oh, I won't be staying to eat. I couldn't—"

"Of course you will!" Sarah exclaimed.

"No, really. I don't want to intrude."

"You're just going to cook and go?" Jesse said.

"That's what you pay me for," Caroline replied carefully.

He snorted at that and renegotiated his position, uncrossing his ankles and rolling his weight onto one hip. "You don't have family to eat with."

"No, but—"

"This is silly," Sarah said to Caroline. "You eat with us every day. You'll either eat with us on Thanksgiving or you won't cook."

"But—"

Jesse pushed away from the counter and retrieved his cup, strolling past Caroline to the doorway. "Give up, Blondie. You're not going to plan and cook the feast and then go home alone to a TV dinner. Nobody here would enjoy the meal that way. So either say yes or we all eat TV dinners. I mean it."

He actually smiled down at her, and her heart turned over in her chest. She whispered, "Yes." Happiness swelled inside her. They really seemed to want her here.

His smile grew satisfied, smug even. "Good," he said, turning away. "I sure don't want to miss my mustard greens." He winked and went through the door, disappearing from view.

Caroline sat very still. Did that wink mean that he really didn't want to miss *her?* The hope she felt was so acute that it was very nearly painful. She could barely pretend to pay attention as Sarah went on with planning the menu, but somehow she managed, and gradually the euphoria hardened into resolve. She was going to be with Jesse and his family and friends on Thanksgiving, a real Thanksgiving. Her first.

She was nervous. It was ridiculous; she'd been cooking for the family and hands for some time now, and she was confident in her abilities. She certainly hadn't had any complaints. Yet she was nervous, nervous and excited and happy. For the first time she would sit at a Thanksgiving table with someone other than her mother and, on occasion, one of her mother's boyfriends. Those times had been the worst, for whenever Irene had a man around, she had no time for anyone else. Dinner had often been eaten in front of the television set on those occasions, with the man in question hollering advice to some football team or other.

It was true that Sarah had scheduled this year's Thanksgiving dinner around a football game, but she'd assured Caroline that she would enjoy the day. Sarah intended to watch the game herself and was happier than Caroline had seen her so far, even though her younger son wouldn't be joining the family for dinner, after all. Maybe Sarah's mood had to do with the fact that Rye had promised to come Christmas and stay for a week or so, bringing his family with him. Whatever the reason, Caroline was glad to see Sarah smiling and hear her humming as they worked together in the kitchen.

"This broccoli torte smells so good!" she said after checking the oven once more. "I love ricotta cheese."

"Think Jesse will like it?" Caroline asked absently, stirring the mustard greens. The aroma wafting up from the pot was enough to clear the most tightly clogged sinuses. Sarah chuckled.

"Honey, after he tucks into those greens he won't be able to taste anything else."

"Look who's here." Haney walked into the kitchen and

brought another man with him. Sarah laughed and opened her arms.

"Kanaka!"

Caroline watched as the man embraced Sarah. Of only average height, he nevertheless gave the impression of being a large, powerful man of quiet dignity. As the two separated, Caroline noticed that his ink black hair was quite long and clubbed at the nape with a strip of painted leather. His facial features were those of one of the area's indigenous Indian tribes. His dark eyes danced merrily as they made a blatant perusal of her.

"Shoes Kanaka," Sarah said, performing the introductions, "I'd like you to meet my good right arm."

Shoes Kanaka folded his hands together in front of him. Inclining his head, he said solemnly, "Hello, Good Right Arm."

Caroline laughed, and Sarah slapped him playfully on the shoulder. "Her name is Caroline Moncton."

"But if you have to give her another name, call her Blondie," said Jesse, striding into the now crowded room. He clapped Shoes Kanaka on the back and cuffed him lightly about the head. "How's my newly married brother?"

"Happy."

"And yourself?"

"Happy for him."

"Me, too. Glad you could make it. Wait'll you taste her cooking."

Kanaka smiled serenely and pushed his gaze back to the "her" in question. Caroline smiled back. "She cooks, too?" he murmured smoothly.

Caroline blushed, while everyone else laughed and Haney said, "According to Sarah she's even more useful than she is pretty."

"She. Her. Blondie. And what name do you prefer?" Shoes asked, his disturbingly discerning gaze never leaving her face.

She shrugged and tried not to look at Jesse. "I'd settle for Good Right Arm."

"Oh, no, you won't!" Sarah exclaimed laughingly.

"Caroline is a beautiful name," Shoes Kanaka said. His dark eyes swept over her. "Blondie is apt. But Caroline suits better."

She smiled at him. "Thank you. Caroline it is. Now, do I call you Kanaka or *Shoes?*'' She let her tone convey her puzzlement at the odd moniker. His smile became a silent chuckle.

"I am a farrier by trade, Caroline. That means I—"

"Shoe horses. I see."

"It makes more sense when you realize that his Chako name is virtually unpronounceable," Jesse said.

Kanaka put on an offended expression. "Only for weak-minded whites," he said mildly, and everyone laughed at Jesse's comeuppance. Everyone but Caroline. Shoes Kanaka noticed. With a smile he said, "Perhaps you should judge for yourself. My Chako name is Wilipikin'ao'oa'nikilswaume."

Caroline blinked, lost after the first half dozen guttural syllables. "Well, we could always call you Willie," she quipped, and the look on Shoes Kanaka's face made everyone laugh.

After his initial reaction, which was something between surprise and horror, Shoes put his head back and roared. Tears were rolling down his cheeks when he finally managed to say, "I think Kanaka, if you do not mind, Caroline."

"All right," Caroline said, chuckling. "It's nice to meet you, Kanaka."

Kanaka took both her hands in his and stacked them one on top of the other, squeezing them flat between his own. "It's nice to meet you, Caroline," he said formally. Then he patted his middle, grinned and asked, "When do we eat?" That set everyone off again.

Sarah eventually got the men out of the kitchen. Caroline listened to their laughter and banter from the den as she and Sarah hurried to put the final touches on the meal. Tiger showed up and was accepted into the camaraderie of his fellows. Finally it was all on the table. Sarah called everyone in and directed them to their seats. Haney and Jesse got the head and foot of the table, with Sarah on Haney's right and Caroline on Jesse's. Tiger sat next to Caroline, Kanaka next to Sarah and on Jesse's left, which put him opposite Caroline.

"Now," Sarah said firmly, "I want everyone here to name at least one thing he or she is thankful for. Haney, you start."

Haney made a face, but then he cleared his throat and said, "I'm thankful Rye is happily settled with Kara in New Mexico."

A chorus of "Here, here!" went around the table. Haney looked at Tiger.

Tiger swallowed and said, "You tell him and I'll deny it, but... I'm thankful for Handsome. He's been a lot of help around here."

"Amen to that," Jesse said, "and anyone who repeats it will answer to me."

Everyone laughed, but then it was Caroline's turn. She couldn't keep her gaze off Jesse's face. "I'm thankful for my job and...for new friends."

Jesse smiled and addressed the table at large. "Well, I don't even know where to begin. Guess I'll sum it all up by saying I'm very thankful for this place and for my family and for friends, old and new." Caroline smiled down at her plate, hoping he included her in there somewhere.

Shoes had the floor, and he was smiling almost secretively. "I echo Haney in this. I've never seen Rye and Champ so happy. New Mexico and Kara have been good for them. Also for me." He said this with some surprise. "We're putting together a new business venture, Rye and I...and a very fierce Jicarilla Apache from the reservation down there."

"I hear she's really something to look at, too," Jesse said meaningfully.

Kanaka grinned. "She can cut your heart out and make you want to watch," he said.

The men hooted, and Sarah announced gleefully, "I smell romance in the air!"

"Maybe," Shoes admitted. "I'm working on it."

"Well, that's something definitely to be thankful for," Sarah said.

"I want to hear more about this business venture," Haney said.

"Later," Sarah told him. "It's my turn now." She looked around the table. "I'm always thankful for my family and for friends, as well, but right now, I'm especially thankful for a recent addition." She looked directly at Caroline, who caught her breath in shock. "You've no idea how much easier you've made my life, dear," she said to Caroline. "I can't thank you enough for all that you do."

"But it's just my job," Caroline pointed out meekly.

"Nonsense," Sarah said. "You go way beyond what we pay you to do, and don't think I haven't noticed."

Caroline blushed. Her eyes filled with tears. She'd been thinking only about Jesse and making him like her when she'd come here. She hadn't counted on this. She gulped and managed to say, "Thank you. I love it here."

"Good," Sarah said, and with a satisfied nod, she turned to her husband. "You can carve up that bird now. I'm starved!"

Caroline bowed her head and blinked back the tears while everyone else got down to the business of filling their plates. To her everlasting delight, she felt Jesse's big, heavy hand gently, briefly pat her knee, but before she could even glance her gratitude to him, he was reaching for the mustard greens.

The meal was a delight for Caroline. She heard her cooking praised by everyone present—even Sarah, who had overseen everything and contributed recipes as well as ample guidance. Conversation focused on the business venture Shoes and Rye were considering, a re-creation of an Old West cattle drive, complete with Indians and chuck wagon for paying tourists. That turned into a detailed account of the very real cattle drive Rye had undertaken in order to save his wife, Kara's, New Mexico ranch. Caroline had heard and read the news accounts, of course, like everyone else, but the details were interesting and sometimes shocking.

It was hard to believe that sheer greed could make Kara's own cousin repeatedly attempt sabotage and even murder to keep Kara from saving her ranch. But thanks to Rye, Kara succeeded, and the hardship of the experience had forged a relationship between the two that had led to love, marriage, and by all accounts, happiness for Rye, Kara and Rye's son by a first marriage, Champ. It sounded as though it might yet lead to romance for Shoes Kanaka, too.

They were all groaning by the time Haney announced that the ball game was about to start, and dessert hadn't even been served yet. The men immediately rose to their feet. Caroline saw Sarah wring her hands lightly, a sure sign that she was hurting, but Sarah gamely began clearing the table.

Caroline snagged Jesse's sleeve as he moved by her. A nod in his mother's direction answered the question that he looked down at her. Comprehension immediately set his face. While the other men headed for the living room, he walked around the table to his mother's side.

"Do you have anything to take, Mom?"

"What?"

"You're hurting, aren't you?" he said softly. Sarah looked up, apologetic and woeful. He put his arm around her. "Stop acting like you've done something wrong. Arthritis is a disease, Mom, not an insult. I want you to take something for the pain and go into the living room and relax. Caroline and I will take care of this." He nodded at the table.

"Oh, no," Sarah said. "You go watch the game. I'll—"

"We won't be a minute," Jesse said firmly. "Now, do you have something to take or not?"

Sarah reached into her pocket and pulled out a small plastic box. "Caroline put them in a flip-top box for me," she said. "I can't get the bottles open anymore."

"We have a lot to thank Caroline for these days," Jesse said, reaching for Sarah's water glass.

"We certainly do," Sarah murmured. Using her thumb to push up the top of the box, she shook out two small pills before closing the box and dropping it back into her pocket. She put the pills into her mouth and reached for the glass Jesse held. The glass wavered and shook in her hand, but she got the pills down, and Jesse took the glass away, returning it safely to the table. He glanced worriedly at Caroline, who was quietly gathering up dishes. "Go on," Jesse said to his mother, gently pushing her toward the doorway. "I want to talk to Caroline, anyway, and this is as good a time as any."

Sarah relented. "Oh, all right. But I'll be in to help you wash up later, Caroline. The hot water seems to do my hands good." Caroline smiled and nodded. Sarah shook a crooked finger at Jesse. "You two hurry up, now."

"We will," Jesse said, reaching for a half-empty bowl of potatoes whipped with sour cream and roasted garlic. "We want to watch the game, too."

"We'll be quick," Caroline assured her. Sarah went off with

a little smile curving her mouth. "You wanted to talk to me?" Caroline asked of Jesse after Sarah was gone.

He shrugged. "I just said that to get her moving, but I might as well tell you how much I appreciate what you do around here. You're right about her being in pain too much, and I appreciate you letting me in on that particular secret."

"Thanks, but I'm just trying to do a good job."

"I don't think we have to worry about that," he said lightly, adding, "I'm looking into getting her help, and my brother is, too. I spoke to him about it the other night."

"I'm glad to hear that, but you don't have to help with the table," Caroline told him. "I'm perfectly capable of handling this by myself. It is, after all, what you pay me for."

"Don't be stupid," he said bluntly. "This is a holiday, and today you're not just the cook and chief bottle washer, you're a guest, too. Now move it. I really do want to watch that game."

Caroline laughed. "What is it about men and football?"

"It's not just men," he said defensively. "Mom loves football. You probably would, too, if you knew anything about it."

"Maybe you can teach me."

"Deal, provided we can get in there before the first quarter ends."

"What's a quarter?"

Jesse laughed and launched into an explanation as they carried dishes into the kitchen. Her head was spinning with football rules, objectives and anecdotes by the time they joined the others in the den, the leftovers put away and the dirty dishes soaking. Jesse was glad to hear that no one had scored by the time they joined the others watching the game. Caroline was relieved to hear that the first quarter had not yet ended. He dropped down on one end of the couch next to Shoes and Tiger. Haney occupied his usual easy chair and Sarah the other. She shoved the comfy ottoman at Caroline with her foot. Caroline rolled it over to the end of the couch and sat down next to Jesse, who was busily and loudly explaining what was taking place while talking encouragement to his team of choice.

Caroline didn't understand a moment of it, but she had great fun just watching the others and listening to Jesse's convoluted explanations and the good-natured arguments they inevitably spawned. She began to realize that watching the game was as much a game as the game itself! And she naturally took Jesse's side in every argument. After all, he was her teacher. His point of view was the only one that made any sense to her or even registered. At halftime, Sarah asked who wanted dessert, and to Caroline's surprise, everyone did.

Shoes raved about the lemon meringue pie. Haney gobbled up two pieces of the pumpkin without comment or pause. Jesse savored a huge chunk of fresh apple cake, which Sarah had told Caroline was his favorite, and Tiger, to Caroline's amazement, ate some of everything. Sarah nibbled pumpkin pie and cake, but Caroline couldn't bear the idea of swallowing another bite. She concentrated on getting everyone served and keeping their coffee cups filled before the game resumed.

As they all trooped back to the den, she was surprised and pleased when Jesse volunteered to trade places with her, saying, "You're probably tired of sitting on that ottoman without anything to lean back against." It was Kanaka who insisted on taking the ottoman, however, and so Caroline wound up sitting right next to Jesse on the couch. When Jesse lifted his arm and stretched it along the back of the sofa at one point, Caroline told herself that it was a casual, thoughtless gesture having more to do with his own comfort than any intention to get closer to her, but she couldn't help the small flutter of excitement that began in her chest and moved lower until she was almost embarrassed by it. No matter what Jesse was thinking—and he didn't even seem to notice that his arm was almost around her—the fact remained that this was the best Thanksgiving she'd ever known, and it was all due to Jesse. She intended to make sure that he knew how happy he'd made her today.

Jesse stretched and inhaled the cold, sharp air. It had been a good day—the company, the food, the atmosphere. His team had even won. What more could a man ask for? The door opened, and Shoes Kanaka stepped out onto the porch with him, shrugging into his coat.

"Hey, chief! You out for a breath of fresh air, too? Or are you leaving us?"

"I'm off. It's getting late, and all that good food is making me sleepy."

Jesse nodded. "You know you're welcome to stay for the night. We always have a bed with your name on it."

"I know, and I appreciate it. You are my second family. But my first deserves some of my time, too. I'm heading out to the reservation. My uncle expects me."

"How is Man Father?"

"Well. Di'wana's death is still difficult for us all, but his faith is strong, and she is at peace. It helps, frankly, that Rye and Champ are happy with Kara now."

"I know what you mean. I worried Rye would never find real happiness, and that would surely affect Champ. I'm glad for them all."

"I, also." He lifted a hand to the back of his neck, slipped it beneath his ponytail and rubbed leisurely. "It's kind of hard to watch sometimes, though."

"What do you mean? What's hard to watch?"

"Rye and Kara," Shoes said. "They're so hot for each other they practically smoke. They kind of eat each other with their eyes, you know? Kind of like you and that little Caroline."

Jesse nearly dropped, his knees suddenly weak. "Are you nuts? You been smoking or something, having visions?"

Shoes chuckled and tucked his fingertips into his jean pockets. "Jesse, that girl hangs on every word you say. She can't keep her eyes off you—and vice versa."

Jesse tried to laugh it off. "She's just a kid. She wants to impress the boss."

"She doesn't look like any kid I ever saw," Shoes commented, "and don't try to tell me you haven't noticed."

"She's a pretty girl," Jesse said tartly, "but she's way too young, and she's not my type."

Shoes sent him a scathing look. "She's every man's type, and you darn well know it. Long silky hair, face like an angel. There's nothing wrong with her figure, either. She ought to be six feet tall with all that leg."

Jesse clenched his hands into fists and bit his tongue. She wasn't a piece of meat, for pity's sake, to be chewed over like a morsel tossed to the dogs. But he knew that any comment would damn him for sure. He managed a shrug.

"So what? The world's full of—"

Shoes cut him off. "Yeah, right, and every one of them hovers around you like a fairy godmother waiting to grant your every wish."

Jesse gulped. He'd feared that he was the one hovering. "Teach me football," she'd said, and he'd taken it as a calling. Had everyone noticed? "You, uh, you're reading more into it than is there," he finally said, hunching his shoulders against the cold. Funny, the air no longer seemed brisk and bracing. It had developed a definite bite rather quickly.

Shoes kept staring at him for a long, awkward moment, but then he sighed and said, "Man, you Wagners have heads like cement." He was smiling when he said it, though, and Jesse chose to laugh it off.

"Well, when that's where you keep landing, you either develop a thick skull or you die."

"We Indians prefer thick souls," Shoes said cryptically, and Jesse shook his head.

"Philosophy, now? What next?"

"War paint and weapons," Shoes quipped.

Jesse threw up both hands. "I give! Just leave the hair."

"No self-respecting warrior would be caught with your hair on his belt."

"Insults are the last resort of a desperate man."

"Naw, just a sleepy one." Shoes rubbed his eyes with both hands. "I'm gone, my friend. See you at Christmas, huh?"

"You bet. Give my best to your uncle."

Nodding, Shoes went down the steps and out into the night. A few moments later, Jesse heard his truck start up. He watched the headlights come on and the sweep of the twin beams as the heavy van made a U-turn and headed for the road, turning right, toward the reservation.

Jesse stared long after the truck was gone around the bend. He kept hearing Kanaka's deep, resonant voice inside his head.

Doesn't look like any kid I ever saw. Six feet tall with all that leg. Hovering over you like a fairy godmother ready to grant your every wish.

He thought about sitting next to her on the couch, her slender form tucked neatly against him. They hadn't touched, but he'd felt her all along his side. It had seemed silly for her to sit anywhere else, right for her to be next to him, and that chilled him more than the cold night. He'd had enough fresh air. He turned toward the door just as it opened and a familiar rabbit coat stepped outside.

"Jesse."

He backed away instinctively. Finding his voice took a moment, but he was relieved to find it hearty and light. "Caroline. Calling it a night? I was just about to go in myself. Eating's real tiring work. Cooking and eating, now, that must be downright exhausting. Rest well. Good night."

He meant to push past her and on into the house, but she pulled the door closed, effectively blocking his way, and suddenly he was scared. Big, brawny Jesse who could control brute horses with a flick of his wrist, scared of sweet little Caroline. She barely came to his shoulder, and he'd never been so afraid of anyone or anything in his life.

"Jesse, I want to tell you something." She stepped closer. He flinched but managed to stand his ground. What on earth was wrong with him, anyway? What could happen here on the porch in the cold? She swayed closer still. "Today was the best day of my life."

The best day of her life. Hell.

"Everyone was so kind to me today, so complimentary. I just wanted to thank you. None of it would have happened if it wasn't for you."

That was one idea she had to get over. "I...I didn't do anything."

"You hired me."

"Mom—"

"But you're the boss. You sign my paycheck. And you invited me today."

"Now that was—"

"So thoughtful," she said, moving closer still. She lifted a gloved hand and laid it lightly against his chest. "And you taught me all about football, and you helped me clear the table."

"That was for Mom," he said, appalled at the huskiness of his voice.

"You're a good son," she whispered, "a good man."

He knew what she was going to do even before she leaned into him and went up on tiptoe. He cleared his throat but couldn't think of anything to say, and then she was pressing her pretty mouth to his, gently, sweetly. Step back, his brain told him. He ignored himself completely. It took all his strength to keep his arms at his sides, and even then his hands reached for her, finding only cold air.

Her hand slid up his chest and around to the back of his head, cupping it lightly, her mouth firm on his. She tasted slightly of pumpkin and coffee and a sweetness all her own. He felt as if he might be dying, everything in him sinking, sinking away, but then he felt heat pool in his groin, and knew his body was not reaching for death by mortification but reacting to desire unlike any he'd known before. Suddenly he wasn't just frightened, he was terrified.

He behaved completely without thought, reaching up and seizing her by the upper arms, pushing and holding her away. When he looked down into her face, he wished he hadn't. Starlight limned her clearly. Her eyes were still closed, her mouth slightly open, her pale, silken hair streaming down her back. She looked enchanted, enchanting, the very essence of woman, Eve awakening to Adam. He jumped back, coming right to the edge of the step, another fraction of an inch and he'd fall. He fought the urge to windmill his arms, but he was more concerned with Caroline touching him again than with landing on his butt in the snow.

She pulled a deep breath through her nostrils and slowly opened her eyes. Her shoulders relaxed. Her hand dropped to her side. Her eyes seemed to take a moment to focus, but when they did they found him unerringly. She smiled, eyes reflecting starlight, and just stood there, looking like everything soft and delicious in the whole wide world. He decided that if she so much as blinked he would throw up his arms to fend her off and leap down into the snow.

She blinked, and he didn't move a muscle, damn him.

"Thank you, Jesse," she whispered.

He opened his mouth and found he couldn't say a word. He nodded curtly, face flaming hot. Sweet heaven, he was thirty-eight years old, and she had him blushing like he was the kid!

She walked toward him, slowly, as if he were a skittish horse and she was taming him to hand. He would never feel quite so smug working a horse again. Poor things, scared breathless. He was poised for flight, but she walked right by and down the steps, saying softly, "Good night, Jesse."

"Mmmmmm." It was all he could get out, more even than he'd expected.

She went down the walk lightly, her hair shining like a fall of moonlight in the night. He stepped back into the shadows beneath the porch roof and watched her move away from him. She went out the gate, and he heard the snick, creak and clump of her car door opening and closing. It was a very old car, not very safe, probably. If she was his, he'd get rid of that car and buy her a shiny new truck, something that wouldn't crumple like a piece of paper upon impact.

If she was his. Good grief, what was he thinking? She was not his. She would never be his. He didn't even want her. He didn't want anyone. He wasn't made for it. He knew that, had accepted it long ago. Even if she hadn't been too young and too innocent and too sweet, she wasn't for him. More to the point, he wasn't for her—or any woman.

Suddenly a great sadness seized him. He'd once believed that marriage and fatherhood would be the culmination of himself as a person, but he'd gradually realized over the course of his marriage that he'd taken a great deal for granted. It didn't just happen because you wanted it to. It required something that he couldn't quite grasp, something he obviously didn't have. And Kay had been the one to suffer for it. He wouldn't put another woman through that, certainly not a sweet young thing like Caroline Moncton.

He'd thought about this more and more lately since Rye had

found Kara, and he'd come to the conclusion that it was different for Rye than for him. Rye had the gift of deep feeling. He felt things right to his core. His failure with Di'wana had crushed him utterly. Her unfaithfulness had shamed and wounded him, cut the heart right out of him. But Jesse couldn't say that. Kay had been the model wife, the perfect woman, smart and pretty and patient, so patient. And it hadn't worked. It wasn't even that he hadn't loved her. He had. He did. But not like he should have. That was his dirty little secret, his awful truth that no one but him had ever known. He hadn't loved his wife as she'd deserved to be loved. He couldn't. He didn't know why, but he couldn't. And it had killed her as surely as if he'd put a bullet through her brain.

No, he was not the man for Carolyn Moncton or any woman interested in more than physical satisfaction. It was sad, but it was true, and he had to live with it.

He shook his head. It was a day of Thanksgiving, and here he was feeling sorry for himself. With all that he had, the ranch, family, good friends, he had no right for feeling maudlin. Nothing would be gained by it. He pushed his mind to other things. Was his mother feeling well? Was she in pain? He'd better go in and see. Level and sure again at last, he turned to the door, opened it, and went inside.

Chapter Five

The moment she heard his footsteps on the staircase at the end of the hall, she went into action. The plate came out of the warming oven, the coffee cup was turned up and filled, even the folded paper napkin beside his plate got tweaked into a truer alignment with the edge of the place mat. When he came into the room, she was sitting in her chair sideways so she could cross her legs and idly swing one foot while sipping her own coffee and lazily perusing the local newspaper. She wanted to look totally relaxed; her pose was somewhat constrained, however, by her clothing, if nothing else.

She was wearing comfortable blue jeans and a plaid shirt that was so small she dared not slump in it. For one thing, the sleeves were too short. In an effort to counteract that, she had opened the cuffs and rolled them back. Once. They were too tight to roll them a second time. The only thing she could do about the snugness across her chest was to keep her shoulders level and her back as straight as a board. That way the front didn't gap between the buttonholes. But let her relax—just a little bit—and the space between the third and fourth buttons gaped prodigiously.

At the time she'd chosen it, the shirt had seemed so Jesse, but she'd been having second thoughts almost since she'd left the apartment, and now it seemed downright absurd. It was too late to do anything about it, though, so she beamed a smile and said, just as she'd rehearsed, "I was restless this morning, so I figured I might as well come in early, but when I got here there wasn't anything to do so I fixed your breakfast." Perhaps it was a little too well rehearsed. It certainly came out too fast.

Jesse stared at her a moment, then looked at his plate. Caroline was relieved to see that the biscuits were still high and fluffy, the gravy thick and white and lightly flecked with pepper, the eggs scrambled to perfection, the bacon crisp and brown. She realized suddenly that she'd forgotten the orange juice and bolted out of her chair, sloshing coffee and scattering newspaper. With a small exclamation, she plunked the coffee cup onto the table and plucked at the wafting leaves of newspaper, all the while scurrying sideways toward the refrigerator. In short order she got the paper sloppily crammed beneath one arm and the refrigerator door opened. Snatching the small glass of juice, she pivoted, swinging it toward the table. Somehow she managed to keep it all within the rim of the glass and deposit it safely beside Jesse's plate.

Only as she straightened from a tense crouch did she realize what a spectacle she had made of herself. Indeed, Jesse's eyebrows had climbed almost to his hairline. She couldn't help noticing that a damp, wavy, rusty brown lock had fallen over one gray-blue eye. She cleared her throat and said softly, as if it wasn't patently obvious, "O-orange juice."

Jesse's head tilted sideways, but then his gaze switched back to the table. After a moment he pulled out the chair and sat down. Carefully he tugged his napkin from beneath his flatware and spread it over one thigh. He picked up his fork and his knife, each movement slow and deliberate as if she was a wild creature he feared startling. He cut into a biscuit, dipped the small portion into the gravy, and carried it to his mouth. He held it in his mouth a moment, chewed, then nodded approvingly. Caroline allowed herself to sink down upon her chair in relief.

Jesse seemed to be fighting a smile as he forked up the second bite. He chewed, swallowed and grinned. "Restless, huh?"

Suddenly her explanation lay exposed for the lame excuse it was. She fought a wave of heat that climbed from her chest to her face. Even her breath felt scalding hot as she exhaled. She watched him eat, painfully aware that he was waiting to see if she was going to be honest with him. Finally she realized there was only one thing to do. Pulling in a deep, cooling breath, she came out with it.

"I wanted to see you. Alone."

He seemed to weigh that and said not a word in reply to it, but merely continued eating.

She didn't know what to say next. A dozen flimsy excuses for why she wanted to see him ran through her mind, but she knew instinctively that he'd see straight through them, just as he had the first. The only option seemed to be hard honesty. She gulped. "I...I wanted you to notice me."

He swallowed, stuck his fork in a chunk of scrambled egg and said casually, "I notice you."

This did not produce tingling excitement or soaring relief in Caroline. Instead, it seemed to put her in the same category as clean socks and the television in the den, things he noticed and then promptly forgot about the rest of the time. Caroline frowned.

"What I mean is, I wanted to do something nice for you, and I especially wanted you to notice it."

He nodded and picked up a piece of bacon with his fingers. "Like when you brought the coffee down to the barn the other day."

She didn't know where this was going, but she didn't seem able to send it in the direction she wanted, anyway, so she figured she'd play along. "That's right."

He bit off the end of the bacon. "See, I noticed."

Frustration seized her. Was he purposefully being obtuse? Did she have to rub his nose in it? She took a thoughtful breath. "But do you know why?"

"Why you want to do nice things for me?"

"Yes."

He shrugged. "Because you like me, I suppose."

"Yes."

"Not just because I'm the boss."

"No."

He nodded and dug into the remainder of his breakfast, polishing it off in record time. Laying down his knife and fork, he leaned back in his chair to gulp coffee, pat his flat middle and say, "That sure beat my rubbery eggs and burned toast."

"I'm glad you enjoyed it."

Nodding, he got to his feet and drained his cup. He set his cup down by his plate, picked up his orange juice and drained it with a satisfied, "Aah." Smiling, he lifted his big hand over her head, saying, "Yes, ma'am, you sure are a good cook—for a kid." His hand descended and ruffled her hair.

Caroline's mouth fell open. For a kid? A *kid!* By the time she was able to speak again, he was walking down the hall.

"O-o-o-oh!"

She sprang to her feet. If he'd been standing there in front of her, she'd have smacked him one. As it was, she very nearly went after him. Only the rattle of the windows as the outside door was opened and closed prevented her from following him and giving him a large, vocal piece of her mind. He had been deliberately obtuse! Well, he wasn't going to get away with it. He would notice her, really notice her, and admit that he was looking at a fully grown woman, if managing it was the last thing she ever did. She brought her hands to her hips determinedly, pressing her elbows back and lifting her chin. A button shot clear across the room. Her shirt gaped open, revealing the lace-edged camisole beneath. Dismayed, she looked down at herself.

The full roundness of her breasts literally overflowed the material into which she'd stuffed them. Her eyes narrowed dangerously. For a kid, he'd said. Well, he was going to eat those words. She'd serve them up herself, right along with breakfast, lunch and dinner. Every time he said them, she'd feed them right back to him, until he had to go searching for evidence to back them up—and that's when she'd have him. Smirking, she tugged the fabric together and went to get a safety pin. Oh, yes, Jesse Wagner was going to open his eyes wide, and she was just the woman to see to it.

He'd skipped supper, sending word up to the house that he had to stay with a horse that might be coming down with something and he would eat later when he had the time. What he'd really meant was that he'd eat when Caroline was long gone. It was no doubt cowardly, but he couldn't face her again just yet, not with her wearing that tight shirt that showed clearly what he'd already suspected: Caroline Moncton wasn't built like a kid of any age, which didn't mean that she wasn't one, just that his body couldn't quite seem to appreciate the finer points of the reality. It was best just now that he kept his distance; so his belly button was kissing his backbone and his cold, tired body yearned for the comforts of home.

He kept his head down as he trudged up the low hill toward the house. The night had an edge to it that made his bones ache and threatened to bite the end off his nose. Welcome warmth flowed over him when he opened the side door and stepped up into the darkened hall. He divested himself of his outer gear, stomped his feet clean on the inside mat and ventured on into the house. The television in the den was on, the volume turned low. His dad was probably watching the evening news. He would join him as soon as he'd found something to eat.

What he found was a heavy stoneware plate heaped with a thick hamburger steak, rice, mushroom gravy and a hot bean salad in the warming oven. A pair of Caroline's tall cream biscuits were wrapped in tin foil. Ravenous now, he ate standing up and washed the meal down with half a glass of cold milk. That second half would sure go good with something sweet. He poked around a bit but found nothing to interest him. Carrying his glass into the den, he noticed that his father's chair was empty, but a rustle of movement told him that someone was stretched out on the couch.

"Any of that chocolate cake left?" he asked.

A feminine gasp was his first clue that he wasn't talking to his father, then Caroline Moncton sat bolt upright on the sofa, blinking her eyes. He leaped back, nearly dropping the glass of milk.

"Oh. I guess I fell asleep," she said thickly.

While he stood there mentally kicking himself for not checking to see if her car was still parked in the driveway, she lifted her arms over her head and stretched like a lazy cat, bowing her back and thrusting forward ample breasts. Jesse's mouth went dry. He couldn't help noticing that her shirt was held together with a safety pin. At the moment the soft flannel fit her like a second skin, and he wondered where the button was and just how long that pin would hold. Finally she slumped forward, sighing, and got to her feet. That was when he realized he'd been holding his breath.

"How's the horse?"

"Huh?"

"How's the horse? Tiger said you had a horse coming down with something."

"Oh. False alarm. H-horse seems fine now."

She beamed him that thousand-watt smile. "Good. Well, I guess you're wanting your dinner."

"No, uh, actually, I've already eaten."

She seemed momentarily disappointed, then her gaze fell on the half-empty glass. "Well, how about some dessert? I made a coconut custard pie today."

"Uh, no. No, thanks."

Her face fell. "Don't you like coconut?"

"I like coconut fine. I just don't... That is, I'm really beat. All I want to do is go to bed. I mean, turn in. I'm, uh, just going to turn in now. Good night." He nearly made it. He had turned and was almost into the hallway when she stopped him.

"Jesse, don't be like this."

He thought about ignoring her words and heading straight down the hall to the stairs, but the sound of her voice, all husky and soft, had brought him to a complete halt. He couldn't very well plead ignorance now when it was so obvious he had heard her. He put on a devil-may-care expression and turned back to face her. Lifting his glass, he took the time to drink his milk before saying with a smile, "I don't know what you mean, hon. I'm just tired, and since you were asleep when I came in, I figured you were probably as tired as I am."

Caroline sighed and folded her arms just beneath her breasts. "You aren't being fair."

"About what?" He was proud of himself; he sounded totally perplexed.

"About me."

He shook his head. "Caroline, don't you realize how much we value your work around here? Why, Mom literally sings your praises. You've worked out real fine. No cause for concern."

She stuck out her chin pugnaciously, her mouth drawn into a pretty pout. "I'm not talking about that."

"No?" He threw his arms out. "Well, I can't imagine what you're talking about, then, but I assure you, everyone here is pleased with everything you've done. Okay?"

She didn't answer him, just stood there, holding him with her eyes. He made himself smile as if she'd given him just exactly the reply he'd expected. "You better get on home now. See you tomorrow."

He attempted to flip her a wave, forgetting that he held the empty milk glass, and covered his unease with a self-deprecating chuckle. He sounded like a duck choking, but he wasn't sticking around any longer to see how she was taking it. With a light-heartedness he surely didn't feel, he turned and went on his way, stopping by the kitchen to rinse out his glass and leave it beside the sink with his plate. She still hadn't left by the time he was finished, so he whistled tunelessly as he hurried down the hall to the stairs. She let him go, but he couldn't help wondering if it was going to be that easy. Just how long could he sidestep her? And just how blatant was she willing to be? He had the feeling that he might have unwittingly declared war and that she had just begun to fight.

Jesse climbed the steps to the loft, appalled with himself and the whole situation. He couldn't believe he was doing this, but what else could he do? She'd lain in wait for him more often than not lately. Mornings, afternoons, evenings, he never knew when she was going to turn up. It was like walking around waiting for an ambush, knowing it was coming, dreading it. Wondering if he could prevail.

The awful truth was that the woman, *girl,* scared him to death.

Even when she wasn't around, she harried him. He wished for the millionth time that she hadn't kissed him on Thanksgiving night, that she hadn't worn that tight shirt the next day, that she wouldn't smile at him with her blue-green eyes all smoky and go out of her way to do sweet things for him: cook his breakfast, bring him coffee, press his no-wrinkle shirts, put extra starch in his jeans just the way he liked. He wished she wouldn't look at him with naked longing in her eyes and that her voice wouldn't go all husky and soft when she spoke. Most of all, he wished he could forget how it felt to stand close and let her mouth work against his, her small hand stroking his skin. He didn't want to think about how she smelled or how she looked with her straight pale hair falling down her slender back. He wanted to sleep peacefully again, without dreaming of a girl much too young and much too innocent for what he had in mind. What he couldn't quite get out of his mind.

Sighing, he looked around him. He hadn't turned on the overhead light, and much of what he saw was cloaked in pure darkness, but he knew this place, like every other on the ranch, as well as he knew his own face. An enormous white freezer, used for storing everything from stud and bull semen to mare's milk and vaccinations, stood at the top of the stairs. Bags of feed were stacked at one end of the long room. Two large round bales of hay took up the other end, one of them more a mound now than a bale. Along the sides were trapdoors set at regular intervals in the floor. The chutes below went straight to the feeding boxes built into each stall on the ground floor of the big barn. In the center of the room stood a long metal table and a pair of mixers, operated much like oversize flour sifters, that emptied into buckets.

He spent part of every day here blending feeds for his horses and dumping them down the feed chutes or, sometimes, carrying them back downstairs to hand-feed a sickly or nervous animal. This was one of his favorite places, redolent of the clean, loamy fragrance of grains and animals. It was always possible to find a warm or cool—as the case might be—corner here. Sometimes he came here just to think and look out across the property at the mountains from the big loading window that faced the house.

He went there now, unlatching and opening the heavy shutter just wide enough to see outside. There in the driveway beneath the untidy glow of a sensored lamp atop a high pole sat Caroline's tiny, decrepit foreign excuse for an auto. Damn. Didn't she ever go home? He closed and latched the shutters, shivering in the bitter breeze.

What was he going to do now? He wished he'd had the foresight to bring a book or a magazine with him, then he grimaced. Why was he hiding out here in the barn like a wayward child when a comfortable chair and a warm, cozy fire waited for him in the house? But the answer to that was all too obvious. He was hiding out here because Caroline waited for him in the house, too. He'd fled immediately after dinner, when she'd told him that she wanted to discuss something with him at his convenience. He'd hoped that "his convenience" would prove so inconvenient to her that she would just let it go, but as usual, Caroline was nothing if not resolute. Well, she wasn't going to wear him down. He had lots more experience at keeping himself out of involvements than she could possibly have at forcing them. Meanwhile, he was stuck here with nothing much to do.

He figured he might as well check on each of the horses personally once more and moved across the floor to the stairwell, unaware that his heavy footsteps clumped loudly enough to be heard below or that anyone was there to hear them. He was halfway down the bare wood steps when she spoke.

"There you are."

He nearly jumped out of his skin, but the instant after that he was angry.

"Damn it, Caroline!"

"Sorry," she said contritely. "Didn't mean to startle you."

Suddenly he felt like a heel, but he wasn't about to apologize. Instead, he said gruffly, "What are you doing here?" Only belatedly did he realize that he'd just opened himself up to conversation. In order to discourage an answer, he pushed by her and went straight to the first stall, letting himself in with the horse. She followed him.

"I told you I wanted to talk to you about something."

"I'm busy, Caroline," he said brusquely, peering into the feed bin. He ran a hand lightly over the bay's sleek back, watching the animal shiver, as if it was the most important thing he'd seen all day. Caroline stood patiently. When he couldn't bear it any longer, he demanded, "Can't this wait?"

"No, it can't wait," she told him softly but firmly, hanging her elbows over the stall gate. "I'm busy, too, Jesse. I have a schedule to meet every day, and tomorrow, along with putting three meals on the table—"

"Two," he retorted without thinking. "You don't have to cook my breakfast every morning, you know."

"That's beside the point. Breakfast or not tomorrow, I still have to do the shopping."

Shopping on Friday. That's right. He'd forgotten all about her system. Laundry on Mondays, floors on Tuesdays, bathrooms on Wednesdays, dusting on Thursdays, shopping on Fridays. The house seemed to stay effortlessly spotless and the pantry fully stocked all the time since she'd come. "What's that got to do with me?" he snapped, uncomfortable suddenly with her surprisingly sophisticated organization of her duties.

"I want to discuss doing the shopping in a different way."

He finally had to stop pretending to work on the horse and give her his attention. "You'll have to explain that."

She gathered her thoughts and did so succinctly. "The first Friday of every month your mother and I sit down and make out menus for every day. Then once a week we go through the pantry to see what we have on hand, make a shopping list, and go to town. Sometimes we have to hit three or four stores to get the best prices, and it's usually too much for your mother. She winds up shivering in the car while I try to finish up at hyper-speed."

"So what's your solution?" He had no doubt that she had one.

"A warehouse store has opened up not too far away. They have a good reputation, excellent products, the very lowest prices, but you have to buy in bulk. Also, they require a membership fee every year. So the initial outlay would be like three times the weekly grocery budget, but I've done the figures repeatedly, and I'm convinced we could get at least a month of meals for the cost of those three weeks, even figuring in the extra meals while your brother's family is here for Christmas and Christmas dinner itself. Now we have the storage space for buying bulk, and it would mean very nearly one-stop shopping but at a greater distance, and the grocery budget would have to be disbursed differently. And before you decide, I should point out that the weather may sometimes rule out the trip, which is just under fifty minutes, meaning that we could find ourselves winging it through the local grocery stores at times, and that could—probably won't but *could*—negate the savings. So, what do you think?''

He had to mull it over. She'd certainly done her homework. Frankly, he'd had no idea food shopping was such a chore. Hadn't given it much thought, really, but now that he did, he realized that she'd been providing all those rich, abundant meals on the same budget on which his mother had been operating with a good deal less results. Obviously his mother couldn't manage the shopping with the same efficiency as Caroline—either because of her infirmity or because she just hadn't thought of doing it Caroline's way or both. He put his mind to the thesis with which she had presented him and came up with a question.

''Could we maybe buy for, oh, two or three months in advance? That way the weather wouldn't be such a big factor.''

She bit her bottom lip, giving his question some thought. ''Two maybe, but not three. We'd have to have a good deal more freezer space, and also, we'd need to run into town every so often for fresh vegetables and such.''

''Won't we have to do that, anyway?''

''Yes, you're right. We will.''

''So, if we had a bigger freezer in the house we could buy in bulk maybe once a quarter and augment that with fresh goods from town, say once a week.''

She nodded. ''You'd sure save a bundle on your grocery budget that way, and your mother wouldn't have to endure the weekly shopping marathon. I've tried to get her to let me handle it alone, but she knows it's really a two-person job.''

''But this way you could handle the weekly shopping by yourself?''

''I don't see why not.''

''Okay, let's do it.''

She stared at him in obvious surprise. ''Just like that? But what about the freezer?''

''I'll trade with you,'' he said. ''There's a freezer upstairs about half-full of various stuff. If it's suitable for your purposes, I'll have it switched with the one in the house.''

She shrugged happily. "Let's take a look at it."

"Okay."

He let himself out of the stall and led her up the stairs to the top. This time he flipped on the overhead light. "It's not real attractive, I know. Pretty scratched up. But it works fine. It's actually newer than the one in the house."

She shook her head. "Nobody goes in the pantry but your mom and I and sometimes your dad. I can't imagine that they'd mind. I sure don't. Can I look inside?"

He fished a key out of his pocket and fitted it into a tiny, round lock beneath the handle. The lock clicked softly, and Jesse nodded. "Go ahead."

She opened the door and poked her head inside. "Shelves are all intact. I like these two big pullout bins here. The door has really deep, keeper space." She straightened and closed the door. "I only see one problem."

"What's that?"

"The freezer in the house doesn't have a lock."

He shrugged even as he put the key in and turned it. "I'll get a padlock. This one really isn't enough to stop a determined thief, anyway."

She lifted her arms and smiled. "Works for me."

He felt rather pleased with himself. "I'll have them switched tomorrow."

"Terrific."

They stood there smiling like idiots for a moment before Jesse remembered that he was supposed to be keeping his distance. He was just about to suggest that she go on her way and let him get back to "work," when she turned away and took a look around the loft.

"Oh, this is great!" she said. "Just like a barn is supposed to be. What are those things in the floor?"

He heard himself answering before he'd even thought about it. "Those are feed chutes. The traps slide open so you can pour feed down the chutes straight into the feed bins in the stalls downstairs. That way you don't have to carry everything up and down the stairs."

"Clever." She beamed him a smile that seemed to say she

credited him with the idea. He had, indeed, thought of it. She pointed at the mixing table. "What's that for?"

"Mixing special feeds. Some cattle have special needs, usually it's horses, though."

"And you do very well by your horses," she said, a touch of something that sounded very like pride in her voice. She walked into the center of the room, trailing one hand along the edge of the table. "What is it about a pile of hay that makes you want to jump in and roll around?" she asked rhetorically.

He chuckled. He couldn't help himself. "I don't know, same thing about a pile of leaves, I guess."

She whirled around to face him, her gestures exuberant. "Did you play up here as a child?"

He shook his head. "No. It wasn't built then. We had a big old tumbledown barn with a loft we weren't supposed to play in because it was too rickety, but did sometimes, anyway. I built this place about seven or eight years ago."

"It must be wonderful here in the summertime with that great big window open," she said dreamily. "I always fantasized about playing in a place like this with my brothers and sisters."

"You don't have brothers and sisters," he said thoughtlessly.

"But I always wanted them," she said. "Aren't you glad you have a brother?"

"Sure. Even when he was a smart-alecky little pain in the butt, I always kind of liked having him around. Frankly, I don't see nearly enough of Rye now."

She nodded, as if she'd expected him to say those very words and did another slow perusal of the loft. "This place needs kids," she said, "a whole bunch of them, running around and playing hide-and-seek, throwing hay all over the place." She looked up at the beams overhead. "You could hang a tire swing from the center of the roof, and they could play out here even in the winter. It wouldn't be nearly so neat as this, though. Kids aren't neat, not usually. But what fun they'd have!"

Something about the way she said it made it come alive for him in that moment. Suddenly he could see a boisterous trio jumping and running and swinging around the room. At least two of them were boys, but the ringleader was a little girl, her long blond hair streaming out behind her as she shrieked and streaked around the room. His heart turned over. The fiercest longing he'd ever known seized him. It knocked him back, staggered him. Children. His children.

But he would never have children. Never.

All at once, he knew who to blame for this dangerous fantasy, this gut-wrenching realization of a loss he'd never allowed himself to ponder. He glared at Caroline. Damn her! Even when she wasn't enticing him with her silent invitations, she was still a needle under his skin, reminding him every minute of what he couldn't have and shouldn't want. Somehow the loft had grown too small for the two of them. He pulled at the neck of the plain white T-shirt he wore beneath his chambray work shirt and coat, feeling the need for a deep breath that he couldn't quite seem to catch. And Caroline, who was entirely too perceptive for his good, noticed.

"Jesse, is something wrong?"

He turned away from her. "I don't have time to stand around daydreaming," he snapped. "I have work to do."

He pounded down the stairs, taking them two at a time. He was surprised that she didn't come tearing after him, but he didn't mind. It gave him time to find some equilibrium and pull some old tack out of storage to keep him busy. He was preparing to rub oil into the old, cracked leather when she finally switched off the light and slowly descended the stairs. He felt her standing at his back for so long that he began to wonder if he was imagining it, but when he turned, there she stood, hugging herself through her shabby coat. "What?" he barked at her.

She lifted her head and looked him straight in the eye, saying softly, "We haven't decided whose names to put on the membership card."

"What?"

She took a deep breath and let it out again silently. "I told you. The warehouse shopping center requires that you buy a membership every year. It's only a few dollars, but without it you can't get inside to shop unless you're accompanied by a cardholder. You can put two names on the card. We haven't decided whose."

He waved a hand irritably. "Put yours and Mom's on it."

"I don't think that's a good idea," she said quietly.

He frowned in exasperation. "Why not?"

"We're talking about shopping for a whole quarter of the year, Jesse. I can't manage that by myself, and your mom won't always be able to go. Besides it's your membership. Yours and your mother's names should be on it. I can always go in with one of you."

He tried to think of a way out of it, but at the moment he just couldn't quite manage to wrap his mind around the problem. In the end, he simply shrugged. "Fine. Whatever."

"All right."

He tried to keep his gaze on what he was doing and not on her sad angel's face. "So we're done here, right?"

"If you say so," she whispered.

It cut across his nerve endings, as elementally heartbreaking as a newborn's first frightened wail, but he managed to keep his head down and his hands busy until she whispered a farewell and left him. It was only afterward that he began to feel petty and ashamed and small. How much of a man was he, after all, if he couldn't let himself speak respectfully and kindly to a youngster with a crush? Because that's all it was, a young girl with a foolish little crush on an older, worldlier man. He ought to be handling this better, instead of running scared. It didn't work, anyway. She was always around, always needing to talk to him.

Actually, for a while there, they'd carried on a pretty normal conversation. He'd enjoyed seeing her pleasure in the loft, hearing her thoughts. She'd missed all the things he so often took for granted, home, family, a special place to play. She should have children. Someday. With the right man. He caught a flash once again of that little blond-haired girl flitting past his mind's eye, and his gut clenched. Not his. Never his.

Disgusted once more with the train of his thoughts, he tossed away the leather tack and capped the oil. This was absurd. The whole thing was just absurd. What the hell was he afraid of anyway? She wasn't likely to seduce him. She was exercising her flirting skills, nothing more. She hadn't asked him to marry her, for pity's sake, just to pay her a little attention. That couldn't hurt anything. Could it? He wasn't sure, but he knew for a fact that he wasn't handling this well.

He cleaned his hands, turned off the lights and struck out for the house. He couldn't help the little shimmer of relief that he felt when he heard her old car clanking and rattling away, but she would be there again tomorrow, and he had to find some rational way to deal with it.

He promised himself that he was going to find a better way to deal with Caroline Moncton. He had to.

For both their sakes.

Chapter Six

Wednesday. She did the bathrooms on Wednesdays, starting with the small bath downstairs and finishing with his. Since it was after lunch, Jesse figured he'd given her enough time to get upstairs before he went in to talk to his mother. Sarah was in the office trying to make sense of his father's ledger entries. She looked up when he quietly entered the room and closed the door.

"Oh, good," she said, "just the man I should be talking to."

"Hey, that's Dad's end of the business," he said, only half teasing as he pointed at the ledger, "and I never could read his writing."

"Well, if you think this is a nightmare," she declared, "wait until you hear what he's up to now."

Jesse chuckled and dropped down onto the only other empty chair in the room. "Do tell."

She leaned forward, elbows braced on the desktop. "He wants to buy a computer."

This was not news to Jesse, and he was surprised that it seemed to be news to her. "Mom, everybody's computerizing. They have lots of programs for farming and ranching these days. We've been talking about it for months, if not longer, and we're agreed that we ought to make the investment before the end of the year in order to get the greatest tax break from it.''

''But we don't know anything about computers,'' she protested.

''We can learn.''

''Speak for yourself. This old brain isn't as trainable as it used to be, you know. Your father's isn't, either.''

''That's not true,'' he countered laughingly. ''You're as sharp as you ever were. Dad, too. All we need is someone to teach us the basics.''

Sarah sighed. ''Frankly, that's not what concerns me.'' She stared at her hands, which were knotted and slightly twisted. ''I doubt I can even use a keyboard now.''

Jesse reached across the desk and covered her hands with his own much larger one. ''You don't have to type to help out,'' he told her gently.

She smiled wanly. ''That's what Caroline said.''

''Caroline?'' Slightly stung, he withdrew his hand.

Sarah nodded. ''She says that there are all kinds of modems and devices to use, but that kind of thing costs money.''

''We can afford it,'' he told her carelessly. ''We're not broke, you know.''

''Actually, I don't,'' Sarah said in an oddly pointed tone. ''Not really.''

Something about that disturbed Jesse, but he couldn't put his finger on what it was just then. He shrugged and said, ''Well, we can certainly afford a computer and someone to teach us how to use it.''

''Oh, Caroline can do that,'' Sarah said dismissively, and Jesse felt a flare of something very close to jealousy.

''Oh, come on. What does Caroline know about computers?''

''Quite a lot, actually,'' Sarah informed him. ''And you needn't take that tone. She agrees with Haney—and you—about the computer.''

''Well, that ought to cinch it,'' he said drily.

''But how do we know what to buy?'' Sarah argued, either ignoring or missing his sarcasm. ''Computers are expensive, and they don't come complete. How do you ever decide what components you need? If you let the salesman decide for you, you'll wind up with a lot of pricey stuff you'll never use.''

Jesse chuckled in exasperation. ''Mom, we have an appointment with a consultant. He doesn't sell anything, he just makes recommendations. Didn't Dad tell you any of this?''

Sarah's mouth turned down at the corners, and she dropped her gaze to the ledger once again. ''Your father never tells me anything,'' she grumbled, ''and he never listens to anything I say, either.''

Jesse usually brushed off such remarks, but his mother's voice had a bitter edge to it this time that he hadn't heard before. ''Oh, you know Dad,'' he said, hoping to lighten the mood. ''He never has much to say. And I know that sometimes he tunes out everyone, but I don't think—''

To his shock, she interrupted and abruptly changed the subject. ''Did you have a specific reason for coming in just now, son? You're not usually in the office at this time of day.''

He sat back in his chair, aware of a creeping unease. ''Mom, is something wrong?''

She flashed him a look. He was stunned to see her eyes gleaming with tears, but then she was flipping through the ledger as if engrossed by the columns of cramped handwriting. ''Don't you have something on your mind?''

''In other words, it's none of my business,'' he said wryly.

She didn't reply with so much as a flicker of an eyelash. Jesse had seen this maneuver before and knew from long experience that she wasn't going to answer, and the truth was that he felt a certain relief. He had never been comfortable discussing his parents' relationship, perhaps because they were not comfortable discussing it. He waited several moments, allowing the former subject to fully close, then sat forward again.

''I've, uh, been meaning to speak to you about something, and we sort of touched on it just now.''

When she lifted her head, her eyes were dry and her expression was pleasant. ''What would that be, dear?''

''Caroline.''

Sarah relaxed back in her chair, her expression at counterpoint with the gesture. "What about Caroline?"

He already regretted the way he'd put it. "Well, it's not Caroline, really. It's me."

"Oh?"

"The thing is, I've been meaning to take on more of the office work myself. This computer stuff kind of intrigues me, and, well, that means that we're sort of renegotiating our positions around here, you and I. I mean, once we get the computer—if I'm going to be taking over more of the office work, and you are doing less of the actual work around the house—I thought maybe it was time that you took over, like, the financial decision-making part, uh, where it comes to the house, that is."

She sat and listened patiently, nodding as he stumbled through what he wanted to say, and then she thought about it, nodding some more and narrowing her eyes, mouth compressed. And then she sat up straight, looked him right in the eye and said, "I don't think so. Seems to me that one person has to make all the financial decisions that fall outside the established budget. That's your job, and it seems to me that you do it well."

He couldn't believe it. For a moment he was absolutely dumbfounded. She'd told him no! "But, Mom, who appointed me boss?"

"No one appointed you. You took over, and your father and I were happy to let you."

"But not of the house! I have my hands full with the ranch and the livestock."

"Don't be silly," his mother said in her best no-nonsense voice. "The house and the ranch aren't separate entities, not financially. We run everything out of one account, one master budget."

"Well, that needs to change!" he countered sharply.

"I don't see why. The arrangement works quite well."

He couldn't think what to say next, then suddenly he was twelve years old again, his mouth running off with him. "But it's not fair!" he all but wailed. "I make all the decisions."

"Will you listen to yourself?" Sarah chided. "You've been

making all the decisions for years. You're good at decisions, especially when it comes to finances.''

"But—''

"Besides,'' she went on firmly. "Caroline wouldn't be happy dealing only with me.''

Caroline! It always came back to Caroline! It wasn't like him to lose his temper with his parents, but then he'd never felt quite so betrayed by one of them before. He came completely out of his seat.

"Caroline! Is she all you think about anymore? She's not even family. She's an employee, damn it! She'll do what she's told or she'll go elsewhere! What is it with her, anyway? Why does she have to talk to me all the time? Why can't she just talk to *you?*''

It had been years since his mother had pulled rank on him, but she hadn't forgotten how. Her tone was every bit as authoritative as it had been in the past, if not more so. She stood, rising regally from the battered old chair behind the small desk, and pulled herself up tall, as tall as she could, anyway. Her chin came up so high that the thick bun that usually sat on the back of her head lay against the back of her neck, as well.

"What on earth is wrong with you, Jesse Dean Wagner?'' she said. "What have you got against that girl? Caroline has brought more care and concern into this house than anyone I can think of. She's fresh. She's bright. She's hardworking.''

"She wangles her way into everything that goes on around here!''

"That's not true, Jesse!''

"I'm sick and tired of tripping over her every time I turn around!''

Sarah rolled her eyes. "That's so petty. She's done everything in her power to please you!''

"I don't want her to please me!'' he shouted, knowing he was being unreasonable but unable to stop himself. "I just want her to leave me alone!''

"Oh, Jesse, grow up!'' Sarah snapped, and Jesse saw six shades of red.

Grow up? She was saying that to *him?* He knew then that if he didn't get out of there, he was going to say or do something he would deeply regret later. He swallowed down the angry, bitter words that were suddenly crowding his throat, turned on his heel, and stomped out of the room.

Caroline was standing in the hallway, her pale hair tied back at the nape, head bowed, a plastic bucket of cleaning supplies hugged to her middle, one shoulder braced against the wall. The look on her face made his heart drop like a lump of lead in water. She'd heard it all, no doubt, every desperate, angry, ugly word. An apology leaped into his mouth, but with it came all kinds of resentful, hateful things that he had just enough sense left to know he'd regret letting loose. He bit them back and headed down the hall as fast as he could go without actually running. Adults didn't run in the house, after all.

Adults didn't shout at their mothers, either. They didn't hide out in cold barns. They didn't pretend, didn't lose control. Adults faced situations head-on, calmly, maturely, honestly. Now if he could just figure out how to do that, everything would be fine! Oh, hell, what was wrong with him? How had this happened?

He crammed his hat onto his head, snatched his coat off the next hook and went out the door slinging it on, his muffler trailing behind him, gloves dropping out of his pockets. He wanted to kick something, punch something and throttle himself all at the same time. And he was no closer to solving his original problem than he had been. Worse, he had a new problem now. Two, actually, because now he had two apologies to make, and that was never easy for him. Lately, nothing seemed easy anymore. No matter how hard he tried.

Wearing that big coat with the collar turned up and a muffler tucked into it, he looked out of place there in his own kitchen.

"I've just been covered up lately," he said, working his way around the brim of his hat with both hands. "Sick horses and what have you. Just a lot on my mind, I guess. Anyway, I spout off about nothing sometimes, and that's what happened the other day here. I've already apologized to Mom, but I wanted to be sure you didn't take to heart all that stuff I said. It wasn't about you."

Caroline nodded, her hands clasped tightly in her lap. "I understand. Don't let it trouble you anymore."

"I just didn't want you to think you aren't appreciated around here. Mom couldn't manage without you now, and I'm real grateful for all you do."

"Thank you."

"No, I'm the one who should be thanking you, Caroline."

She nodded, smiling weakly. He'd behaved these past few days as if nothing had happened. He'd been charming, polite, aloof. Caroline hadn't expected the apology—she'd been the one caught listening to a private conversation, after all—and now that she had it, she wasn't sure what she was supposed to do with it. She'd pushed too hard with Jesse. No wonder he was sick of the sight of her. In all fairness, she supposed she owed him an apology, too. But that wasn't what he wanted, and she knew it. What he wanted was to be left alone.

She had been dazzled by him as a girl and even more so as a woman, and she had let that convince her they could be more to each other than merely employer and employee. She'd done just what she'd hated to see her mother do all these years. She'd built a fantasy around air and tried to make it reality. Why was she surprised that it had come crashing down? She'd been a fool. He wanted no part of her, and she had to accept that. She took a deep breath, squared her shoulders and lifted her chin, meeting his gaze.

"I want you to know that I'll be staying out of your way from now on," she said. He opened his mouth, but she shook her head, bowed it and went on. "You're too busy to hold my hand, and I...I figure I know the ropes around here pretty well now."

"Caroline, I never meant—"

"It's all right," she told him kindly, looking up again. "You've all been so good to me. I've got no complaints, not about the job."

He nodded and shuffled his feet. She could feel him straining against the compunction to get out of there, now that it had all been said, but he stayed his ground and worked at small talk.

"How're things at home?"

She shrugged. "Fine."

"Your landlord's not found a buyer for the duplex yet, then?"

She skimmed a gaze over him. "Well, maybe. I mean, some family's made an offer, but I think that's as far as it's gone."

Jesse nodded. "I see."

"It's no big deal," she said, lying through her teeth. "I'm thinking of finding someplace else anyway, someplace nicer. You know?"

"Yeah," he muttered.

She knew he was thinking about her hope of moving in here and hurried to put his mind at ease. "There's a place with a heated pool and a kind of clubhouse. You know, that new apartment complex on the west side of town. I was thinking I'd look into that. It'd be nice to have a real apartment, for a change."

"Isn't that place kind of expensive?" he asked.

She shrugged. "I can always find a roommate. I'm not used to living alone, anyway." She knew that wasn't going to happen. For one thing, even with a roommate, she couldn't afford an apartment in that building. For another, she hated the idea of living with another single woman. She'd had her fill of that lifestyle.

Jesse said something about keeping him informed and left her to her thoughts. She was relieved. She didn't want him to see how worried she was about finding any place that she could afford. Certainly she would find nothing as cheap as the shabby apartment that was her home. She'd probably have to be satisfied with a room in someone else's house, unless she defaulted on her school loans or took a second job. Or she could leave this job and find one that paid better. Maybe that would be for the best, but she hated the thought of leaving Sarah to find someone else to help her. Besides, she loved what she did here, even though she knew now that she had been stupid to take this job. Stupid? She'd been downright self-delusional.

She'd convinced herself that there was something special, something almost magic between her and Jesse, when the truth was that he hadn't even known she existed. Jesse wasn't going to fall in love with her. He didn't even like her. She was just some kid who had insinuated herself into his family and proceeded to make a pest, an embarrassment, of herself. She was

Irene's daughter, after all. She sighed deeply and set her chin on the heel of her hand, feeling small and alone. So very alone.

True to form, however, she did not let herself dwell long on her disappointments. She had laundry to begin and lunch to start, and she wanted to talk to Sarah later about an article she'd recently read. The author had contended that some arthritis could be halted and even reversed by proper nutrition and certain supplements. Caroline wasn't certain that she approved of a radical application of the author's theories, but she thought Sarah ought to at least know about the alternative. And it was a way to keep herself busy, to focus on someone else's difficulty.

Keeping herself busy was not a problem. For several days she found so much to do that she often skipped lunch. She continued to come in early to make Jesse's breakfast. She figured that she owed him that much, and besides, she enjoyed doing it, but she no longer hovered nearby hoping for a kind word. Instead, she got on about her work.

Over the weekend she found an ad in the local paper requesting a sitter evenings for a busy mom anxious to finish her Christmas shopping without her children in tow. The ad requested references, and Sarah was glad to furnish them after Caroline assured her that it was only temporary, a way to earn a little extra cash. She let Sarah think that the extra money was for Christmas, but in reality she was desperate to put away funds for her impending move. It was a done deal now. Just after the first of the year, when she returned from her honeymoon, Nancy would sign papers closing the sale of her duplex house to a young family intending to completely restore it. They were to take possession by the middle of January.

The baby-sitting job also had another purpose, though. It gave her a good excuse to rush away from the ranch right after getting dinner on the table. Some days she managed not to see Jesse at all, but whenever she did, he was polite and friendly in a very proper, very distant manner. Caroline tried to follow suit, but sometimes just looking at him produced an ache so deep that it was pure torture. She tried harder to stay out of his way.

Sarah worried that she was overdoing it, but Caroline knew that she would have to do much more if she was going to move into any of the apartments about which she had called so far. She would have to take a second job permanently, most likely as a bookkeeper, and the irony that it would probably pay as much as her full-time job at the ranch was not lost on her.

December continued dank and dark, much like her mood when she wasn't consciously fine-tuning it, and the bitter cold brought added burdens, the worst of which was the fact that Caroline's old car did not suffer it well. She had to let it warm up twenty or thirty minutes sometimes before the gearshift would properly work, and so she had developed the habit of getting dressed, running out to start the car, and letting it warm up while she applied a little makeup, brushed out her hair and gulped down a cup of coffee. When she allowed herself to do so, Caroline worried that the old car wasn't going to hold out much longer, but since she could do nothing about it anyway, she tried not to waste her time or energy in pointless panic. Then came the dark morning when it simply didn't start.

She usually left the transmission in neutral the evening before because it was getting increasingly difficult to wrestle the gearshift into position after it had sat in the cold all night, and this morning was no exception. As she put the key into the ignition, she planted one foot on the emergency brake and hovered the other above the gas pedal. Pumping the pedal just as required, she turned the key—and absolutely nothing happened, not a grind, not a shudder, not even a click. When repeated efforts yielded nothing more, she accepted the inevitable and considered her options, which seemed to consist of waking Nancy and Bud, who was now in residence, in order to call out to the ranch or walking down to the convenience store on the corner to use the phone there. With a sigh, she went back into the apartment, pulled on an extra pair of leggings and a sweatshirt over what she was already wearing and set out down the block.

Haney answered the telephone, sounding gruff and sleepy. He said little when she explained her problem, and she didn't ask to speak to Sarah. Might as well let her sleep if she was going to have to manage on her own that day. Caroline accepted a cup of coffee from the clerk behind the cash register and warmed herself inside before hiking back up the block. Thanks to the bitterness of the weather, it was too cold in the living room to sit and work on the Christmas gifts she was knitting, so she stripped off a layer of clothing and crawled back into bed, hoping she would be able to get a little extra sleep herself.

She woke sometime later to weak sunshine and a sense of disorientation. By the time she figured out why she was here, someone was knocking insistently on her front door. No doubt that was what had awakened her in the first place. Groaning, she shook off the heavy lethargy and crawled out of the bed. It was cold in the little bedroom, which meant that it would be freezing in the living room. Shivering, she grabbed her coat and threw it on, then shoved her stocking feet into house slippers so old that all the fluff had worn off the toes.

"Coming!" she called out as she opened the bedroom door. The wind rattled the windows, and she wished that she had tacked up the heavy plastic sheeting that she and her mother had used to keep them warm in the winters past. Nancy had requested that she not do so this year so she could show the house to best advantage. Now that the house was sold, surely it would be all right to seal the windows until she was ready to leave. It would certainly cut her fuel bill, and she'd be much warmer into the bargain. With that in mind, she pushed back the curtain to see who waited on her doorstep. It took a moment for her mind to register what her eyes clearly saw. She jumped back and wrenched open the door. "Jesse!"

He didn't wait to be invited inside, just backed her up and shut the door. "Mom sent me to get you."

Caroline put a hand to her rumpled hair, aware that she looked a mess. Jesse's gaze swept over her. "Let me, uh, brush my hair and put on some shoes," she mumbled.

He nodded, his gaze skittering around the room. Caroline hurried back to the bedroom to get ready. She hadn't expected anyone to come for her and certainly not him. Now that he was here, she didn't want to keep him waiting. She kicked off her house shoes and dropped down onto the edge of the bed to pull on her half boots, then quickly applied some mascara to her pale lashes, grabbed a hairbrush and hurried back to the living room, pulling it through her hair in long, hard strokes. Jesse was still standing just as she'd left him. She grabbed her small handbag and slung the strap over one shoulder.

"Ready."

He turned an incredulous face to her. "How can you live like this?"

Shame flooded her. Ignoring the flush of embarrassment, Caroline lashed the brush through her hair vigorously. "It's not so bad. It's clean, and it's cheap. Besides, I told you I was thinking of getting a nicer place."

"That's not what I'm talking about. It's freezing in here!"

Caroline shrugged. "It's usually warmer than this, but Nancy didn't want me to put up plastic sheeting until she was through showing the house. I'll get it up tonight."

"I don't think so," Jesse said.

"Yes, I will," she retorted. "Mrs. Henderson's always home by nine-thirty. I'd have done it already, but I haven't been spending much time here except to sleep, and it's warmer in the bedroom."

"It would have to be, wouldn't it?" he said roughly. "Otherwise, you'd freeze to death!"

She blinked at him, uncertain if he was angry or just concerned. "I told you—"

"You never said anything about the wind blowing through the walls!" he roared. "Sweet heaven, it's a wonder you haven't died of exposure!"

Angry and concerned. Thrilled despite herself, she murmured, "The walls are sound. It comes in around the windows."

He lifted off his hat and ran a hand through his hair. She happened to adore the way it waved back from his forehead, undulating softly as it shaped his skull, and she watched unabashedly as he tamped down his temper and resettled the hat.

"You should have said something about the shape this place is in," he grumbled.

She looked at the hairbrush in her hand and said, "I thought you knew. Nancy's apartment isn't much better."

"Nancy's place is at least warm. She has rugs on the floor and decent furnishings. The windows have been caulked and the doors weather-stripped. I should know, I did it myself," he added uncomfortably. "She never said anything about needing it done over here. I always assumed she was putting money back into the rental at the expense of her own quarters."

"She doesn't have any money to put back into this place, Jesse. We barely pay her enough to cover the taxes and insurance. It's all any of us could afford. Don't blame her. It's not her fault my mother didn't find someone like you to take care of what we couldn't."

He turned his head away from her. After a moment he swept a hand around, indicating the furnishings in the room. "Any of this stuff yours?"

"No. No, it's not. I think most of it belonged to an elderly aunt of Nancy's. She said once that her cousins gave her everything they didn't want themselves."

He nodded. "Okay. Well, you'd better pack a bag."

She really wasn't certain she'd heard him right. "Pack a bag?"

He turned a hard, flat look on her. "That's right, pack a bag. We'll pick up everything else later, including the car, for what it's worth."

Pick up everything else later? Caroline stared at him. "You're taking me home with you to stay?"

"Where else are you going to go? Even if you could find something you could afford on short notice, it wouldn't be any better than this."

Caroline blinked, not bothering to feel insulted. "Jesse, I've lived here more than four years now. Besides, when I suggested that I move into your house, I wasn't thinking about how crowded it would be when your brother and his family came to visit. You really don't have room for me."

"There's an attic room," he said, his tone clipped. "It might need some fixing up, but you can stay in the guest room until it's done. There's no closet, but my grandmother's wardrobe should do unless you've got dozens of dresses to hang."

She smiled at the absurdity of that. "Not hardly."

"The furniture's old, but it's good stuff, real antiques, some of it."

"I like antiques," she said softly. "They have a kind of continuity, you know. I always think about all the other people who must have used them down through the years.''

He nodded, but she could tell he wasn't really thinking about what she'd said. He cleared his throat. ''You'll have to use the hall bath on the second floor,'' he said.

''That's fine.''

''When Rye comes, he and Kara can share the bath with me, just as we did when we were boys.''

''Whatever. I don't mind sharing.''

''Maybe Kara can go in with you, then, and Rye and Champ and I can use the bath that joins our rooms.''

''Sounds good.''

He stuffed his gloved hands into his coat pockets. ''Go on. No use standing around in here freezing.''

She dropped her purse and brush on the seat of the chair and rushed to do as he'd said. The relief that she felt was almost overwhelming, and she dashed away grateful tears as she threw together clothing, toiletries and the few cosmetics she used. In afterthought, she added some books she'd picked up at the library. They were due soon, and she didn't want to chance forgetting about them. As she worked, she could hear Jesse clumping around in her kitchen, rattling pots and pans and poking around in her cabinets. Let him look, she thought. She had nothing to hide.

When she wagged her suitcase out into the living room, he was standing in the kitchen staring at all the stuff he'd pulled out onto the counter. ''We'll pack this up later. I can find someplace to store it until you're ready for it again.''

''All right. It shouldn't be too long. I've been intending to find a part-time bookkeeping job after the first of the year.''

''We'll see,'' he said. ''Ready?''

She nodded. He walked across the room and pulled the handle of the suitcase from her hand.

''Do you want to speak to Nancy before we go?'' he asked.

''No, I'll call later from the ranch. They tend to sleep in kind of late when they're not on the road.''

He didn't blink an eyelash at her use of the plural pronoun. ''Her husband should have done something about this place.''

''They're not married yet,'' she said. ''They're planning a Las

Vegas wedding next week, followed by a Las Vegas honeymoon. Besides, I don't think he's thought about it. They aren't here much, and when they are I don't see them. They're sort of all wrapped up in each other.''

The look he gave her said that wasn't excuse enough to his way of thinking, but he let it drop. ''Doesn't matter now,'' he said. ''Let's make tracks.'' He laid a hand at the small of her back and literally pushed her forward.

She didn't know exactly what she was letting herself in for, but she knew that the ranch house was warmer and more comfortable than this place. She'd gotten over the stupid idea that Jesse was attracted to her; she wasn't stupid enough to keep freezing her toes because of that disappointment. No matter how kind he was, he wasn't falling in love with her, and as long as she kept reminding herself of that fact, she ought to be fine. She didn't even pause for one last look before she closed the door and locked it.

Chapter Seven

He needed his head examined. What on earth had possessed him to move her into the house? But he knew the answer to that. He couldn't leave her there in that ratty apartment to freeze to death. Didn't the little idiot know that the coldest part of the winter was still ahead of them? True, this one was turning out to be one for the record, but he couldn't believe that even in a normal year some plastic sheeting stapled over the windows could make that place livable. Still, she'd lived there four years, so desperate to hold on to it that she'd apparently refused to leave until her mother's abandonment and the sale of the place had given her no real choice. It boggled the mind and made him feel small, pampered and ungrateful.

But to move her into the house! Why hadn't he just given her a raise so she could find someplace better? Well, it wasn't too late for that. He could still offer her the raise and promise to help her find a permanent place.

Yet, try as he might, he couldn't seem to find the words to broach the subject on the drive back out to the house, but he promised himself that he would bring it up soon. As for Caroline, she seemed strangely quiet. She stared out of the passenger side window of his truck as if she'd never seen snow before. He told himself that was good, but he couldn't quite convince himself that he liked it. This distance between them, the false politeness, felt even stranger than the avoidance. In an odd way, he missed that wide-eyed, determined youngster who had pursued him so shamelessly. Was that vanity, he wondered, or something else?

He wished she would just smile, maybe bat those thick eyelashes at him. Even without mascara her lashes were long and silky. He hadn't been able to help thinking in that moment when she'd opened her door to him that he was seeing her face just as it would look first thing in the morning, skin fresh and as glowing as pale gold, mouth a dusty rose, eyelids heavy with sleep, lashes like corn silk. He imagined her hair spread out on the pillow beneath her head, a lazy smile curling her lips. He rubbed a hand over his face, alarmed at the train of his thoughts.

Just this once, he wished fervently that he was the sort to indulge in pickups and one-night stands. Maybe sexual release would get Caroline out of his mind. Of course. Why hadn't he thought of it before? All he needed was a good workout between the sheets. But that would mean finding a willing woman who wouldn't expect more than sex and simple friendship—not an easy endeavor. Besides, he hated the so-called "singles scene." That was why he'd carried on so long with Nancy. The last thing he wanted to do was sit in some loud bar drinking booze he didn't want while pretending that he wasn't like the other randy fools looking over the available females, trying to figure out who was most likely to put out with the least trouble and expectations. The whole exercise was distasteful to him.

That was why Nancy had been such a gift. She hadn't balked when he'd stated bluntly that he wasn't interested in loving anyone or having anyone love him. All he'd wanted was privacy, sex and friendship, in that order, and she'd given it to him. And yet in all honesty he couldn't say that he really missed her. He hadn't even thought about her in months.

Maybe if he slept with Caroline he could stop thinking about her.

The very idea knocked him back in his seat. He was mad to

even think it. Caroline wasn't like Nancy. She wasn't world-weary and content just to survive, and she shouldn't be. She was too young for that, too lovely, too loving, too bright and giving. Caroline was like Kay, the kind of girl a boy could proudly make his wife, but he wasn't a boy anymore, and he'd been down that road; he knew better than to try it again. One Kay was enough. He couldn't bear a second. It wasn't fair, not to him and not to Caroline. He would just have to get over this unfortunate fascination with the lovely Miss Moncton. She was too young for what he had to offer. Too young. And he'd damned well better not forget it.

Caroline whirled, arms flung out, laughter bubbling up in her throat. "Oh, I love it! I just love it!"

Jesse bent and placed the last box on the floor in front of the old dresser. He closed the wardrobe door and waved a hand at the red-on-white vertically striped wallpaper. "Hope you don't mind the faded paper."

"Oh, no." She shook her head, rushing over to smooth a hand across the mellowed wall. "Your mother told me that you and your brother picked out this pattern."

He chuckled. "We thought it looked more 'soldierly' than the baby stuff she wanted to put up, you know, alphabet blocks and trucks, that kind of thing. I was all of nine, and I called it a game room, not a playroom."

Caroline laughed. "Whatever you called it, you and your brother must have had some good times up here."

He nodded, smiling. "Yeah, we fought some pretty fierce winter battles in this room. Usually it was the cowboys and the Indians banded together against the intergalactic warlords of outer space."

"I envy you that," she said softly. "You don't know what I'd give for a little sister or brother."

He lifted his arms and tucked his fingertips into the back pockets of his jeans. "I can guess."

She smiled doubtfully at that and spun away to run a hand over the arch of the footboard on the old iron bed she'd placed in the center of the long wall.

"Furniture's pretty old," Jesse said.

"Your mother said this was your grandmother's bed."

He nodded. "My grandfather bought it for her on impulse the very day it appeared in the mercantile window. She never slept on any other bed after that. My mother and both her brothers were born right there."

And no doubt conceived there, Caroline thought. Sighing dreamily, she pointed to the bedside table. "That was your grandfather's, wasn't it?"

"That's his smoking table," Jesse confirmed. "The holes in the top are for his pipes. He kept his tobacco in that tin-lined drawer, and that thing on top held his matches. There's a pumice stone inside for striking. Granny took it into her bedroom when he died, saying she wanted it close. That chair, too."

Caroline turned to the old rocker, its horsehair upholstery was faded and worn, but she wouldn't have changed it for the world. Jesse's grandfather had sat in that chair of an evening, rocking and smoking his fragrant pipes, perhaps reading some journal or other. "I'm going to knit a pretty throw for this," she said. Her books were stacked on the old-fashioned braided rug beside it, and she intended to sit here on cold evenings, snuggled warm in her throw and reading. Mornings she would curl up on one of the storage benches built into the dormer windows and gaze out at the snowy world, warm and snug in her attic room. A sense of belonging enveloped her. It was something she hadn't expected to feel, not after all that had happened—or hadn't happened— between her and Jesse.

"You know," Jesse said, scuffing one boot against the floor, "you've really made Mom's life a lot easier. She can't say enough good things about all you do around here. The fairest thing would be for me to give you a nice raise so you could get that apartment with the covered pool."

Caroline laughed. "Jesse, to tell you the truth, I can't afford that apartment until my school loans are paid off. Even with a fifty percent raise, I'd still have to get a second job or a roommate. This lovely room, right here in a real home with people I care about, is more than I've ever had. I can't tell you how happy I am with it."

He bowed his head. When he lifted it again, he was smiling. "I'm beginning to see how you kept your roving mama here four years after she wanted to be gone."

Caroline laughed again. "It wasn't easy, let me tell you. But she wanted me to be happy, she really did. Does, I mean. And I want her to be happy, too."

"Well, I'm glad you're happy now," he told her softly.

Impulsively she floated across the room to stand before him. "I know who I have to thank for it," she told him. Her arms flew up, but she checked the impulse to hug him, just barely, hanging on her tiptoes, arms sinking. "Thank you, Jesse."

Laughing, he threw out an arm and looped it about her. "You're welcome."

She laughed, too, and let her arms surround him, hugging tight just for a second before letting down her weight and stepping back. It felt so good to stand close to him, to feel the heat emanating from his big body. She smiled up into gray-blue eyes, surprised to find them reflecting a smoky warmth that momentarily stopped her heart.

His arm still hung loosely about her shoulders. His feet shuffled lightly as they moved against the hardwood floor, inching closer. His gaze dropped to her mouth, and she knew she wasn't mistaken.

"Jesse," she whispered in delight, placing her hands against his chest and sliding them upward onto his shoulders.

He made a small sound at the back of his throat, his arm sliding downward and tightening in the small of her back. His free hand came up to cup the back of her head, pulling her against him once more. His mouth came down on hers, his eyes squeezed tightly shut. She opened her mouth and coiled her arms around his neck, elated. He did want her! As if providing further proof, his tongue stabbed deep into her mouth. She cried out, the sound lost in him, as she felt that joining right through the center of her body. She crushed herself against him, reveling in the feel of his hard chest. He held her so tightly that she could barely breathe, and yet it wasn't tight enough.

Everything about that kiss was a revelation for Caroline. She had sensed it, suspected how it would be, could be, when two people wanted each other. It was addictive, this heady need, this swirl of sensation. Every touch felt extraordinarily rich, shockingly intense and not nearly rich or intense enough. She wanted, needed, more. She ground her mouth against his, and he responded by cupping the mounds of her hips and pulling her tight against him. The hard ridge pressing against her belly told her how much he wanted her and woke an inexplicable need in her to wrap her legs around him. She didn't have the slightest idea how to go about it, but her leg just naturally curled around his, unbalancing them both slightly so they teetered and then stumbled.

Suddenly he was pushing her away, his big hands clamped around her upper arms. The expression on his face said clearly that he hadn't intended to kiss her, that he was even more shocked by what they had done than she was. She smiled reassuringly at him, wanting to do it again, hoping to do it again. His grip tightened, and for an instant she thought he meant to pull her close again, but then he abruptly released her, stepping back at the same time. One hand went to his waist, the other swept through his hair while his gaze bounced off everything in the immediate vicinity but her.

"Jesse, I—"

"No." He sliced a hand through the air. "That was my fault. I apologize. It won't—"

"Don't apologize!" she pleaded. "I don't want you to apologize. I want you to want me."

His eyes blinked wide in obvious alarm. "Caroline, you don't know what you're saying."

"But I do, Jesse. I've wanted you from the beginning."

He literally backed away. "Don't be stupid. What I'm feeling isn't sweet or romantic. It's pure lust, nothing more, and you're too young for those kinds of games."

She curbed the impulse to stomp her foot. "I'm not too young!"

"Don't argue with me! I know what I'm talking about."

"Stop treating me like a child!"

He pointed a finger at her, his mouth already forming the sharp words he would say, but then he stopped, gulped and bowed his head. The pointed finger became part of a fist and then, gradually, an open hand. He sucked in a deep breath through his mouth, pushed it out again and lifted his head. "It won't happen again," he insisted flatly.

Caroline swallowed the arguments crowding her throat and folded her arms across her middle. It would do no good to try to make him see reason now. Stubborn, stubborn man! But he wasn't going to convince her that it was nothing, either. Didn't he see that they could have something grand between them? Well, he would. She would make him see that she wasn't too young to love him the way he needed to be loved. Then he would feel more than simple lust. She knew it. She had always known it, but he had made her doubt for a little while. That wouldn't happen again.

After a moment Jesse cleared his throat. She looked up, finding him perched near the opened door to the narrow stairwell. He leaned a hip against the doorjamb and mimicked her stance, folding his arms. She knew instantly that he was trying to foster a feeling of normalcy, move them back to that place where they'd been before the kiss. Well, let him try.

"The, um, computer came today."

She took her time, responding only after a long pause. "Oh?"

"Umm-hmm. Haven't had a chance to look it over yet or anything. I figure after the holidays..."

She nodded and looked down at the floor, letting him know that she considered the subject exhausted. He rubbed his nose and shifted his weight.

"Oh, by the way, Rye's doing some Internet research on that arthritis clinic in Denver. He's getting all the information he can and bringing it with him when they come for Christmas."

Caroline forced herself to relax. Strolling over to the bed, she swung down to sit near the foot, saying, "What does Sarah think about it?"

"I...I haven't mentioned it to her yet. Didn't know whether I should without all the information."

"Oh, I think you should," Caroline told him. "And while you're at it, why don't you encourage her to visit the hot springs north of town? Mrs. Henderson told me that she knows several people who go there for relief when their arthritis is bad. In addition to the springs, they offer some sort of herbal massage. They sell all sorts of supplements and things there, too, but Mrs. Henderson wasn't so sure they work. Still, it can't hurt to try it, and it's close.''

Jesse nodded. ''It might not be much more than a good rub-down and a hot bath, but at least it'll give her something else to look to while Rye's checking out the clinic.''

''That's what I thought, too.''

Nodding again, he pushed away from the doorjamb and threw a hand at the box on the floor. ''Well, that's the last of your stuff. I found a safe place in the barn for the rest.''

Caroline rose from the bed, her hand gripping a fanciful curl in the wrought iron footboard. ''Thank you again, Jesse, for everything.''

He flashed her a guilty glance, nodded once and went out the door. She listened to his footsteps on the narrow stairs, a slow smile moving across her mouth. If he really thought they could just forget that kiss, pretend it hadn't happened, then he was in for an especially difficult time. Poor darling. He thought he was dealing with a precocious child who didn't, couldn't, know what or who she wanted. But he would see. He would see that she was a woman with as much to offer him as she needed from him. He would see that no one could love him better than she could, be better for him than she could. He would see that he needed her, too, and then she would have him. They would have each other. Always.

''I don't know,'' Sarah said. ''Denver is so far away.''

''Mom, we've been through this,'' Jesse said patiently. ''Don't decide now. Wait until we have all the information.''

''Meanwhile, there's the hot springs,'' Caroline said hopefully.

Sarah looked at her husband, who sat at the kitchen table, hunched over his coffee cup. ''What do you think, Haney?''

Haney shook his head. ''My uncle had arthritis,'' he said in his gravelly voice, staring down at his cup. ''He was eighty-four when he died and still throwing a loop.''

Sarah's mouth flattened. Jesse rubbed a hand against the back of his neck. Caroline studied Haney thoughtfully. Didn't he realize the seriousness of his wife's disability? Now that she thought about it, Caroline was sure that he didn't. But how could he not? Unless he just didn't want to. She lifted an eyebrow at that, wondering if Jesse realized that Haney was doing his very best to ignore the seriousness of his wife's condition. Jesse, it seemed, was too concerned himself to notice.

"It won't hurt anything to check out the spa," he was saying. "Why don't you make an appointment?"

Sarah's hand fluttered stiffly around the roll of hair on the back of her head. "I don't know. It's been years since I last wore a bathing suit."

Caroline laughed. "You don't have anything to worry about there. I bet you'll look great."

"I don't know," Sarah said again. "I wouldn't want to go by myself."

"Of course you wouldn't," Jesse said.

"I'll go," Caroline volunteered. "I've always wanted to. They say it's very relaxing."

"What about you, Haney?" Sarah asked lightly, and Caroline knew suddenly that it was a very important question for the older woman. Haney, however, didn't seem to get it.

"Not likely," he scoffed, getting up from the table. "If I wanted to loll around in scalding water, I'd do it in my own bathtub upstairs. For free."

"It's more than the heat from the waters," Caroline said gently. "It's the natural minerals and these special creams they massage you with. It's a whole treatment."

"Sounds goofy to me," Haney said, shaking his head. "But you all do whatever you want. I've got work to do." With that he left the room.

The naked pain and disappointment in Sarah's eyes shone clearly before she turned away, busying herself at the sink. Caroline looked at Jesse and saw her own concern mirrored on his face. "I'll go," he said a little too enthusiastically. "Heck, a little relaxation never hurt anyone. I might even make a standing appointment."

Sarah sent a smile over one shoulder. "You don't have to go just for my sake."

"No, I want to go," he insisted. "I really do."

Sarah turned away from the sink, interest sparking in her eyes. "All right. If you want to go, then I will, too."

"Great!" Jesse said. "You make the appointment and just tell me when."

"All right," Sarah decided firmly. She looked at Caroline. "Do you have the number?"

Caroline nodded. "I'll make the call, if you want."

"Fine. An appointment for the three of us then."

"The three of us," Caroline echoed, sneaking a look at Jesse. He was smiling, but she could tell that he was regretting this already. He would go, nevertheless, for his mother. And Caroline would make the most of it. Oh, yes, she would.

Jesse tossed his small bag into the back seat next to Caroline and closed the door, then walked past his mother sitting in the passenger seat and around the front end to the driver's side door. He opened it and folded himself into place behind the wheel. His mother's car was a full-size top-of-the-line domestic model, but he still felt as though he were packing himself into a sardine can whenever he settled down into it. He preferred stepping up into his truck, but he didn't want to subject his mother to climbing up into her seat, and it would have been close quarters with Caroline tucked in between them. The last thing he needed was to be in close quarters with Caroline. So they were making this short trip in his mother's car.

Spreading his arm out along the back edge of the seat, he backed the car away from the garage and into the drive, guiding it carefully around Caroline's pitiful little pile of junk in the process. He'd had a new battery installed for her, but he had his doubts that would do much. A few minutes later they were driving through Durango and heading north. Twenty minutes after that, they turned into the icy lot of a low, unimposing brick-and-glass building and parked near the door.

"I don't know about this," Sarah said, gripping the armrest with her knobby hand.

"What's to know?" Jesse said lightly. "You're going to have a nice massage, and then we're all going for a relaxing swim."

"I don't know," Sarah said again, as Caroline got out of the car.

She walked around to Sarah's door, opened it and stooped down to look inside. She took one of Sarah's hands in hers. "I'll be right here with you the whole time," she promised warmly. "You'll feel better after. At the very least, your back won't bother you so much."

Her back? Jesse looked a question at Caroline. He hadn't known about his mother's back. Caroline telegraphed a silent message with her eyes. Don't worry, it said. She'll be okay.

Sarah nodded and released her safety belt. Caroline helped her out of the car while Jesse let himself out and pulled the two bags out of the back. They were whispering together when he came to open the door to the building for them, but stopped as soon as he drew within hearing distance. Sarah went in first, moving a little stiffly, with Caroline right behind her, her hand on his mother's shoulder. Sarah identified herself to the attendant behind the counter and was told politely to wait a moment while her masseuse came for her. They spent the time looking at the array of products on the shelves around the room. Caroline noticed they were big in aromatherapy here, as well as herbal teas and creams. Some of the supplements were pretty silly sounding: mugwort and lady's mantle, evening primrose and marigold. What on earth was saw palmetto?

A very strong-looking middle-aged woman in a pale green lab coat arrived with a clipboard. She led Sarah to a rattan chair and asked a few questions, after which she felt the joints in Sarah's hands and neck. She promised no miracles, but assured Sarah that she would feel better after the treatment.

"If you'll follow me," the masseuse said to Sarah, "we'll get down to work." She looked at Jesse and Caroline. "The two of you can change and enjoy the waters if you want. We won't be long, only about twenty minutes."

Sarah said haltingly, "I think I ought to visit the ladies' room first."

She sent a desperate look at Caroline who immediately said to the masseuse, "I'd like to come along for the massage if you don't mind. Maybe you can show me something I can do to help at home."

The masseuse nodded. "That's fine. Room six in, say, five minutes?" She pointed down a hallway next to a door marked "Ladies' Locker Room."

"Great," Caroline said, and Sarah nodded, obviously relieved. Caroline smiled at her as the masseuse walked away. "You go on. I'll meet you in room six in a minute."

Sarah nodded and hurried toward a sign that pointed toward the rest rooms. Jesse noticed that her shoulders were a little more stooped than usual. Caroline turned to him.

"She's feeling self-conscious. I helped her try on her bathing suit yesterday, and she said she looked like a dumpy old lady. I told her she has a great figure, and she does, but she says that she's getting old while Haney remains youthful and strong. Jess, I know it's none of my business, but I know you saw how Haney acted the other day. He doesn't seem to realize how hard this is for her. I think you should talk to him."

Jesse sighed. "And say what exactly? That he ought to pay more attention to Mom's aches and pains?"

"That he ought to pay more attention to her, period. She needs to feel attractive, Jesse. She needs to know that having arthritis doesn't mean she's turning into a little old lady. And one more thing."

He almost groaned aloud. She didn't expect much! Take Mom to the spa. Talk to Dad about something that was clearly none of his business! Now what? "Let's hear it."

"I'm going to try to get Sarah to go for a makeover, nothing dramatic, just some subtle makeup and maybe a haircut. That bun has to go."

Jesse barked a laugh. "Good luck! Mom's had her hair like that forever."

"Well, forever is too long in this case," Caroline said militantly. "I mean it, Jesse. She needs a younger look, something more sophisticated. Something that will make your father sit up and take notice for a change."

Jesse shook his head. "I'll speak to Dad if you think it'll help, but I wouldn't count too heavily on that makeover stuff, if I were you.''

"But you're not me," Caroline said confidently. "You just do your part and let me worry about the rest."

Taking one of the bags from him, she marched off as if to battle. Chuckling, he shook his head. A makeover! Cut her hair, put on makeup. It would never happen. As for the other, he would speak to his father about his mother's feelings, but he doubted he would be telling Haney anything he didn't already know. Still, it couldn't hurt if he kept it casual and light.

He carried his bag to the men's locker room, changed into a pair of navy blue shorts, which were the closest thing he had to a bathing suit, looped a towel around his neck and walked out to the pool.

Actually, it was plural. There were three pools. An attendant came to meet him, explaining that the temperature in the pools were cool, warm, and hot. The springs spilled into the hot pool. The water in the cool pool was piped in and mixed with water from the springs in the warm pool. Swimmers took them in different order, depending upon their objective. For first-timers they recommended ten minutes in the warm pool, followed by five minutes in the hot pool and five minutes in the cool, but he had a full hour and could do with it what he pleased. Jesse figured he might as well follow the recommendation, and the attendant assigned him a timer.

The air was chilly in the big room, despite the tendrils of steam rising off the hot pool, and the warm pool was a welcome change. It felt just like a big bathtub with too many people in it, not that it was actually crowded, though there were more swimmers here than in the other two pools. The smell of sulphur was fairly strong at first, but he quickly adapted and began to relax. He was feeling pretty good by the time he moved to the hot pool.

Hot was no overstatement, and the deeper he waded, the hotter it got. By the time he reached the middle, he felt as though his toes were boiling and his sinuses were as open as the barn door after the horse had bolted, but the few other bathers in attendance seemed perfectly at ease, and he figured if they could handle it, so could he. He waded back to the edge and hung his arms over the side, letting his body float upward. Either the water was cooler at the top or he was adjusting quickly. Nevertheless, five minutes was plenty. He still felt toasty warm as he padded the short distance to the cool pool and slid in.

It was all he could do to stay put. The water felt icy cold on his superheated skin. No wonder the warm pool was the most crowded! Before the five minutes were up, he'd gone from chattering teeth to fairly comfortable, but he didn't hesitate to get back to the warm pool. It felt glorious on his skin, and he actually felt his muscles relax and soften. He was floating at the edge, feeling rather like a human puddle, when Caroline and his mother came through the double glass doors.

They were both wearing bathrobes and carrying towels, which they laid on a bench next to his. Caroline looked around, spotted him and waved, then casually took off her robe and tossed it aside. Jesse sank straight to the bottom of the pool, gasping and choking as acrid water flooded his mouth and throat. When he surfaced, Caroline was standing with both arms raised, pinning her long, sleek hair atop her head. He gulped, expecting the top of her bikini to split at any moment. Made of faded blue-and-white-checked cotton, it was at least one size too small. Those perfect pale breasts literally spilled out of it. Conversely, the bottom seemed to fit perfectly, even if it did stop much too far below that unbelievably tiny waist. What really stopped his heart, though, were those legs. It was physically impossible to pack all those curves and that much leg into only five feet five inches.

She motioned sharply with one hand before he realized that he was obviously staring. A repeat of that action told him that he should be looking at something else. He switched his gaze in the direction she indicated and lifted both eyebrows as he took in what she'd been trying to show him. His mother, too, had laid aside her robe and was walking smoothly toward the warm pool, her chin tilted up. He recognized instantly how self-conscious she was—and with no cause whatsoever. Her shoulders were square, her back straight as a rod, her legs slim and shapely. He was greatly surprised by the amount of firm curve in her figure. The sly old girl had been hiding a treasure behind those shirtwaist dresses and baggy pants.

He went to meet her, stopping when the shallower water threatened to reveal more of his body than was wise, and reached out a hand to her. She came gracefully down the steps, putting her hand in his, and he drew her forward with a low, soft whistle.

"Gosh, Mom, you look great!"

Her cheeks pinked, and her chin came up a notch higher. "Don't be silly."

"I mean it! I always knew you were pretty, but I never realized what a figure you were hiding behind that apron of yours!"

She rolled her eyes, but a smile tugged at the corners of her mouth. Caroline's arrival commanded his gaze. She was beaming at him as she waded through the sultry water. He quickly switched his attention back to his mother. "Are you feeling as good as you look?"

Sarah laughed and lifted a hand to the back of her neck, rolling her head gently side to side. "Better, I'm sure. The massage was heavenly!" She turned to Caroline. "I'm tingling!"

"That's the cream," Caroline said.

Sarah put her hands to her hips and carefully bent at the waist. "I do believe my back is better, too."

"That would be the massage and those spine-elongating exercises she put you through," Caroline surmised.

"Just what is this with your back?" Jesse asked worriedly.

Sarah made a face and flashed a slightly censorial look at Caroline. "The last time I saw the doctor," she said reluctantly, "he told me that the arthritis is in my spine."

"And lately she's been having a good deal of pain there," Caroline revealed unrepentantly.

Jesse sighed and wrapped both arms about his mother's shoulders. "Mom, why didn't you say something?"

Sarah looked away. "Your father doesn't like me to talk about it," she said softly. "It doesn't help, anyway."

Jesse looked at Caroline. Right again. What else was she right about? He looked down at the top of his mother's head, at the heavy wrap of hair atop it. He tightened his hold a bit, absolutely certain what he should say next. Whether it would help or not was anybody's guess, but he knew he had to try. "You know," he said thoughtfully, "you really ought to update your look a bit."

Sarah stared up at him in shock. "What?"

"I'm serious. Get yourself a haircut and a new outfit or two. Stop hiding behind that apron all the time. Heck, I'm thirty-seven years old, and I just realized my mom's a babe! I think it's time you strutted your stuff a bit."

Sarah's mouth fell open. Then she laughed and swatted him playfully with her hand. "Jesse Dean, what has gotten into you?"

He hugged her a little tighter. "A guy can be proud of his mom, you know, even of how she looks, and you look great. Why not let everyone know it?"

Sarah waved away the idea. "I'll settle for feeling better." But as she lowered herself further into the water and began to swim away, the glimmer of interest sparkled in her eyes. Caroline stepped closer to Jesse through the swirling water. Her eyes seemed bluer than normal, shining with something deep and frightening. "Thank you," she said softly.

He shrugged, trying desperately not to react to her nearness. He told himself that he'd gotten over his shock at seeing all that luscious female skin. "When you're right, you're right," he said lightly.

"And when you're wonderful, you're wonderful," she told him huskily, her hand brushing across his chest as she moved after his mother. That was all it took. Suddenly, he was hard as stone again.

As soon as her back was turned he gulped a deep breath. "Yeah, I'm a saint," he muttered through his teeth, and immediately headed for the cool pool, hoping he could get there before anyone noticed that his shorts were suddenly much too tight.

Was it selfish of him to wish he'd never laid eyes on Caroline Moncton, even when she was undisputedly the best thing that had happened to his mother in a very long while? Sarah was much better, even if it was only temporary. Jesse could see it in her posture and face. Without Caroline, he would never have known that the arthritis had been found in his mother's spine, he wouldn't have seen her silent suffering, at least not until it had become unbearable for her. Without Caroline, that time would have come much sooner than it would now, if they couldn't prevent it, and he meant to try. Caroline took the burden of the household chores off Sarah and ran the house as smoothly as silk into the bargain. Their meals had never been better balanced, tasted finer or cost less. He had just seen a sparkle in his mother's eye that he had never seen before. Yes, it was definitely selfish of him to wish he'd never laid eyes on Caroline Moncton, but couldn't he at least have been spared the sight of her in that bikini bathing suit?

And now she was living right there in the house with him! Thank God his parents were there, too. He didn't want to think what might happen if he and Caroline spent too much time alone. One thing was certain, he had to get a grip on himself where little Miss Moncton was concerned. Otherwise, he was going to get a grip on her, and then heaven help them both.

Chapter Eight

Jesse let himself into the house and stomped straight down the hall without bothering to first divest himself of his outerwear. He went straight to the kitchen and found there just what he feared he would. His mother stood at the sink, her back to him, tightly hugging herself. He didn't have to see her face to know that she was crying. Caroline stood helplessly to one side, her expression stricken, her lower lip trembling. Jesse curbed the impulse to go to her and instead asked of either of them, "Where is he?"

"Upstairs, I think," Caroline whispered, but Sarah rounded on him.

"What did you say to him?"

Jesse tamped down his temper. It wasn't her fault, bless her. "Nothing that should have brought on this." He backed out of the room, muttering, "Stubborn, hardheaded, stupid son of a—" He was heading down the hall when he heard Sarah and Caroline follow him into the hall. He stopped and turned. Sarah's face was contorted with worry.

"Leave him alone, Jesse. You can't talk to him when he's like this. Just leave him alone!'' She lifted her hands to hide the tears trickling down her face.

In that moment Jesse could have stomped his dear old dad right into the floorboards, but he knew that would accomplish nothing. Haney's overreaction to Jesse's careful admonition to treat his mother with more concern and appreciation told Jesse that there was more going on here than one partner in a long-term marriage taking the other a bit for granted. Haney had erupted in a blaze of anger, shouting that he knew a sight more about Sarah Wagner than anyone else. He had told Jesse, among other things, that he'd loved ''that woman'' for forty years, that he was an excellent husband, that all she could think about anymore was her ''little aches and pains,'' and that even if it had been any of Jesse's ''goldarned'' business he wasn't about to take ''no lessons'' from him! Then he'd stormed off to the house, muttering about their business being their business, ''by damn!'' Jesse had been left to stable a horse before he could follow, and in that short a time, the harm had been done. And it was clearly up to him to smooth it all over again.

Jesse addressed himself to a morose Caroline. ''Take care of her.''

Nodding, she slid both arms around Sarah's shoulders and turned the other woman back to the kitchen. Jesse went straight down the hall and up the stairs. At the landing, he turned right toward his parents' room rather than left toward his own. The door was standing open, and he paused on the threshold long enough to see that his father was sitting on the edge of the bed still wearing his coat, his hat in his hands, head bowed and jaws working. Jesse walked into the room and stopped.

''Ready to talk instead of shout?''

Haney waved a hand at him but didn't look up. ''Nothin' to talk about,'' he said, that gravelly voice rife with pain.

Jesse unbuttoned his coat. ''Yeah, right. You go ballistic because I suggest Mom's feeling a little vulnerable and weak right now and—''

''She's not the only one!'' Haney barked, leaping up off the bed. ''Hell's bells, Jesse, you don't think it pains me to see her hurting? What do you expect me to do about it? I'm afraid to even touch her! All I know to do is to put it out of mind and go on!''

''Dad, I understand what you're saying, but—''

''You don't understand nothing! You haven't slept in the same bed with one woman for more'n half your life!''

For some reason that rocked Jesse back. It touched something hot and tender deep inside of him, something sore and aching that he hadn't even known was there. It must have been apparent, too, because Haney's face suddenly fell.

''I didn't mean that the way it sounded,'' he said more sedately.

Jesse shook his head and tried to put a normal face on it. ''No, you're right. I don't know what it's like to be married for a long time. But I do know Mom, and I know she's suffering right now.''

Haney looked away. ''I never said she wasn't suffering. I only said she ought to keep what's between us where it's always been and where it belongs, between us. She shouldn't have said nothing to you. She should've talked to me about it.''

Jesse finally understood the problem. ''Dad, she didn't say anything!'' He wouldn't tell him that it was Caroline who had pointed out the problem to him, only that the problem had become obvious. ''I just realized that she seemed to be needing a little special attention, that's all.''

Haney sent him a sharp look. He shifted his weight nervously, wiped his palms on his pants legs and looked away again. He swallowed, his Adam's apple bobbing up and down in his throat. ''You figured I didn't notice that?''

''Frankly, yes. Otherwise, you'd have realized that she wanted you to go to the spa with her the other day. She needed your support for that.''

Haney made a face. ''Jesse, I don't buy no snake oil. You ought to know that!''

''No one's saying that it's a cure, Dad!'' Jesse pointed out. ''But it did make her feel better, and right now that's about all we can do for her. She has a right to feel better, doesn't she?''

'''Course,'' Haney said dismissively.

''Besides,'' Jesse said, taking another tack, ''you should've gotten a load of her in that bathing suit.''

Haney stabbed him with his gaze. "You think I don't know how she looks in a bathing suit?"

Jesse disciplined a grin. "If you did, you'd have been there to look again."

Haney frowned. "That ain't no way to talk about your mother."

Jesse chuckled. "You're just sorry you weren't there."

Haney lifted a hand to the back of his neck. "Better I wasn't," he mumbled. He looked up at Jesse from beneath the crag of his brow, the message in his eyes telegraphing clearly. He didn't want the temptation. He really was afraid to touch her. Jesse understood suddenly why his mother was feeling self-conscious and old and why his father was short of temper. Was she that delicate? Or was it that Haney couldn't handle the situation? Whichever, Caroline had seen it, not him.

Rattled, Jesse stepped back, but he said, "Dad, Mom needs you more than ever just now."

Haney stared at him for a long moment as if trying to decide something, but then he nodded. "I know. I'll go down and apologize in a minute if you'll get Caroline out of the way. I've embarrassed myself in front of her enough."

Jesse nodded. It seemed that there ought to be something more to say, but for the life of him he couldn't think of it. He backed away, slowly, struck by how sad his father seemed to be just standing there with his hat in his hands. For the first time that morning, Jesse felt perfectly helpless, and he didn't know why.

"Just give me a minute," he mumbled, backing toward the door. Haney didn't reply and didn't look at him, though Jesse knew he'd heard. Jesse turned and walked out of the room, even more troubled than when he'd entered, just in another way.

He went lightly down the stairs and up the hall to the kitchen. Caroline was speaking to Sarah in a low voice as she thumbed through a cookbook. Sarah's eyes were dry, but she looked up the instant Jesse entered the room. For the first time, Jesse took off his hat. "Dad will be right down," he said with a tight smile. Relief flooded Sarah's eyes. She nodded and turned away. Jesse looked at Caroline, aware of the trepidation in her gaze. He kept his voice carefully neutral. "Caroline, can I talk to you for a few minutes?"

She closed the cookbook and laid it on the counter. "Sure."

She lifted her chin, but he knew dread when he saw it. He tried a smile, but it didn't seem to make much difference. He led her to the living room, where he set aside his hat, tugged off his gloves and slipped out of his coat. She trailed a hand along the back of the couch, but he noticed that the other was knotted into a fist. He ran a hand through his hair and opened his mouth to speak, but at the last instant she beat him to it.

"It's all my fault, I know. I never should have said anything to you. It wasn't any of my business, and if I hadn't convinced you to—"

"Whoa! I didn't bring you in here to bust your chops."

She looked up in surprise. "You didn't?"

"No! Dad just asked me to give him and Mom a little privacy so he could apologize."

"Oh." She sagged against the couch, obviously overcome with relief. "Thank God!"

He couldn't help a chuckle. "You didn't really think I was going to be that tough on you, did you?"

She made a face. "I wouldn't blame you if you were, but that's not what I meant." She put a hand to her chest and closed her eyes. "I felt so sorry for her! He was so angry, and I couldn't even tell what it was about at first." To his dismay, she burst into tears.

"Here now!" He stepped forward impulsively. She twisted her face away as if in shame. He lifted his arms, lowered them, lifted them again. Damn! He mentally slammed off the alarms blaring inside his head and did what seemed best under the circumstances: he stepped up and took her into his arms. She turned her face to his chest, sobbing like her heart was broken. "Caroline, honey, don't. There's no reason to cry. Come on now."

She looked up then. Her eyes were moss green, with tiny shards of blue in them. His heart constricted. "I thought I'd ruined it for them," she said through her tears.

He chuckled but not because it was funny. It just seemed terribly important that he make her feel better somehow. "Sweetheart, one shouting match doesn't make much dent in a forty-year-old marriage. Besides, you didn't do anything wrong. Neither did I, come to think of it. No, there's more here than either one of us realized, I think, but they'll work it out. You'll see.''

Her breath came in shudders. "You're sure?"

"Absolutely."

She closed her eyes, sighing in relief. "There's such pain there, Jesse. It breaks my heart. I couldn't bear it if I were the cause!"

He could see very clearly that she meant that, and it touched him deeply. "Sugar, you've done nothing but good around here. Your concern for my mother is obvious and helpful—to her and to me. Even to Dad."

She sniffed, a smile starting. "Really?"

"Really. Now dry those tears."

But instead of drying up, fresh tears welled again. She shook her head. "I can't help it," she whispered, a smile wobbling on her lips. He knew then that he had to kiss her. There just wasn't any other way.

It was as natural as breathing, bending his head to hers, covering her mouth with his. At first it was all comfort given and taken. She tasted of honey and salt, the saltiness of her tears, the honey beckoning him deeper into her mouth. It might have ended just the way it had started if she hadn't gone up on tiptoes, her hands lifting to his head, fingertips brushing lightly through his hair then splaying to cup his head and press his mouth harder to hers. Suddenly, even knowing that he was going to regret it, he desperately wanted that honey and plunged his tongue into her mouth for it.

She shuddered and tightened her hands in his hair, lifting against him. As she pressed against his chest he thought of her breasts spilling over the top of her bathing suit and groaned. Her hands slid down the nape of his neck to his shoulders, briefly massaging the muscle there before her arms slid around his neck.

He tightened his arms, and that leg curled around his again. At the same time, her tongue dueled with his and slid into his mouth, nearly blowing the top of his head off. Another moment and she would completely wrap herself around him, taking him between her legs. He quivered at the thought, achingly aware of the hardness in his groin and the softness of her belly. Then she pulsed against him. It was just the barest rocking of her hips, the tiniest tilting of her pelvis, the slightest rub against him, and he very nearly exploded. Once more and he would, like some randy schoolboy copping a feel.

Thoroughly disgusted with himself, he pushed her away, held her off, really, the length of his arms between them. The hardness in his groin knotted painfully, but it served him right. Damnation, what was he doing? He had to get control of this! The dreamy look on her face didn't help him one bit. Eyes glazed, mouth parted and moist, she showed him naked desire. It was all he could do not to pull her against him and finish what he had so stupidly started. But he wouldn't. Hell, no, he wouldn't. He hoped. He stared at one hand, willing the fingers to unwind and release her. To his relief, they did. He jumped back about a yard.

She stayed there, swaying lightly, and a slow smile curled her lovely lips. She took a deep breath and reached out a hand for him. "Jesse."

The sound of his name skittered over his nerve endings. He shuddered and shook his head defensively. "No. No, no, no, no, no!"

She languidly put both hands to her hair, still looking at him like she could eat him up in a single gulp. "Jesse, don't you see? It's perfect. You're perfect for me. You're everything I've ever wanted, and I know you—"

"Caroline! Stop right there!" He didn't think he could bear more. He sucked air and searched for the words. He knew they were there somewhere, buried under all those images of her in that swimsuit, wrapping herself around him.... Oh, Lord, he was losing his mind! She took a step toward him. He jumped, putting out an arm.

"Caroline, this is all my fault! I'm sorry! I know I said it wouldn't happen again, and it wouldn't have if—" He gulped. Better not go there. "What I mean is, I...I took advantage of a w-weak moment, and I'm thoroughly ashamed. I give you my word, it won't—will not—happen again."

She actually stamped her foot. "Jesse! Why don't you get it? I want it to happen again! And again! And—"

"No!" He made a slicing motion with his hand, cutting her off. Realizing that he had shouted, he lowered his voice to a rumble. "I mean it, Caroline! I won't have an affair with a girl young enough to be my daughter!"

She made a sound somewhere between a growl and a screech, a warning clear enough to make him backtrack to complete factuality.

"All right, almost old enough to be my daughter! That's not the point!"

She put her hands to her hips. "No, it's not the point, Jesse! Age doesn't have anything to do with this."

"You're saying that because you aren't old enough to know any better!"

"I'm saying it because it's true!" Her voice rose alarmingly. "I know you want me as much as I—"

He shushed her with one eye on the doorway. "Keep your voice down!"

"I know you want me as much as I want you!" she hissed, hands knotting into fists. "You can't deny your feelings, Jesse, not with me! Not after that kiss!"

"You let me worry about my feelings!" he hissed back, punctuating it with a jab of a forefinger. "I mean it, Caroline! This has got to stop! I will not...become involved with you!"

"You are so stubborn!" she said, stamping her foot again.

"That's right! So just forget about it! Confine yourself to my mother's feelings and forget about mine! This is the end of it. Understand me?"

She folded her arms, head cocking to one side. "Oh, I understand you, Jesse. Now you understand this! I'm not some teeny-bopper with overactive hormones! I'm a woman with a mind of my own, and I know exactly what—and who—I want. If you just give us a chance, we can be really good for each other."

"No, we can't, baby," he told her sorrowfully. "That's what you've got to get through your pretty head. I'll never be any good for you. Never."

She straightened her spine and looked him square in the eye.

HOW TO PLAY

"PINBALL WIZ"
and be eligible to receive
THREE FREE GIFTS!

1. With a coin, carefully scratch the silver circles on the opposite page. Then, including the numbers on the front of this card, count up your total pinball score and check the claim chart to see what we have for you. **2 FREE** books and a **FREE** gift!

2. Send back this card and you'll receive brand-new Silhouette Special Edition® novels. These books have a cover price of $4.25 each in the U.S. and $4.75 each in Canada, but they are yours to keep absolutely **FREE**!

3. There's no catch. You're under no obligation to buy anything. We charge you nothing for your first shipment. And you don't have to make a minimum number of purchases — not even one!

4. The fact is, thousands of readers enjoy receiving books by mail from the Silhouette Reader Service®. They like the convenience of home delivery and they like getting the best new novels before they're available in stores...and they love our discount prices!

5. We hope that after receiving your free books you'll want to remain a subscriber. But the choice is yours — to continue or cancel, anytime at all! So why not take us up on our invitation, with no risk of any kind. You'll be glad you did!

FREE
MYSTERY GIFT!

We can't tell you what it is...but we're sure you'll like it! A free gift just for accepting our **NO-RISK** offer!

The Silhouette Reader Service® — Here's how it works:

Accepting your 2 free books and mystery gift places you under no obligation to buy anything. You may keep the books and gift and return the shipping statement marked "cancel." If you do not cancel, about a month later we'll send you 6 additional novels and bill you just $3.57 each in the U.S., or $3.96 each in Canada, plus 25¢ delivery per book and applicable taxes if any.* That's the complete price — and compared to the cover price of $4.25 in the U.S. and $4.75 in Canada — it's quite a bargain! You may cancel at any time, but if you choose to continue, every month we'll send you 6 more books, which you may either purchase at the discount price or return to us and cancel your subscription.

*Terms and prices subject to change without notice. Sales tax applicable in N.Y. Canadian residents will be charged applicable provincial taxes and GST.

If offer card is missing write to: Silhouette Reader Service, 3010 Walden Ave., P.O. Box 1867, Buffalo, NY 14240-1867

BUSINESS REPLY MAIL
FIRST-CLASS MAIL   PERMIT NO. 717   BUFFALO, NY

POSTAGE WILL BE PAID BY ADDRESSEE

SILHOUETTE READER SERVICE
3010 WALDEN AVE
PO BOX 1867
BUFFALO NY 14240-9952

NO POSTAGE
NECESSARY
IF MAILED
IN THE
UNITED STATES

"I don't believe that, Jesse Wagner. I don't believe one word of it!"

It was obviously no use. It was going to be totally up to him to protect the little fool from herself. If only he was up to it!

"Hell!" he swore, grabbing his coat and hat.

She wrapped her arms tighter and narrowed her eyes at him, as if to say that she wasn't about to give up.

"Hell and damnation!" He crammed the hat on his head and got out of there, slinging on his coat only as he tore out of the house into the cold, gray day.

That woman was going to be the death of him! How did she get so aggravating in just twenty-one years? How did she get so— No, she was not irresistible. Tempting as heaven, but not irresistible! He wouldn't let himself even think it. Because he would resist the fetching Caroline. He would resist her until she forgot all about him. And then she'd be safe. They'd both be safe. And life could get back to normal again.

Why was it that normal had never seemed so bare? Or so lonely.

It took far less careful prodding than Caroline had anticipated to convince Sarah that the beauty makeover was a good idea. Even though Sarah and Haney had kissed and made up Caroline sensed an uncertainty there, a silent worry too personal to be shared, but whether or not that had anything to do with Sarah's receptiveness to change, Caroline couldn't be sure. She did not doubt, however, that Jesse was ultimately responsible for Sarah's decision to go through with the makeover, and she blessed him for making the suggestion in advance of her own—even if she did want to wring his neck these days.

He had gone right back to his polite, charming, very distant old self, as if he had never kissed her and she had not declared herself and nothing had changed. But two could play that game. Let him think that he had her at a safe distance. She was right here in the same house, and there would be plenty of opportunities to prove her point. Meanwhile, Christmas was coming and Caroline loved her attic room. She would be content for the moment if not for Sarah's brooding.

At least Sarah's arthritis seemed less painful for several days after their visit to the springs. She actually managed the Christmas shopping in good time and enjoyed a little window shopping along with it. Caroline talked Sarah into a few purchases for herself and in the process gathered a decent understanding of Sarah's personal taste and private wish list. Then came the appointment at the beauty salon.

They were like two giddy girls. Caroline went along to pave the way and lend a helping hand. Mostly she helped Sarah decide to do all that the stylist suggested and then held her hand while more than a foot of hair was chopped off, the remaining was shaped, colored a buttery blond highlighted with silver and brushed into a full, classic style that would be easy to maintain. In the end, it swung sleek and straight from a side part to her collar, where it curved under gently, framing her patrician face. It remained long enough to sweep into a short, simple ponytail or a sophisticated twist, the color bringing a glow to her supple skin.

Sarah was thrilled. She went into the makeup session with heightened enthusiasm. The cosmetician used a touch of plum shadow to bring out the color of her gray-blue eyes, a bit of pencil to darken the natural arch of her brows, and a subtle touch of mascara. A soft blush on her cheekbones accentuated their height. The final touch was a rich pink moisturizing lipstick for every day and a dramatic blue-red for dressy evenings. In the slim jeans and soft pink sweater set that Caroline had convinced her to buy, Sarah looked fifteen years younger.

"Only my hands look old!" she said in amazement, prompting a lavish manicure that left her with oval, pearl pink fingernails and soft, elegant hands.

Caroline could hardly wait to show her off. Heads literally turned as they walked down the street together arm in arm. A woman whom Sarah had known the better part of twenty-five years failed to recognize her when they passed by. Then, after Sarah went back to speak to her, she gushed on and on, finally leaving with the name of the shop and stylist and a personal recommendation. Sarah was laughing and gay in a way that Caroline had never seen her. She bought a pair of earrings and a frivolous pair of bedroom slippers before they headed home—and gave Caroline another delicious idea.

Half an hour later they were chattering like a couple of magpies while hurriedly preparing dinner. It was almost on the table when Caroline heard the side door open. Excitement sped up her heart, but a glance at Sarah found her calmly arranging tomatoes and sliced onions on a small plate. As footsteps clearly belonging to Jesse moved down the hallway, however, Sarah sent an apprehensive glance at the doorway, then quickly swept off her apron, draping it over the back of a chair. When Jesse arrived, she was poised, placing the plate of fresh vegetables on the table.

For a long moment, Jesse simply stood in the doorway and stared. Then slowly his jaw dropped and he stepped into the room.

"Mother?"

Sarah swept back one side of her hair, then looked at him. Suddenly her face broke into a smile. "You like, huh?"

Jesse came forward, staring wondrously. "Holy cow!" He began to laugh, then swept her off her feet, swinging her around, his hands at her waist. They were all laughing and he was just setting her back on her feet when Tiger and Handsome crammed into the kitchen together.

Their conversation stopped dead as they saw Jesse and Sarah. They looked a question at Caroline, who merely smiled. As one, they took a second look. As one, they dropped their jaws. As one, they both exclaimed, "Mizz Sarah!" And then they were babbling about the change in her, how pretty she was, how young. They were both touching her as if they couldn't quite believe their eyes, and she was smiling, inclining her head, accepting their compliments with graceful, almost regal, ease.

"Wow-ow!" Handsome exclaimed as Haney came into the room. Like the others he paused in the doorway. Silence and stillness contained them all. Haney looked around the room, a mild question in his eyes. Then those eyes came to rest on Sarah, and he froze. After a moment he blinked. An instant later he started calmly across the crowded room, the others parting to let him through. He walked straight to her and stared. His strong jaw seemed to soften, his mouth moved slightly. One strong, leathery hand came up and skimmed over her hair as a slow smile creased his face.

"Looks like that girl I married is still right here with me," he said gently, and Sarah laughed deep in her throat, leaning into him. His arm slid around her waist, and he pulled her close, bending his head to kiss her temple.

The moment was so poignant that no one else seemed quite able to touch gazes, but then Jesse sent a smile and a wink at Caroline, and she rocked up on her toes, beaming. Tiger thumped Haney on the back, and Jesse turned a grinning Handsome toward his chair. Suddenly everyone was talking and laughing again as they hurried dinner onto the dining room table.

"Tell. Tell all," Jesse demanded when they'd all taken their seats, and Sarah did, laughing about the ghastly moment the scissors had first whacked through her thick hair. Caroline described how the look on her face had gone from appalled to pleasantly amazed as the mirror revealed the transformation.

Haney covered Sarah's hand with his on top of the table, saying, "Never thought I'd be glad you cut your hair."

Sarah smiled almost seductively, and then she broke the moment by preening comically, tossing back her head and sweeping her hair from her neck with a flick of her hand.

It became a celebration, laughter and merry conversation making pan-grilled hamburgers, potato chips and barbecued beans something special. Afterward, Tiger and Handsome each kissed Sarah's cheek before taking their leave, and Tiger spared Caroline a conspiratorial wink. Handsome had never warmed up to her after her initial rejection of his flirtatious overtures, but even he nodded in acknowledgment before leaving the room. Haney complimented Sarah on an excellent meal, ignoring Caroline completely, much to her delight. It was Jesse who offered to help Caroline clean up, however, freeing Sarah to accompany her husband to the den.

Sarah firmly refused, however, and made a big show of pulling on a pair of rubber gloves over her manicured nails before starting the dishwater. She hummed as she did the washing up. When they were finished, she led Caroline to the den, where she stood a moment watching the television before announcing casually that she thought she'd take a warm bath and turn in early, it having been an eventful day. Haney said nothing, but he slid to the edge of his chair and seemed to perch there, his attention apparently trained on the television even as his posture indicated a certain impulse to follow his wife. Caroline deemed it the perfect moment to put into motion her latest idea.

Looking at Jesse, she said evenly, "Would you mind if I spoke privately with your father for a moment?"

Jesse was clearly disgruntled and curious, but he got up off the couch with a slow nod and left the room. Caroline sat down in his place, leaning forward earnestly, her elbows on her knees. Haney looked straight at her.

"Something on your mind?"

She nodded. "Sarah and I have had the opportunity to do some window shopping lately, you know, because of Christmas, and I thought you'd like to hear what she's been looking at with such longing for herself. It doesn't seem appropriate for anyone else to give her."

He nodded, hands folded together as he mimicked her pose. "I've kind of had something picked out, but if there's something special she really wants..."

Caroline mentally crossed her fingers. "It's a peignoir set, you know, a nightgown and robe. Dove gray silk chiffon and lace, full-length. It's really elegant and also rather expensive. She said it was the most beautiful thing she'd ever seen, but she wouldn't spend the money. Instead, she bought herself a pair of matching bedroom slippers. When I held it up to her, the color was just spectacular, and the gown... Frankly, it's a little, well, sensuous. So I thought if you were, you know, embarrassed to go into the boutique and buy it yourself, I would be glad to do it."

It was impossible to read his expression, or lack of one. She couldn't tell if he was interested at all until he shrugged and said, "No, I'll take care of it."

He looked away, and she sat back, telling herself that the rest really was up to him. Jesse reentered the room then, a challenge on his face. She waved him over and curled her legs up beneath her, preparing to turn her attention to the television. He walked to the end of the couch and paused.

Haney sat on the edge of his chair, staring pensively at nothing whatsoever. Jesse cleared his throat, and Haney started. Then very casually he rose, placed a hand at the back of his neck and muttered, "I think I'll turn in early, too. Not as young as I used to be."

He smiled lamely and moved past Jesse. Just as he reached the end of the couch, he paused and laid a hand on Caroline's shoulder, gripping it lightly. She looked up at him and smiled, satisfied now that she had done the right thing. He went out of the room, moving rather quickly for someone "not as young as he used to be."

Jesse looked down at Caroline, his hands on his hips. She raised an eyebrow, and a smile twitched at the corner of his mouth. Suddenly they both began to chuckle. Jesse sat down in his father's chair. "Can you get over it?"

"The change you mean?"

"In both of them," he said. "Mom looks fabulous. Well, I don't have to tell you. You're the mastermind. But somehow Dad seems...rejuvenated, too."

Caroline put her head back and laughed joyously. "Do you blame him? She's really a very beautiful woman, and he'd have to be half-dead not to catch the lures she was casting out."

He smiled and came right out with it then. "What was the private confab about, may I ask?"

Caroline leaned forward conspiratorially and told him. He pursed his mouth, lifted a brow and inclined his head in approbation. "You sly girl, you. What will you come up with next?"

"Actually," Caroline said, "I have a couple of suggestions for your Christmas list, too."

"Do tell, Miss Moncton."

"We saw a four-piece wardrobe set the other day, skirt, sweater, a classy jacket-coat, slacks, all in a perfectly beautiful plum-colored wool blend. It suits her to a T. I know she'd love it. She wears an eight, by the way, maybe a ten on top." She gave him the name of the boutique, and he actually took out a slip of paper and a pencil and wrote it down.

"All right, Miss Christmas Elf. What else?"

She spread her hands. "That ought to do it."

He studied her a moment and asked bluntly, "What are you going to get her?"

She smiled. "The hot springs seemed to help, don't you think?"

He nodded. "I don't think she's cured by any means, but she seems to feel better."

"Exactly. So I thought, why not the full spa treatment? Really pamper her, you know? Facial, massage, mud bath, manicure, pedicure, steam room, the works."

"That's pretty costly, isn't it?"

She shrugged. "It'll be worth it. She'll be a whole new woman by New Year's. Besides, I've had a raise recently."

"Oh? Funny, I don't remember that."

"I'm not paying rent, remember?"

Jesse nodded. "Ah. Still..."

"It'll be fun. I want to do it. I'll economize with the rest of my list. Actually, I'm a pretty good knitter, so I'm making everything else, and I only have one more gift to finish. So don't worry about it. Other than my school loans and a few small debts, that old heap of mine and some personal things, I don't have much else to spend my money on."

Jesse nodded reluctantly. "Okay, if you're set on this."

She hunched her shoulders, as excited as she'd ever been about anything. "I am. I can't wait, actually. She's going to have a wonderful Christmas!"

He folded his hands in his lap and looked at her. "You really love my mother, don't you?"

She was surprised. "Of course I do. Why wouldn't I?" Then she shook her head. "You don't know how wonderful she is. She's just the perfect mother."

Jesse looked down at his hands. "Sometimes you make me feel so unappreciative and clueless."

She laughed and moved to the edge of her seat, reaching out a hand to swat his knee lightly. "Jesse! That's not true. You do everything for her that you know how to do."

His gaze was sudden, sharp. "But I'm the one who's had it all, Caroline—mother, father, brother, home, even the ranch. My boyhood was a delight, rich in every way. Yet you're the one who sees every need and takes steps to meet it. And you've had none of those things.''

"That's not true.'' She inclined her head in partial capitulation. "Okay, my own mother isn't exactly the conventional sort of parent, and we have flitted from pillar to post for almost my whole life, and I've missed having a real family and a real home. But at least I know exactly what I want, Jesse. And look, my mama didn't raise no idiots, as the saying goes. I'm smart enough to know I can have it all and to go after it. Haven't you figured that out yet?''

He opened his mouth, closed it again and seemed to pull back. "This conversation's getting a little deep,'' he said carefully, "and I'm really too tired for it. I think I'll call it an early night, too.''

Caroline sighed and shook her head as he rose to his feet. "You left out something earlier, Jesse, when you were talking about yourself. You said you'd had the perfect childhood, parents, home, brother. You even mentioned the ranch. But you left out your wife, Jesse. Why is that?''

He stared down at her, his face going rigid. "Good night, Caroline,'' he said tightly, and walked away.

Caroline braced one arm on the back of the sofa and put her hand in her hair. "Why is that, Jesse?'' she whispered. "If you loved her so much, why did you leave her out? And why are you trying to leave me out, too?''

Chapter Nine

The light rap of knuckles on the office door skittered up his spine, punctuating the state of his nerves. Nevertheless he steeled himself and called out in a steady voice, "Come in."

She opened the door, peeked around it and beamed an electric smile before slipping inside and closing it behind her, just as he'd intended. Jesse sat back in the creaky old desk chair and measured out a friendly smile of his own. "Caroline. Thanks for taking the time for this. I'll keep it short and sweet." He picked up the envelope and transferred it to the front edge of the desk. Cautiously she stepped up to the desk and reached out a slender hand. "Merry Christmas," he said, tucking his hands behind his head as he leaned back in the chair.

Caroline looked over the plain white envelope carefully, turned it and flipped up the flap, extracting the check with the tips of her fingers. Impassively she read the number printed on the check face, and her eyes widened briefly. Then she merely slid the check back into its envelope, smiled wanly and said, "Thanks."

She made no effort to hide her disappointment, and Jesse made no effort to hide his exasperation.

"For pity's sake, Caroline, that's a generous Christmas bonus if I do say so myself."

"Yes, it is," she conceded baldly. "Too generous. Frankly, I'd be happier with a pretty scarf or a nice wallet or, God forbid, cheap perfume, anything personal."

"Personal," he echoed, wanting to kick them both, her for being so damned difficult, himself for caring. He slammed forward in his chair and snatched up an ink pen, fixing his gaze on the forms spread out before him. "Yeah, well, personally I'd appreciate it if you'd keep your disappointment to yourself," he grumbled. "That's considerably more bonus than I've given either of the hands, and they've been here a hell of a lot longer than you have."

He assumed that would be the end of it, and only then realized just how much pleasure he'd taken in setting down the amount. Stupid little hen. Didn't she realize that it was her own generosity that had prompted his? He knew perfectly well what a full day at the local spa was costing her, but he knew, too, that she would take as much joy in the gift as his mother would, perhaps more so. He wanted to aid that, dope that he was, and look what it got him. But then, what had he expected?

He pushed that question to the back of his mind, even as he became aware that she had not moved away from the desk, merely around it. He turned his head toward her just as she settled herself on the corner of the desk next to him. Leaning back again, he put a little distance between them and waited while she studied the envelope in her hand.

"Sorry," she said finally, her voice pleasantly husky.

Jesse waved a hand negligently, ready to forgive her anything and not nearly as upset by that fact as he ought to be. "Forget it," he said.

She folded her arms, tapping the edge of the envelope against her chin. "I've told myself for a lot of years that money isn't anything important, and it isn't, unless you don't have it when you need it, but it sure can make important things seem easy at times, like being able to give somebody something you want them to have." She tossed the envelope down in front of him and leaned back slightly, her upper body weight balanced on the heels of her hands and braced on her arms. "I like to be extravagant sometimes," she said.

He chuckled indulgently. "Doesn't everyone?"

"Probably. You obviously do."

"Aw, it's not that," he said. "I just—"

Suddenly she leaned forward. "You just wanted to make it easy for me to be extravagant in my giving. You're giving me this money because you're afraid I'm spending too much on your mother's Christmas gift."

He cleared his throat, quite as pleased with himself now as he had been when he'd inked in the amount on the front of that check, and dismayed at the same time. Was there no winning in this situation? Must her understanding and gratitude come with such awareness? How could he hope to please her and not heighten this damnable attraction between them?

"I made a snap judgment," she said. "I thought you were trying to avoid any personal involvement."

"I am," he said honestly, running a hand through his hair in frustration, "or I would if I could just figure out how."

She slipped off the corner of the desk and gently, determinedly inserted herself between it and him. As she levered herself up onto his lap, he groaned, partly in outright fear, partly in helpless delight. Sweet heaven, had a woman ever felt so good? Had doom ever felt so close at hand? She placed her arms around his neck and pressed her weight against him, forcing the chair to lean back with both of them.

"I won't let you," she whispered. "I can't, Jesse. You're too perfect. I want you too much."

He was shaking his head slowly side to side. "I'm not perfect, honey, and that you could think so just proves that you don't know—"

She didn't let him finish. Catching his head between her hands, she molded her mouth to his with exquisite precision. He couldn't have kept his hands to himself then if his very life had depended on it. He didn't even try. When touching her was as much punishment as pleasure, what was the point? One hand went to her waist. The other settled on her thigh. Then he took them both where he really wanted them, reflexively cupping one breast and inserting the other between her legs to rub gently at their apex. She closed her hands in his hair and worked her mouth over his, her tongue lashing and licking and finally driving between his teeth. Within moments he felt her dampness, confirmation that she did, indeed, want him there. He couldn't bear any more.

He dropped his hand from her tightening breast and pulled the other from between her thighs, clutching the arms of the chair. Gradually, the heat of her mouth on his cooled as she broke the kiss and laid her forehead against his. He enjoyed holding her on his lap a few moments longer, then firmly, determinedly set her off. She stood over him, one hand on her sweetly rounded hip, the other delicately sweeping across her lips, a wealth of unspoken desires in her eyes. He nodded in complete understanding. Then with a strength of will he hadn't even known he possessed, he pulled his chair a little closer to the desk and looked around for his pen. Where had that thing gone? He didn't remember letting go of it, dropping it, swallowing it. Spontaneous combustion, perhaps? He wouldn't doubt it. She brushed a hand against his cheek, picked up her check and, mercifully, left him to try to bully his mind and body back into compliance with his battered, besieged mind.

Eventually he gave up looking for his pen and simply faced the facts.

He didn't have a snowball's chance in hell. The attraction was simply too potent. Before this was over, somebody was going to get hurt, both of them probably. The only question now was how bad it was going to be. But he'd do his best. He'd go down fighting, by God. He couldn't live with himself any other way—and maybe not even then.

They laughed at her but not with derision. Haney shook his head and said that he'd never seen anyone have such fun with pine boughs and string. Jesse said he wouldn't know he was indoors instead of out if not for the warmth and the furniture. Sarah just marveled at her energy and inventiveness, saying that it had been years since the house had been truly decorated for the holiday season. What they couldn't understand, of course, was that it was a dream come true for Caroline: a family Christmas in a

warm and loving home. Even if she wasn't a m
family, she wanted everything to be perfect. So she
house in boughs gathered for her by the men and the finer
lected over Sarah's lifetime, each piece placed with careful, joy
deliberation.

The tree was a special joy. Jesse and Tiger took her out with
them on a Sunday afternoon to choose and cut it. They hauled it
home in the back of an old ranch truck, shook the snow from its
swaying boughs and wrestled it into the house. It was an immense
thing, seven feet tall and fat. Sarah had a place cleared in front
of a living room window, and they stood it there, taking forever
to get it straight in the special stand that Haney had constructed
when Jess and Rye had been boys. With Sarah's direction, Haney
and Jesse outfitted the tree with strand after strand of multicolored
lights, then sat back to gobble popcorn and tease Caroline about
the meticulousness with which she hung the ornaments over
which Sarah rhapsodized.

Sarah had a memory for every bulb and snowflake, some of
which had belonged to her great-grandmother, but the antiques
and other beauties weren't closest to her mother's heart. Every
crudely shaped and sloppily painted, grade-school-era clay Santa
brought out a story about one of her boys. Every poorly carved,
semipolished lump of knotty pine elicited a teary reminiscence
that Caroline soaked up like a sponge. Her own personal favorite,
however, was the delicate bisque and velveteen angel that claimed
the place of honor on the tip of the tree. Passed down through
the family for generations, it had been fashioned by some long-
dead maiden aunt. Caroline considered it a work of art, a priceless
family treasure. She sat late at night after everyone else had gone
to bed, watching the lights blink and staring at that ageless angel,
hoping that the one who had fashioned it still shared in the joy
it brought and praying for good things for this special family.

She baked every festive goody in Sarah's Christmas cookbook.
Haney teased her by saying that she'd used a crate of sugar and
a barrel of food coloring. Jesse said that Haney ought to know
since he'd eaten half of it himself, though Jesse said it as he
munched the leg off a cookie reindeer.

Gaily wrapped gifts appeared beneath the tree as if by magic.

...oaking in rum and spices. Sarah put on ...he place was packed to the hilt and fairly ...the time Rye and his family arrived for ... evening of the twenty-third.

...ve been more thrilled if they'd come ex-...s it was, she stood back, watching with delight ... ...ers affectionately greeted family. Rye, Kara and Champ were ... what she expected. For one thing Rye was not so large as his older brother and father, and his thick, wavy hair was almost completely gray. In some ways he was almost a throwback to the cowboys of old, from his drooping mustache to his run-down boots. But his gray-blue eyes were pure Wagner. Kara was a big, busty blonde as cowboy as he was. Completely free of artifice, she wore both her jeans and her femininity with a casual self-assurance that Caroline admired and with which she identified. Champ's Native American blood dominated his appearance, making him seem a miniature version of Shoes Kanaka, his late mother's cousin. They seemed an odd mix, those three, gray Rye, blond Kara, Indian Champ, but they were happy and very much a family despite the short time they had been together as one.

Rye made much over his mother's appearance, exclaiming that she now looked more like his sister than his mother, given his gray hair and her new soft blond. The glance he shared with Jesse said that he didn't miss the increased stiffness of her movements, however. Kara gave hugs and kisses to everyone but was especially exuberant with Jesse, so much so that Caroline admitted to herself that she felt an unaccustomed spurt of jealousy, but only a spurt, for it quickly became evident that Ryeland Wagner and his bride could not keep their hands off each other. Every glance required a touch, as did every change of subject, every smile, every shift of weight, every breath, it seemed. Those two were so in love that they ached with it and made Caroline ache for it.

When all the family had been greeted, Sarah called Caroline forward and made the introductions. Champ spared her a polite wave and busily began perusing the gifts beneath the tree; Rye and Kara, however, each captured one of her hands and held it between their own.

"So this is the amazing Caroline," Rye said.

"That we've heard so much about," Kara added.

"Mom and Jess both say you're the best thing since sliced bread," Rye went on.

"And too pretty to look at," Kara continued.

It was as if they spoke—and thought—as one. Caroline laughed, delighted with the pair of them. "Gross exaggerations," she said demurely.

Sarah had joined Haney in helping Champ ferret out his gifts from those beneath the tree. Rye cut a look at his mother, and Kara followed suit. "I don't think so," he said. "I've never seen Mom looking better."

"The spa must have helped the arthritis some," Kara said.

Caroline sighed. "For a time it did, but she's hurting again, though she'll do her best not to let it show."

Rye nodded. "That's just what I expected. I've done some research, and I think we've found a place that can help her. Dad actually mentioned it a while ago, and it turns out he was right."

"Jesse told me. I'm so glad."

Rye smiled. "He told me how fond you are of her. I appreciate that, Caroline."

She shook her head. "No one seems to understand how good Sarah's been to me. All the Wagners, really."

He chuckled. "Glad to hear it." He looked around the room then. "Man, this place looks and smells great. It's like every Christmas I've ever had here all rolled into one."

"That would be Blondie's doing," Jesse said, joining the group and tugging teasingly at Caroline's hair. "She's decorated this place within an inch of its life and baked her little heart out into the bargain."

"Sounds like my mom," Kara said wistfully. "I think she stripped half the trees in New Mexico this year. Looks like I'd have gotten some of that, doesn't it? The cooking and nest-feathering just isn't my thing, though."

Rye slid an arm possessively around her waist and pulled her hard against his side. "Girl, are you beating that mule again? You're all the woman I can handle now and twice the cowboy as any ten men I know. Besides I'd rather have you riding next to me wielding a rope than a frying pan anytime.''

Kara wrapped both arms around him and squeezed. Rye kissed her nose. Jesse shook his head and said to Kara, ''Speaking of your mom, how's Pogo doing?''

It was Rye who answered. ''Happy as a tick on a fat dog.''

''That's a honeymoon that's definitely not over yet,'' Kara said meaningfully.

Jesse chuckled. ''Must be catching.''

''No, really,'' Kara said, hanging on Rye, who was rubbing a hand up and down her back. ''I think they were happy to get rid of us so they could have the place to themselves for a change.''

Jesse just grinned. Caroline knew what he was thinking. These two were oblivious to the fact that they weren't alone! She was happy for them—and so envious that she could barely contain it. How often did she have to clasp her hands together to keep from touching Jesse? Did he ever want so desperately to reach out to her? Would the time ever come when they would do so as unself-consciously as Rye and Kara?

Sarah and Haney were exclaiming with Champ over the size and weight of a certain package with his name on it. They called Rye and Kara over and set about wheedling Rye into allowing Champ to open the gift early. Of course, they were successful. Champ whooped when he saw the electronic game inside. Then everyone spent the rest of the evening trying to get the thing hooked up to the television in the den.

Caroline mulled cider for Champ and wine for the adults, and soon everyone was pleasantly warm and relaxed. Champ went to sleep sprawled over his grandparents' laps, and Caroline hopped up, saying she'd get his bed ready. Rye got up to carry his son upstairs, but Jesse did, too, saying, ''No, let me. I don't get the chance to do this kind of thing much.'' So Rye sat back down and wrapped his arms around his wife, and Jesse gently gathered up the boy.

Haney tucked Champ's arm over his chest so it wouldn't dangle uncomfortably, while Sarah smoothed his raven black head and pressed a kiss on its crown. Jesse turned toward the hallway, and Caroline ran on ahead to ready the bed in the guest room by the light from the landing through the open doorway. It was ready when Jesse got there with the boy. He brought Champ in and laid him gently on the bed, then began tugging off his boots. Caroline joined in, helping him remove the boy's shirt, jeans and socks. Champ slept through it all, a gently snoring deadweight. Leaving the boy in his lightweight insulated underwear, Jesse folded the covers up and tucked them around him before placing a tender kiss in the middle of his forehead.

Caroline smiled as she watched Jesse bending over the boy. What a wonderful father he would make. Jesse looked up then and caught the shimmer of her smile. "What?" he whispered.

She quietly said, "You should have a son of your own."

His expression instantly hardened. He straightened abruptly, turned and walked from the room. Caroline quickly followed. He was waiting at the top of the stairs, his big hands gripping the banister. Caroline went to him and placed a concerned hand on his shoulder, but to her shock he flinched away. "Jesse, what is it?"

"There's something you should know," he said, visibly forcing himself to relax. He lifted his head and looked her straight in the eye, but she felt what it cost him to do so. "I'm never going to be anyone's father," he said flatly. "Never."

She couldn't believe her ears. "Jesse, how can you say such a thing? You don't know—"

"Yes, I do," he said. "It's a decision I made a long time ago, and that's all you have to know."

"But Jesse—"

"All these games of yours, Caroline, they're just that," he said abruptly. "That's all they can be. You need to understand that."

She blinked at him. Didn't he know? Didn't he understand yet? She folded her arms. "Jesse, I'm not playing any games with you," she told him. "And you ought to know me better than that by now."

He stared at her for a moment longer, a world of worry in his eyes. Then he swung around the end of the gracefully carved banister and hurried down the stairs, back toward the safety of the living room. Caroline sighed. What was she missing here? How could a man like Jesse, a man made for marriage and family, just decide never to allow himself such fulfillment? She knew he wanted it. She saw how he had looked at his nephew, the silent longing, the quiet love. What was it that made Jesse think, mistakenly, that he shouldn't have what Rye had—a family of his own? He'd meant to warn her that he wasn't what she wanted, but Caroline knew better. The question was, Why didn't he know? And how could she help him?

Christmas Eve was a revelation to Caroline. She should have realized that she wasn't the only one who saw what a great group of people the Wagners were, but she was surprised, nevertheless, when the doorbell rang just after eleven that morning and the house was suddenly full of people. They came and went steadily for the next five hours, sometimes bearing gifts. At some point during the hubbub Sarah laughingly explained that an old tradition in which they had indulged for years would not die, that of the Christmas Eve Open House. It had been years since she'd sent out invitations and laid out a hearty spread, but people still came.

"And you still love it," Caroline surmised correctly, happy to see Sarah so happy. "Next year we'll lay out a buffet that will have them taking up residence. We'll have to throw them out."

Sarah laughed heartily, only the slight hitch in her breath revealing that the pain in her back had caught her unaware. When Caroline offered to get her something for it, Sarah assured her that she had already taken an analgesic, which should kick in soon. Then she went on about her role as hostess, smiling and chatting and alternately preening and blushing under the welcome weight of compliments.

Shoes Kanaka arrived late in the day and stayed on after everyone else had gone. He brought with him gifts from Champ's Chako grandparent, Man Father, and a request that the boy be allowed to visit him on the reservation for the ceremony marking the formal end of mourning for Champ's mother and Man Father's daughter, Di'wana, who had succumbed some weeks earlier to a brain tumor. The whole story had brought tears to Caroline's eyes when she'd first heard it at Thanksgiving, but as Shoes explained the traditional ceremony and its meaning to the family, Caroline took comfort in the fact that the Chako would celebrate

Di'wana's passing to a simpler life on a higher plane of existence. Champ seemed to understand the significance and to want to participate. It was decided, with little discussion, that he would be allowed to do so. When Shoes then extended an invitation for Rye and Kara to observe, that, too, was quickly accepted. With that somber duty out of the way, the family was free to enjoy the light supper which Caroline had prepared for them and to get down to the real fun, what Sarah called "having the tree."

They began with a simple reading of the Christmas story. Haney read it himself out of the family Bible, his gravelly voice imbuing the words with special meaning. Afterward, Rye produced his guitar and led the family in a number of familiar carols so sweet that Caroline wanted them never to end. Finally, Sarah got out the many cards that had arrived during the previous weeks and passed them around, so everyone would know who had sent season's greetings. At long last it was time to hand out the gifts.

This last, most fun part of the evening was a laughing, messy kind of free-for-all, with everyone talking at once and passing gifts back and forth until the tree was stripped and all were rewarded. They ripped into the bounty with happy abandon.

Man Father had sent interesting blessing or good luck holders to the family, small hand-painted and beaded bags filled with pretty polished stones, feathers and other items of potential magic or "medicine." Caroline was thrilled beyond words to find that she had been included. It was a small thing, but a thoughtful one, and she knew that she had Shoes to thank for it. In addition to the blessing bag, there were other unexpected gifts for her: a pair of bright yellow galoshes from Haney, which elicited laughter from those in the know; a beautifully tailored navy wool coat from Sarah; an intricately carved wood keepsake box from Rye and Kara. Tiger and Handsome, who weren't even present, had slipped in turquoise button covers and a set of pretty hair combs for her, and most surprising of all, a long silk scarf from Jesse. Caroline was overwhelmed.

Others received far grander gifts, of course, and Caroline took as much pleasure in those as her own. Rye and Kara were giving Sarah and Haney a trip to Phoenix to see old friends who had retired there. For Jesse they had chosen a set of classic novels about the Old West, bound in hand-tooled leather. For Shoes they had bought an elaborately dyed and inlaid deerskin vest. Champ got new boots to replace those he'd outgrown and a pair of games for the much-coveted electronic gizmo his grandparents had bought him. Shoes gave him a woven Chako belt that identified him as a member of Man Father's clan.

Even though Caroline had had a strong hand in the gifts chosen and purchased for each other by Sarah, Haney and Jesse, she still enjoyed seeing those things presented and received. Haney took a good deal of ribbing over the gown and robe, but he didn't seem to mind since Sarah was thrilled, so much so that she rewarded him with a steamy kiss in front of the whole family. He blushed but otherwise seemed unaffected.

Caroline dispensed her own gifts with mingled delight and trepidation. Most of them were small in comparison to others', but she'd poured her whole heart into them. Sarah exclaimed happily over her proposed day at the spa, but protested the cost until Caroline whispered to her how generous Jesse had been with her Christmas bonus. In addition, Caroline gave her a pair of red gloves. Sarah couldn't get over the fit of her gloves, the roomier fingers made getting them off and on much easier than the old ones, and the tight cuffs assured that her hands would stay warm. "You have to tell me where you got these, Caroline," she said. "I'll want another pair for certain."

"I'll make you another anytime you want," Caroline declared happily. That elicited gasps from the whole gathering.

"You made these?" Kara asked, carefully examining the tiny red wool stitches encasing Sarah's hand.

"You couldn't have made *these*," Haney said, holding up the socks she'd given him.

"Oh, those are easy," she said dismissively. "They're just tubes."

"But they're padded on the bottoms!"

"Look at the hat Caroline made me!" Champ demanded, proudly holding aloft a simple, cuffed, knitted cap dyed to look like faded denim.

Everyone oohed and aahed appropriately, as much for Champ's benefit as in admiration of the silly cap, Caroline was sure, but then Shoes unfurled the muffler she'd made for him, and everyone abruptly fell silent. For a long, awful moment, she was afraid she'd done something dreadful, but then Shoes smoothed his hand over the narrow strip of colored wool and looked up at her. "Caroline, this is incredible."

She didn't quite know what to make of that. She ran her palms over her thighs nervously. "I don't know what you mean. I just copied the pattern in that painted leather tie you wear in your hair."

"That pattern is Shoes' personal Chako identification," Rye explained. "It's like a personal signature."

"Oh, dear." Caroline looked at Shoes in apology. "I should have asked permission. I'm so sorry."

Shoes raised a hand to stop her. "No, it's all right. Actually, it's quite wonderful. I'm amazed you could copy it so accurately. You enlarged it instead of repeating it."

She shrugged. "I noticed that it was enlarged but not repeated on your belt."

He nodded. "Very observant. I thank you."

"My pleasure."

"A most talented young woman," Shoes mused. "Isn't that right, Jesse?"

But Jesse didn't answer. He was too busy staring down into the box on his lap that he had been carefully opening. Seeing this, Rye wandered over to stand behind Jesse and peer down into the box himself. "Wow."

"What is it, Jesse?" Sarah asked. "What did Caroline make for you?"

Jesse picked up the sweater by the shoulders and gently shook it out, turning it so that everyone could see the front. The grayish blue body was a perfect match for his eyes, and the geometric yellow, red, and black pattern across the chest was derived from a published Navajo pattern. She had carefully worked a single black silhouette of a horse like a kind of badge over the right breast.

"The horseman," Shoes pronounced sagely. "It suits you, Jesse."

"Oh, Jesse, it's beautiful," Sarah said. "Caroline, you've out-done yourself."

Rye smiled knowingly, slipping a look between Caroline and his brother. "Try it on," Kara urged.

Wordlessly, Jesse set aside the box and wrapping, stood, opened the bottom of the sweater and thrust his arms inside, quickly pulling it down over his head and shoulders. It smoothed into place flawlessly, the perfect length, the perfect width, the perfect everything. He ran his hand lightly over the front, then held out his arms, gamely modeling. When his eyes finally met hers, Caroline knew that she had done well. "Thank you," he said simply, and it meant more to Caroline than all the effusive praise coming from everyone else.

Suddenly Kara gasped aloud and unfolded the small afghan that Caroline had made for her and Rye, letting the box and wrapping fall away. Her gaze flew to her husband's, and together they looked at the melange of pastel colors and laughed.

"I figured an afghan would always come in handy," Caroline explained.

"You have no idea," Kara told her meaningfully. "But what made you choose pastels?"

Caroline shrugged. "I don't know. I just like that particular multicolored thread."

"I think you must be psychic," Rye teased as he moved to stand next to his wife, his arm slipping around her shoulders. He bent his head to Kara's, and they whispered together a moment before Rye looked up, shrugged and said, "Actually, we've been saving this announcement, but it seems Caroline has given us the perfect opening."

"Rye, what on earth?" Sarah said curiously.

Everyone stared at them expectantly. Rye cleared his throat and said through a wide grin, "We're having a baby. Kara's preg-nant."

The room erupted in chaotic joy. Sarah was on her feet in an instant, but Haney was right behind her. Jesse was already up so he beat them both to Rye and Kara, enveloping the two in a bear hug. Even Champ, who evidently hadn't been privy to the infor-mation before the announcement, was on his feet and jumping up and down. Only Shoes and Caroline hung back, enjoying the celebration from afar. Shoes got up from his perch on the arm of the sofa and wandered over to stand next to Caroline. She smiled at him, surprised by the tears that suddenly spilled down her cheeks. Hastily, she wiped them away. It was then that Shoes leaned close and said, "The longings of your own heart make you especially sensitive to the needs and joys of others. Eventually it will come back to you."

There wasn't time to ask him what he meant by that cryptic pronouncement, as he moved away then to add his quiet congratulations to those of the others. Kara looked over at Caroline, the afghan clutched in her arms. "This will be perfect for the baby," she said.

Caroline smiled. "I'm so glad. I'll make him some booties before you go. I have some leftover yarn."

"Him!" Sarah exclaimed. "Why not *her?* I'd like a granddaughter, too, you know."

Haney snorted. "Naw, it's another boy. Wagners breed boys."

"You never know," Shoes said solemnly, playing the inscrutable Indian. The beauty of the whole day suddenly overwhelmed Caroline. This laughing, loving, generous family was the embodiment of everything of which she'd ever dreamed. Just being here with them was an untold joy that threatened to destroy her composure and expose her deepest longings. Quickly she turned and slipped away, fleeing down the hall and up the stairs to her very own room tucked beneath the rafters. There she let the teardrops fall and hugged tightly to herself every lovely memory, stowing them away for all time deeply within her heart.

Jesse eased back down the stairs and crept along the landing, denying the urge to go up and knock on her door and offer her the comfort of his arms. Just as he reached his own doorway, a form shifted away from the shadows and stepped forward. Jesse knew he shouldn't have been surprised that Ryeland had followed him.

"She okay?" he asked softly.

Having no doubt about whom he spoke, Jesse nodded. "Yeah,

I think so. She's not used to all this craziness. She grew up pretty much alone.''

"That's what Mother said. She's really something, though, isn't she?''

Jesse nodded again and smoothed a hand over the sweater he still wore. Rye had no idea what a wonder Caroline Moncton was, what she had come from, how accomplished she really was, especially for her age. He'd been torn between embarrassment and amazed delight when he'd opened the box containing this sweater. He couldn't imagine the time and expertise it had taken to fashion such a thing, and he knew that it was as good as an announcement to the group at large that she considered him something special. In the end, he could do nothing but marvel and enjoy, but he was worried, too. He was worried for her. He didn't want to see her hurt. He didn't want to be the one who hurt her. But if he didn't manage to get control of their personal situation, it was bound to happen sooner or later. It was with profound relief that he accepted the change of subject which his brother introduced then.

"Jess, I need to tell you something about the baby.''

A ready smile burst across Jesse's face. He clapped a hand over his brother's shoulder. "That was grand news, Rye. I'm thrilled for you both.''

Rye nodded, smiling to himself. "Thanks. We're real excited, but, um, well, the fact is, the baby's going to be a little 'early,' so to speak.''

Jess beat his smile into submission and folded his arms across his chest, playing the welcome and familiar role of big brother. "You mean Kara was already pregnant when you married her.''

Rye shifted uncomfortably. "We didn't know it at the time, but yeah, she was.''

"That doesn't say much for your self-control, does it?''

Rye tugged on his earlobe. "What self-control? Hell, where Kara's concerned I don't have any. But you ought to know what that's like yourself.''

Jess instantly flashed on that kiss in his office only days earlier. Rye was so right. If he had any real self-control he'd never have let Caroline climb into his lap and fit herself so perfectly against him. He'd never have... Suddenly something that Rye said pricked Jesse. He jerked out of his reverie, asking sharply, "What?"

Rye lifted an open palm. "I said, you know what it's like. You were in love once. You've been married, after all."

Jesse literally reeled. He put out a hand to steady himself, flattening his palm against the wall. Kay, not Caroline. Rye, naturally, was referring to Jesse's late wife. But Jesse had thought only of Caroline. Appalled with himself, he could find no way to cover his distress. Rye clamped a hand down over his shoulder.

"Jesse, what is it? What's wrong?"

Jesse shook his head. "I-It's nothing. I thought you were talking about something else."

Rye's grip tightened, then fell away. "Kara's right then. She said something was going on with you and Caroline even before we saw that sweater."

Jesse made himself stand a little straighter, speak a little lighter. "Caroline's just a girl," he said. "She has a crush. She'll get over it."

"A crush," Rye echoed. "Caroline doesn't seem the type for that to me. She's too mature for it."

"Mature!" Jesse exclaimed, scoffing. "She's just twenty-one, and I mean just as of last month!"

"Age doesn't always relate to maturity," Rye said carefully, "and I think it's more mutual than you want me to believe it is."

Jesse laughed, or tried to. It was a pretty miserable attempt. "She's too young," he said harshly, but Rye shook his head.

"I don't think so."

Jesse stared at his brother in the half-light. He couldn't believe his ears. Rye might as well have said that he approved of Jesse and Caroline as a couple. "Love has turned your brain to mush, little brother," he said flatly, and Rye laughed.

"Probably. God knows I love Kara. I never knew what it meant, Jess, to love someone like this."

And you think I do. Dismayed, Jesse threw an arm around his brother's shoulder. It was both the shame and the tragedy of his life that he didn't know what it meant to love as Rye did, never had—and never would. But that was his personal cross to bear.

"I'm glad for you, Rye," he said huskily, "and this new

baby's a huge blessing, no matter when conception took place. Don't you worry if it comes a little early, just love your family with all your heart, and everything will be fine.''

Rye actually seemed relieved. He relaxed a little. His smile grew a little wider. He threw his own arm up over Jesse's shoulder, and together they went back down to the celebration, arm in arm. Jesse hoped that Rye would never know how very much he envied him, how empty and pointless his own life seemed by comparison. He hoped no one ever knew, for he didn't deserve the pity such knowledge would bring. He didn't deserve what Rye had, and no one knew it better than him.

Chapter Ten

"So the problem is that he thinks you're too young," Kara said, shaking her head. "Well, these Wagner men are nothing if not hardheaded, but take it from me, there's hope for them."

"I can see that," Caroline said. "Rye adores you."

"It's mutual," Kara replied, dropping down into the rocker. "But it always was, and it still took him some time to come around, which goes right to my point. Give Jesse some time. The feeling's there, I'd bet on it. He just has to work his way around to it. It's funny, though, because these brothers are so different."

"How so?" Caroline asked, sitting down on the side of the bed.

Kara took some time to marshal her thoughts. "Rye's a complicated sort, real emotional and not very comfortable with it— but growing more so as time goes by. He internalizes everything, just swallows it down and buries it deep. Jesse's more easygoing, more open. And then there's the difference in the first marriages, too. Rye was hurt real bad. Truth is, I guess they hurt each other real bad. From what I can tell, the marriage was a disappointment to them both. She saw him as her ticket off the reservation. He cared for her, his best friend's cousin, but it wasn't what it should've been. Frankly, he said that it—sex—was like making love to his sister. I can imagine how that made her feel. Anyway, she started sleeping around. The whole thing was just a terrible mistake, and Di'wana's illness forced them both to face up to it, make a kind of peace with it. But Jesse's story is just the opposite.''

''Someone once told me that he was still in love with his late wife,'' Caroline said, her head bowed.

Kara rocked back and forth thoughtfully. ''Maybe. But it's been nearly ten years since Kay died. Looks like he'd be ready to get on with his life by now, even given the tragic circumstances.''

''What do you mean? How did she die? You seem to know.''

Kara nodded. ''Rye told me. She and Jesse were out to dinner at some romantic little place up in the mountains. It was springtime, and a storm came up, a real bad one, apparently. It knocked out the electricity. Anyway, what they didn't know was that it had blown down a power pole in the parking area. I guess there were mud puddles everywhere, and so she took off her shoes. She stepped into a puddle with a live wire lying in it.''

''Dear God,'' Caroline whispered. Kara nodded understanding of her feelings.

''Apparently they were holding hands,'' Kara went on. ''Jesse was wearing rubber soled boots, but the jolt knocked him off his feet, anyway, and their hands were like burned together or something. The ambulance attendant told Rye that he had to pry them apart.''

Caroline sucked in a deep breath, arms folded across her middle. No wonder it had taken Jesse such a long time to get over her death. It must have been horrible for him to lose her like that. ''Poor Jesse,'' she whispered.

''Caroline, it was a long time ago,'' Kara pointed out. ''And I've seen the way he looks at you when he doesn't think anyone is watching. It must be just this age thing.''

Caroline slumped in mock defeat. She hoped that was the only problem, not that it solved anything. ''I still don't know what to do about it,'' she said. Looking down at herself, she tugged dispiritedly at the baggy white sweater that she wore over a black turtleneck and the familiar old matching leggings. "Maybe I should be dressing more maturely."

"I don't know," Kara quipped. "Maybe you should do the opposite. My mother says that nothing ages a woman more than dressing too young."

Caroline sighed. "She's probably right. Think footed jammies would make the point in my case?" she quipped wryly.

Kara laughed at the idea. "I'm not sure I'd go that far." Suddenly she narrowed her eyes at Caroline. "Maybe we shouldn't be coming at this from the direction of age at all. It's not something I could pull off myself, but on you a plunging neckline and a short skirt might make the impression you're after."

Unbidden, memories came to Caroline. Suddenly she was seeing Jesse and the way he had looked at her the day she'd worn the too-small flannel shirt. She felt his hand at her breast and between her legs, pressing against her, his mouth meeting hers hungrily. She shivered with remembered sensation so delicious that her tongue darted out to taste him on her lips. That little action jolted her back to the moment, and she glanced self-consciously at Kara, who seemed to have noticed nothing untoward. Caroline lifted an eyebrow in consideration. It couldn't hurt to kind of "showcase the equipment," as her mother would say. Could it? She supposed she could always try it the other way. Anklets and petticoats, maybe? She shook her head. Ridiculous was not the effect she was after. Decided now, she looked at Kara. "Irene would be proud," she muttered drily.

Kara shook her head. "You'll have to explain that."

Caroline smiled. "My mother is the queen of provocative dressing, and I'm about to put to the test everything she ever taught me by example."

Grinning, Kara slid to the edge of her seat. "Well, let's see what you've learned."

Laughing, Caroline went to throw open the doors of the wardrobe. Soon they were rummaging through her dresser drawers, too, happily planning a wardrobe to make Jesse Wagner sweat bullets.

* * *

"Man, I'm almost sorry I even brought it up," Rye muttered.
Jesse pulled his gaze away from Caroline long enough to
glance at his brother. "What?"

"I said, I'm almost sorry I even brought up the clinic now."

"Uh-huh."

"They haven't stopped arguing about it for days."

"Okay."

"But I have to say, I don't know why he won't go with her.
Do you?"

"Do I?"

The sudden sharpness of his brother's elbow aimed at his ribs
made Jesse jump and yowl. "Ow! What'd you do that for?"

Rye rolled his eyes. "You haven't heard a word anybody's
said for days now. What's wrong with you? Mom and Dad are
making a rare public display over there, and all you can do is
stare in a kind of trance at Caroline's butt!"

Suddenly the temper that seemed to be simmering just below
the surface all the time now erupted hotly. "Watch your mouth!"

Rye held up a hand defensively, the action belied by the knowing little smile that crooked up one side of his mustache. "Calm
down. I don't have any interest in Caroline's butt, not that she
doesn't look pretty hot in that skirt, mind you."

Automatically Jesse's gaze went across the living room, where
Caroline continued to bend over the coffee table, plucking up
crumpled paper napkins and brushing away crumbs with her fingertips. The long, slender length of her legs was exposed right
up to the hip, almost, by that indecently short red skirt that she
wore, if skirt was an apt description for a swatch of fabric that
barely covered her shapely rear end. Their impromptu New
Year's party had been her idea, and as always she'd filled their
plates with delicious food and their glasses with festive drink. He
noticed Tiger staring at the expanse of her chest displayed by the
scooped neck of her tight spangled sweater and felt his hands curl
into fists. He wanted to pound Tiger right into the ground, and
he wasn't even angry with him.

As unobtrusively as possible, he took several deep breaths
through his mouth, calming himself. Finally he swallowed and

said, "Somebody ought to take her in hand, dressing like a little tart, flaunting herself. If I was her father I'd paddle that sweet butt until she couldn't sit down for a week!"

Rye laughed, rocking back on his heels. "But you're not her father. And don't even try to tell me that you're feeling fatherly right now."

Jesse felt his face heat. What he was feeling was so far from fatherly that it shamed him. "What does she hope to accomplish with this?" he hissed. "She's been dressing like a tramp for days now, skirts the size of postage stamps, jeans so tight she can barely move, blouses cut down to here!" He poked himself just below the breastbone with a jabbing forefinger.

Rye nodded, in complete and gleeful agreement. "And she's been all over you like stink on a hog. Hmm, now, what could that signify, I wonder? You don't suppose she's trying to get somebody's attention, do you?"

Jesse glowered a warning at Rye. "This is embarrassing enough without you making jokes about it!" Rye turned his face away, struggling with a smile, but Jesse was already staring at Caroline again. "What does she think this is going to accomplish?"

Rye cleared his throat, saying in a strangled voice, "I can't imagine."

Jesse didn't even hear him, neither did he hear the raised volume of his parents' voices across the room. He barely even noticed when Rye muttered that he'd better get over there and see if he couldn't change the subject. Somehow Jesse just couldn't see or think of anything or anyone but Caroline anymore, and his thoughts alone were driving him stark raving mad.

Finally she finished rearranging the coffee table to her satisfaction and straightened, one hand smoothing her "skirt," the other holding the small paper bag in which she had deposited the refuse. Briskly, she strode out of the room on heels so high that Jesse fluctuated between marveling at her dexterity and fearing she'd break her fool neck. For maybe a full minute his blood pressure returned to something near normal, and then she reappeared, carrying a full bowl of champagne punch in anticipation of the New Year. With every careful, wobbling step the sparkling drink sloshed to the very rim of the bowl—and just feet in front of her lay the throw rug, one forward corner thrown back on itself by some careless passerby.

Murmuring words best left unsaid aloud, Jesse launched into action, hurrying forward from his place by the window to kick down the corner of the rug and relieve Caroline of her burden. Champagne and fruit juice sloshed over his left hand as he roughly palmed the huge bowl.

"Careful!" she exclaimed, as if splashing himself with champagne was the height of disaster.

"Me?" Jesse scoffed. "You'll be lucky if you survive the night in those ridiculous shoes." Turning away, he carried the bowl in two long strides to the side table against the living room wall where Caroline had laid out her feast, depositing it inelegantly on top of some greenery. Caroline elbowed him out of the way, arranging the bowl perfectly in the center of the ring of greenery and fruit that she'd fashioned as decoration.

"Don't be silly," she said mildly. "Women everywhere wear these shoes every day. Besides, they make my legs look good, don't you think?" This last she said while pointing her toe and looking down and around until her gaze reached the shoe itself.

Jesse couldn't stop his eyes from following hers and taking in the smooth, graceful length of that leg. The sheer black stocking literally beckoned his hand, and he just barely restrained it, fingers curling in on themselves. "This is a dangerous game you're playing, Blondie."

She gave him a look of such smug innocence that he wanted to shake her. "Jesse, I've told you before, I'm not playing any kind of game, and by now you ought to understand that." She pivoted on one of those ridiculously high heels and swayed away. He felt like screaming and tearing his hair in frustration. Instead, he dipped himself a paper cup full of potent champagne punch and drained it, crumpling the cup so he couldn't down another in short order. God knew that if he needed anything right now, he needed a clear head.

He picked a corner and guarded it, watching the room and taking silent inventory of its occupants. Champ had been carried up to bed some time ago. Kara sat in an armchair, speaking animatedly with two couples. George Marshal and his fiancée, Wanda, were friends of Rye's from his rodeo days and shared the chair at Kara's side. Wesley Randal and his wife sat next to each other on the sofa, arms entwined. Like George, Wesley had ridden the trail drive with Rye and Kara, the last leg of it, anyway. He'd brought his wife down from Sky Creek, Colorado, to get to know them. Insurance agent or not, Wes was one hell of a cowboy in Rye's estimation, and that was good enough for Jesse, but he couldn't seem to make conversation with anyone tonight.

The fact was that he felt apart from the group gathered here in his own living room. Hell, he felt apart from the whole damned world these days. It seemed he no longer knew himself or anyone else, not even his own parents, and he couldn't figure out how that had happened. They'd been bickering a lot lately, ever since Rye had brought up the residential treatment program at the Denver arthritis clinic that his own father had mentioned long ago. Haney was perfectly willing to drive Sarah all the way to Denver for a single appointment or two, but now that the family doctor had recommended the weeks-long residential program of tests, treatment and therapy, Haney had dug in his heels. Sarah could go but without him. Jesse couldn't figure out why that was so. Actually, he couldn't seem to grasp the problem at all. He couldn't do anything but lust after Caroline Moncton, who was sixteen years his junior. Sixteen years! God in heaven, what had happened to his brain?

He put a hand to his head, feeling every second of his thirty-seven years. Lord, where had his life gone? One day he'd been Caroline's age, and the next he was lost somewhere near forty, alone and losing what little sense he'd had to begin with.

Suddenly, the New Year was upon them. Caroline began passing out cups of punch. Rye turned up the radio so they could hear the countdown to midnight, then walked over to sit on the arm of Kara's chair. She laid her head on his chest and tilted her face upward, smiling. Wanda wrapped her arms around George's neck in blatant anticipation. Wesley Randal draped his arm around his wife's shoulders. Sarah reached for Haney's hand. Tiger moved over to stand next to Shoes, both clearly spectators. Jesse told himself to join them, throw a comradely arm around each and enjoy the show, but even before he turned his head and saw Caroline moving purposefully toward him, two cups in hand, he knew he wasn't going to do that. Instead he stayed right where he was, lounging back against the corner as if he had not a care in the world. When she stopped right before him and set aside the cups, he knew what was going to happen, and he could have pushed past her and gotten himself out of harm's way then, but something held him. It was just a kiss, after all, a traditional way to welcome the new year. He never dreamed she'd take it as far she did, though.

Even before the countdown reached three, she lifted her arms and wrapped them around his neck. At two, she leaned into him. At one, she lifted upward while sliding her body against his, tilted her head, and fitted her mouth to his. It was the hottest public kiss he'd ever received. It scorched his lungs, sizzled against his lips, rammed a hot rod into the pit of his belly, and still he managed to keep his hands to himself until something—he would never know what—told him that this very hot kiss had become the spectator sport of choice for everyone else in the room. It was then that he put his hands to her waist and literally set her back, sweeping a look around the room. Sure enough, every pair of eyes but his own were trained squarely on him and Caroline.

He dredged up a smile from somewhere, put his hands on his own hips and said a hearty, "Happy New Year!"

The wish wafted around the room. Attention shifted, and he looked at Caroline, intending a stern, low warning—and got mad suddenly, ragingly, tear-somebody-limb-from-limb mad. It would have been different if she had preened, laughed, challenged him, anything. But instead she stood with her head cocked and her eyes closed, a smile curling softly at one corner of her mouth. The satisfaction on her face stood as counterpoint to the frustration riding Jesse at full spur. Here he stood, his guts in knots, embarrassment glowing just below the surface of his skin, the hardness in his groin trapping him, his entire body hungry for more while he fought for sense enough to deny it, and she was utterly satisfied with a New Year's kiss!

Suddenly he promised himself that he was going to give Miss Moncton a hard lesson in life. Sometimes you got just what you asked for, and by golly, he was going to give her a taste of that, enough to convince her that she was indeed playing a dangerous game and that she'd best quit while she was ahead. Then maybe life could get back to normal around here and he could sleep nights again without sweating out the adolescent kind of fantasies that had him twitching like a Mexican jumping bean.

Just making a concrete decision felt good, lifted his spirits, filled him with resolve. The smile he fashioned for her came together easily. He ignored the hope glinting in her eyes and concentrated on the twin swells of her breasts as she pulled in a quick breath. Damn if she wasn't wearing a pushup bra. Well, this was a game he had played before, and even if he did hate it, he had reason to believe he was pretty good at it. *Out of your league, little girl,* he told her with his eyes, *but come on and get it.* She smiled, rising to the challenge, just as he'd known she would. He leaned forward and lifted a hand to sweep a lock of pale hair off her shoulder. She had rolled up the sides, leaving the back to fall straight between her shoulder blades and float about her face. It was a very clever style, sophisticated and sexy, and it suited her. He let his appreciation show.

The party wound down pretty quickly after that. His parents were the first to plead fatigue and head for their beds. Shoes and Tiger headed out next. George and Wanda clearly had a private party planned and were eager to get to it. The Randals had booked a hotel room in town and would be spending another couple of days. Rye and Kara had arranged to meet them for dinner the next evening. They made a point of thanking Caroline for all she'd done and exited gracefully, a really nice couple from all indications.

Kara quickly moved to help Caroline clean up, and Rye pitched in, too. Jesse added his own hands, making it quick work to clear the living room. When Kara started running dishwater, however, he took over. "Now, none of that. Take your husband to bed and leave the rest to Caroline and me."

Kara shot a look at Caroline and headed for the kitchen door. Rye did the same with Jesse, his grin declaring that he figured big brother had everything well under control finally. Jesse returned his grin easily. Oh, yeah. He finally knew what he was about. Before he was through, Blondie would be running fast in the opposite direction, and he'd be able to breathe comfortably again. He pulled a dish towel from the stove handle and held it out.

"Wash or dry?"

A coy smile widened her red lips. She reached out and slowly pulled the towel from his grasp. "Roll up your sleeves, big guy, and plunge in."

He hadn't really expected to have to wash, but so be it. He turned on the hot tap water and began unbuttoning his cuffs. Caroline tossed the towel over one shoulder and helped him with the right sleeve, slipping free the button and folding back the cuff. Her bright eyes glowed warmly. It was so easy to smile at her, to let his eyes sweep hungrily over her face. Seeing her breath catch and her lovely neck arch in reaction was not exactly hardship, either. He cautioned himself. It was a game, a lesson, nothing more.

He began moving the dishes into one side of the double sink, swabbing them and setting them in the other side, where Caroline rinsed them under running water before wiping them dry and putting them away. Even working slowly, they were through in little more than a quarter hour. When the last dish had gone into the cupboard and the water had drained from the sink, Caroline passed the towel to Jesse, and he dried his hands while she leaned back against the counter and watched him.

"Good party," he said.

She nodded. "Thanks for helping me clean up."

"My pleasure."

She stood there a moment more, the heels of her hands braced against the edge of the counter. He knew that she was waiting, and he let her wait, until finally she pushed away from the counter and said, "Well, good night."

"Sleep well."

She bit her lip, then headed toward the door. He fell in right behind her, and just as she reached the doorway, he lifted one hand and hit the wall switch, shutting off the light. The other arm he threw around her waist, hauling her up against him, her back to his chest. She squeaked in surprise, then laughed deep in her throat.

"Jesse! What are you doing?"

"Giving you what you want," he said huskily, letting his breath gust against her ear, "what we both want."

Her head fell back against his shoulder, her hands reaching back for him, his name a sigh of delight on her lips. He was hard in an instant. He let his hand sweep down to splay across her belly, pressing her against him, feeling her gently rounded softness against his palm, the delicate jut of her pelvic bones against his fingertips. He ground against her hips, unbearably aroused by their firm mounds. He closed his eyes, nuzzling the gentle hollow of her temple, and forced out the words.

"I give up. I—I tried to do what was right, but I just can't resist any longer. I want you."

"Oh, Jesse!"

She turned in his arms, hugging him. He tightened his embrace and lifted her. Laughing, she kicked up one leg and held on. He couldn't help laughing with her as he carried her to the counter and set her atop it. Pushing between her legs, he let his hands wander over her back and shoulders, up the elegant column of her throat and downward again, skimming over her breasts and dropping to her thighs. "I can't wait to get inside you," he said. "I know you're tight and wet. You'll feel so good."

She gasped a little in shock. "Jesse!"

He wanted to kiss her but wasn't sure he dared. This was tricky enough. He knew that playing with fire meant getting his fingers burned, but he wasn't willing to scorch anything else if he could help it. He laid his forehead against hers and pushed up the hem of her skirt, such as it was. His voice was hoarse even to his own ears as he said, "I don't know why I waited so long. We'll have to be careful, of course. I don't want my parents to know. We'll use your room. Everyone should be settled down soon."

She had stiffened when he'd mentioned his parents, but he felt her relax again. Maybe he wasn't making himself clear enough. He was deciding what to say next when she lifted her hands to his face and kissed him. If that public New Year's kiss had been hot, this one was molten. She'd turned on the blast furnace for this one. Sliding to the very edge of the counter, which effectively left the hem of her skirt around her waist, she wrapped those long legs around him, raking his thighs lightly with those damnably sexy heels as she pressed her hot core against him and seduced his mouth with her own. When she reached around him and grabbed his buttocks with her hands, he cried out in mingled shock and arousal, instinctively rocking against her. He had to place his own hands flat on the countertop to keep from overbalancing and toppling her backward, possibly cracking her skull against the edge of the overhead cabinet. Not that she seemed the least bit worried.

She was all over him, practically eating him up. Another minute and she'd have him pumping into her. What the hell had he gotten himself into? Conversely, he was aware of a burgeoning sense of disappointment. He really hadn't believed she'd go for it. Maybe he was right to think she hadn't quite got the idea yet. He wrenched back, breaking the kiss but not the hold of those legs. She leaned back slightly, balancing her weight on the palms of her hands, arms braced against the countertop.

"What is it, Jesse?" she asked breathlessly. "Change your mind?"

"Uh, no. I, um, just thought we ought to settle the details first."

"What details?"

He settled his hands at her waist and swallowed a surprising lump in his throat. "I—I'm just wondering if m-mutual satisfaction is enough or, um, if we should maybe renegotiate your pay."

With only the dim light from the doorway laying a lopsided rectangle across the table on the other side of the room, he couldn't read her expression, but there could be no doubt what she was about when she reached down, grasped the bottom of her sweater and peeled it up and off over her head. The air left Jesse's lungs in a painful whoosh as he took in the soft glow of her pale skin against the black shadow of her demibra. His hands slid up her slim torso of their own accord. She reached for him, threading her arms about his neck and lifting herself upward to rub those delicious breasts against him. He found his hands at the clasp of her bra as she breathed hot, openmouthed kisses against his throat and chin, across his cheek, rough now with several hours' growth of beard, to his ear.

"Mutual satisfaction was enough for Nancy, wasn't it?" she whispered.

He froze. Nancy? Seconds ticked by before the name slid into place. Nancy! It hit him then that Caroline was equating herself with Nancy, putting herself in Nancy's place. He was shaking her before he remembered that it was not part of the plan.

"You stupid little—"

Those legs dropped, and suddenly she pushed him away. He stumbled backward, terribly aware that he'd somehow lost control of this particularly ugly little game and damned mad. How dare she lower herself to Nancy's level? Her sweater flicked against him as she swept it off the counter and strode across the room. The light flashed on, and she rounded on him.

"I'm not the idiot here!"

He gaped at her. She spilled out of that bra, her breasts bare almost to the nipples. "Put your damned sweater on!" he ordered. Instead she threw it on the floor! "What the hell do you think you're doing?"

"Calling your bluff! Did you really think I'd fall for that pathetic act? Of all the asinine, ignorant *loobies!*" Tendrils of her hair had come down, and she shoved them out of her face, seething.

All of a sudden he felt like a *looby,* whatever that was. "Caroline, I was only trying to point out—"

"Give me some credit, will you? Do you honestly think I'd set my heart on some rutting stud? I could get laid on any street corner in America! But that's not what I'm after and you know it! Just for the record, though, I want it all, love, marriage, home, family, everything, and I want it with you!"

His heart, traitorous deformity that it was, leaped inside his chest. How did she do it? How did she manage to all but reduce him to tears while standing there on those ridiculous high heels, wearing that little rumpled skirt and the most erotically constructed bra, her pale hair falling about her face, chest heaving with anger? Very justifiable anger. God, what he wouldn't give to throw his arms around her and sweep her off her feet just as she wanted and deserved, but he knew that he was not the man for it. If only he could make her understand that.

"Caroline, sweetheart, no matter what either one of us wants, I'm just not what you think I am. I'm not who you need. I'm—"

"Yes, you are!" she insisted. "You're everything I want and need, and somehow I've always known it. What I don't understand is why you can't see that I'm as good for you as you are for me!"

He couldn't believe she'd said that. "Caroline, you're everything any man in his right mind could want, but—just for starters—you're too young for me and—" She threw up her arms, rolled her eyes and spun away. He caught her by the shoulders and turned her back. "All right, then, I'm too old for you."

"Stop it!"

He closed his eyes and tightened his hold on her, resisting both the urge to shake her and the very real need to pull her against him, when what he really needed to do was to make her understand. But how was he to do that?

She shrugged and knocked his hands away, demanding, "Is it Kay?"

He nearly fell over. Kay! Well, why not? Every secret had its day, after all. He took a deep breath. "Yes. It's Kay, more or less."

She wrapped her arms around her middle, seeming deflated and, for the first time, a little self-conscious. He bent and snagged her sweater, handing it to her. She took it and pulled it on over her head.

"Kay is dead," she said softly, almost defensively.

"Yes," he said.

"But you're still in love with her," she accused glumly.

He knew he could let her think that. He should let her think that, but suddenly he wanted very much to tell someone, to tell her, the truth. He rubbed a hand over his face, thinking twice about what he was going to say, but then he just said it. "I was never in love with her."

She looked every bit as shocked as he expected her to look, as anyone who knew him would look. "But you married her!"

"Yes."

"Why?"

He licked his lips, searching for the words. "I thought what I felt for her would be enough, that it would grow with time, change into everything it should be."

She was astounded. He could see it in her face. "But, Jesse..."

He nodded. "I know. I'm not sure I can explain it, but I did love her. She was as precious to me as my very own life, but it wasn't... It was never what it ought to have been, what she needed it to be." He flapped his arms helplessly. "It was perfect. We were perfect for each other. We grew up together, you know. Her parents used to live not far from here. Kay and Rye and I were the Three Musketeers of the Wagner Ranch, playmates, buddies, as close as any three people could be. When I got out of college, I wanted to be married. I really did. It was the next step."

"And Kay was there waiting for you," she surmised correctly.

"It was perfect," he said again. "We had so much fun together." He shook his head, remembering. "She had the most adventurous sense of humor. She just loved everything about life."

Caroline cleared her throat and asked softly, "What went wrong?"

He shook his head. "Nothing. Everything. I knew on our wedding night that I'd made a mistake, but I just couldn't walk out on her, call it off. Wasn't fair."

"What'd you do?"

"My dead-level best," he said, his voice shaking.

"What happened?"

"Nothing."

"I don't understand."

He sighed. "I know you don't. She didn't. I didn't, either. But... I couldn't touch her, couldn't..." He gulped, closed his eyes, opened them again, but he couldn't look at her. "Even when I finally managed it... Well, let's just say that it was always less than satisfactory for both of us."

For a long moment she said nothing, but then she stepped forward and lifted a hand toward him. He recoiled, ashamed and, yes, afraid. "It isn't like that for us. You know it isn't."

"Of course not," he said. "You're forbidden fruit. So was she.

Until I married her.'' Caroline gasped. He didn't blame her. ''Pretty sick, isn't it?''

She shook her head. ''It's not that. You just mistook one kind of love for another.''

''Did I?'' he asked brutally. ''It's true that we weren't all over each other all the time, but I had too much respect for her and her family and mine to push anything. I just tried not to think about it, but the anticipation was there, had been for a long time. Believe me, I had a real active fantasy life going with just about every female that crossed my path. But with my wife...'' He didn't think it necessary to say anything more. He'd revealed enough of the awful truth about himself. He took another deep breath. ''She was dying by inches even before that last night,'' he said quickly. ''I tried, but it just wasn't any use, and I think that night she finally came to accept that I would never be what she needed, what she wanted. If she hadn't taken off her shoes to skip through the rain puddles—'' he coughed away the lump in his throat and finished ''—we would have divorced.''

''But instead she died,'' Caroline said softly.

He nodded bitterly. ''I ruined her life, and then, before she even had a chance to fix it, she was gone.''

''And you were trapped with a load of guilt you don't deserve.''

Jesse looked up sharply. ''No. I was trapped with a load of guilt I very much deserve, and believe me, it's heavy enough to keep me from ever making the same mistake again. Now go to bed, Caroline, before I'm tempted to take what I'm not entitled to and build that load even higher.''

She made an aborted effort to touch him again, then backed away. He saw the mingled regret and dismay and heartache that she hugged so tightly to herself, and he shared it, but that was all they could ever share. She had to understand that now. Like Kay, she deserved more than he could give her, and he wouldn't let her settle for less than she deserved. She was young, after all. She still had a chance to make her dreams come true. With someone else.

Finally she turned around and walked out of the room, a last wave of her hand in his direction. He waited until he knew that she was well out of reach before he slowly followed, alone. Always alone.

Chapter Eleven

Rye clasped his father's hand and pounded him on the back. "You made the right decision, Dad. Mom needs you to help her deal with this."

Haney nodded, but his expression said that he remained unconvinced. Rye turned away, giving Jesse his full attention.

"Well, big brother, guess this is it."

"Guess so."

"It's been a good visit."

"It has."

Together they strolled toward Rye's double-cab pickup truck, their boots crunching on the packed snow.

"When you get a chance," Rye said, "come down to New Mexico and we'll show you a real ranch."

"Yeah, right. Lucky for you I won't be going anywhere anytime soon, not with Dad taking Mom to Denver."

"It's for the best, Jesse," Rye said, serious now.

Jesse sighed inwardly and agreed as lightly as he could manage. "I know."

Rye chuckled and shook his head, not fooled in the least.

"Staying home alone with a sweetheart like Caroline isn't exactly a fate worse than death, old son."

"She's not my sweetheart."

"Not 'cause she doesn't wanna be."

"It's not that simple," Jesse snapped.

"You forget where everything goes?"

"Damn it, Rye!" Jesse hissed, coming to a halt. "She's not like that!"

"Not like what?" Rye retorted innocently.

Jesse yanked the front sides of his coat together, strangling the heavy, sheepskin-lined, plaid wool, and cast a careful look over one shoulder, checking to be absolutely certain that no one else was close enough to hear. The women were chatting together animatedly in the shelter of the porch, as though it wasn't eighteen degrees on this bitterly cold morning, while Haney stood by, huddling inside his coat. "Caroline's not fooling around," Jesse said, keeping his voice low. "She wants to get married."

"And?"

Jesse's mouth dropped open. "What's that supposed to mean?"

Rye shrugged. "Nothing. Just..."

Jesse clamped his mouth together, knowing he wasn't going to like this. "Just what?"

Rye cleared his throat. "Don't you think it's time? Life eventually has to go on, Jess."

"My life's not on hold!"

"I'd like to see you happy."

"I'm happy!"

"I mean really happy," Rye went on stubbornly, "like me."

Jesse rolled his eyes. "You and Kara are in love."

"And you feel nothing for Caroline?"

Jesse clamped down on the roar trying to burst out of his chest. "It's not what you obviously feel for Kara," he said with some difficulty. "I'm not like you, Rye. I never have been."

"True," Rye admitted with a smirk. "While I was out getting under every skirt I could find, you were running the home farm."

"You were just sowing your wild oats," Jesse mumbled. To his surprise, Rye clamped a hand down on his shoulder.

"When did you sow yours, Jess? Never mind, I know the an-

swer to that. You never did. You're not like that. You never were.
Yours is a settled soul, Jesse. You were born for marriage and
family.''

Jesse laughed bitterly. "How little you know me, baby
brother.''

Rye's grip on Jesse's shoulder intensified, then became a kind
of massage. "I know you better than you think, Jess. I've never
seen you fight anything so hard as you're fighting your feelings
for Caroline, and frankly, I'm puzzled.''

"Nothing puzzling about it," Jesse muttered. "She's too
damned young.''

Rye chuckled. "I'd say she's old enough for anything the two
of you might have in mind.''

"You don't know what I have in mind.''

"Yeah, right, and babies grow under cabbage leaves.''

Jesse turned his head away. "It's not as simple as you make
it sound, and don't pretend you know what I'm saying because
you don't. No one does. Just take it from me and shut up about
it.''

For a moment Rye said nothing, but then he squeezed Jesse's
shoulder once more and let his hand fall away. "All right.''

Jesse fought the sudden urge to spill his guts. Again. For all
the good it would do him, had done him. What was wrong with
Caroline, anyway? Why couldn't she get it through her head that
he was not the man she thought him to be? The only explanation
he could come up with was her youth. She was just too young to
understand that sometimes life couldn't be made to fit the shape
of one's dreams and expectations. He, on the other hand, knew
it only too well. He pushed those thoughts away and concentrated
on his brother.

"Listen, you drive careful.''

"Don't worry. Precious cargo.''

Jesse felt a stab of intense jealousy, but the next moment he
couldn't be anything but happy for his brother. God knew that
Rye had suffered plenty with his first marriage. He deserved this
happiness. Awkwardly Jesse hugged him, keeping it quick. "Stay
in touch.''

"You know it. And, Jess...''

"Yeah."

"Maybe you ought to take your own advice."

"And what advice would that be?"

Rye brought his hands to his hips. "Remember when you brought the extra horses out to meet the cattle drive, what you said to me that day you left? You said I should just let Kara make me happy for a while. That turned out to be good advice, brother. I wish you'd do the same, even if it turns out only to be temporary for you and Caroline."

Jesse nodded just to get Rye to shut up. He knew he couldn't do what Rye suggested. Caroline deserved better, not that Kara hadn't, didn't, deserve everything Rye could give her, but then that was the point: Rye could—and Jesse had felt certain even back then that he would—give Kara his heart. That was a luxury in which Jesse himself did not dare indulge. But Rye couldn't know that, and that, too, was for the best. Jesse drew himself up tall and put on a pleasant face.

"Glad you came, Rye. Take care of everyone."

"You know it."

Rye glanced at his wristwatch, then, and grimaced. "Kara, honey, time to go."

She called back that she'd get Champ. Two minutes later hugs had been exchanged all around, Rye's family was loaded in the big truck, and Jesse stood aside as his parents and Caroline hurried back into the house out of the cold. He stood on the edge of the drive, watching as Rye drove away with his expectant wife and son. What he wouldn't give to be in Rye's boots. What he wouldn't give to be different from the way he was.

He told himself that a lesser man would ignore what he knew about himself and take another chance on love, but he didn't really believe that. How could he ever forget that his was not the only heart and life he risked? One woman had already died, her dreams destroyed. He couldn't let it happen again, not to Caroline. Especially not to Caroline.

"Don't worry about anything," Caroline said. "Just concentrate on getting better."

Sarah pressed her cheek to Caroline's and laughed. "Oh, I

know I'm leaving everything in good hands. I know you'll take care of Jesse and the boys.''

''Mom!'' Jesse protested. ''I'm not helpless, you know. I've been taking care of myself for a long time now.''

''Of course you have, dear,'' Sarah said, the twinkle in her eye telling Caroline that she knew very well how Jesse would fare without her. ''Nevertheless, I feel better knowing that Caroline is here with you.''

Jesse grumbled and stomped toward the garage with the last of the bags. Haney was already warming up the car, a fact attested to by the white plume of exhaust fluttering on the crisp morning air. Sarah turned to Caroline again with a smile on her handsome face and a mock sigh.

''I did my best, sugar, but he's still a man, God bless him.''

Caroline laughed. ''We'll do fine. Don't worry.''

''I won't,'' Sarah said, squeezing her hand. ''Do you mind one final bit of advice?''

''Not at all. What is it?''

Sarah pursed her lips. ''There's an old saying. Make hay while the sun shines. Well, the sun's shining, dear, if you take my meaning.'' The gleam in her eye left little doubt.

Caroline gulped and returned the pressure of Sarah's hand. ''I do love him, Sarah. I can't help it.''

Sarah slipped an arm around Caroline's shoulder. ''I know you do.''

''But it's complicated.''

Sarah nodded then said, ''I don't know why he's so fixated on the age thing.''

''It's more than that,'' Caroline said.

Sarah shook her head. ''I can't imagine what.''

Caroline bit her lip consideringly. She had the feeling that Jesse had told no one else what he'd told her, but she didn't know that. Until she did, she wasn't certain what she should say. She decided on a careful foray. ''I—I think it has to do with Kay.''

Sarah straightened and put her arms around Caroline. ''Oh, I don't think so, not really. That was so long ago. He has to be over it by now. I think he's just set in his ways, stubborn, and— I've been thinking a lot about this lately—Haney and I have always been here to share the load, you know, and maybe that hasn't always been for the best.''

"Now, that is nonsense," Caroline said firmly. "This is your ranch, yours and Haney's and Jesse's.''

"Umm, but there comes a time to retire," Sarah said. "Maybe Haney and I have pushed that boundary.''

Caroline was shocked. "Sarah! That is the arthritis talking. That's all that is, and once it's under control—and it will be under control—you'll be raring to go again, you'll see.''

Sarah nodded and smiled. "I suppose you're right.''

"You know I am.''

Haney appeared at the end of the garage then. "What're you waiting on, for pity's sake? It's time to go.''

"Oh, all right!" Sarah called. Then she turned to Caroline for a hug and a kiss on the cheek. "You take care of yourself, too, now, young lady, while you're taking care of everyone else.''

"I will. Don't worry!''

"I won't," Sarah assured her, carefully setting off down the path. Jesse appeared to help her, his arm encircling her waist protectively.

"Have a safe trip!" Caroline called, waving.

Sarah waved back while moving down the walk and speaking quickly to Jesse, who nodded and nodded, though obviously more concerned with seeing her safely to the car than whatever instructions or advice she was imparting. Caroline watched, huddling inside her coat on the small stoop, until they disappeared into the garage. A few moments later, Jesse reappeared, stepping back into the snow as Haney guided the car out of the garage and onto the front driveway. With a single look over his shoulder in her direction, Jesse trudged off toward the barn. Caroline squinted up into the bright glare of a mid-January sun and turned her thoughts to making hay.

What was it about a man's stocking foot that made a woman want to rip his clothes off? It shouldn't mean a thing, that he was sitting there fully dressed except for his boots, which he had removed and placed neatly beside the couch, but for some reason she couldn't keep her gaze off his feet where they rested on the ottoman. The movie they were supposed to be watching on the television had gone by in a tumble of meaningless sounds and sights. Meanwhile, his every move registered physically with her, even though he never touched her, keeping carefully to his end of the long sofa.

A commercial came on, the increased volume penetrating the almost sexual stupor in which she found herself. Caroline sat up straight, aware suddenly of a hollow rumble in her midsection. "I think I'll make some popcorn. Would you like some popcorn?"

"Yeah, sure, if you want."

"Fine. I'll make some popcorn."

She got up and went into the kitchen, mechanically going through the steps of popping popcorn in the microwave. At this rate, she told herself, she would be insane by the time Sarah and Haney returned from the Denver clinic. She and Jesse were banging around this big old house like a pair of haunts, each trapped in his or her own dimension. They ate at the same table, sat on the same couch, climbed the same stairs, but they might as well have been doing those things on separate planets; and yet, at the very same time, she was painfully aware of his every movement and expression when he was near. She didn't doubt, couldn't doubt, that it was the same for him, but she was beginning to understand that he'd slit his own throat before he'd admit it. Somehow she was going to have to force his hand. But how?

She returned to the living room a few minutes later carrying a bowl of popcorn and two canned colas, only to find that Jesse had moved to his father's recliner. Well, he wasn't getting off that easily. Handing him the bowl of popcorn and one of the sodas, she pushed the ottoman over beside his chair and plopped herself down, reaching a hand into the popcorn bowl in his lap. Grudgingly, Jesse balanced the bowl on the arm of the chair and stared at the television. Caroline popped the top on her soda and pretended not to notice when he sidled away from her, squashing himself into the far corner of the recliner.

The television had been giving them a little trouble the past couple of days. Without warning it would start to hiss and continue doing so until someone tapped the end of the sound knob.

As chance would have it, the thing chose just that moment to start sounding like a roomful of angry snakes. "Oh, for pity's sake!" Jesse grumbled, rocking his chair forward.

"I'll do it," Caroline said, getting up.

Just as she passed in front of the recliner, he kicked back again, sending the footrest up and out. The edge connected sharply with her knee. Crying out, she pitched forward and found herself face-down in Jesse's lap, one hand sinking down between the seat cushion and the side of the chair, the other between his legs, popcorn flying. Awareness jolted through her. An instant later, he was practically climbing the back of the chair to get away from her. Disgusted with them both, she groped for the arms of the chair and pushed herself up.

"Stop acting like I'm going to bite you!" she snapped at him, regaining her feet. *Stop thinking about biting him!* she told herself.

Jesse settled back down into the chair. "Sorry. I just— It was my fault."

"Yes, it was," she agreed. Reaching across to the television, she slapped the end of the volume knob and the hissing stopped.

Jesse muttered something about shopping for a new television. Caroline folded her arms and looked down at him. "Why don't you just get it fixed? There's nothing wrong with it but the volume."

He nodded, not even looking at her. "Damn it, Jesse, this isn't fair!"

He gaped at her. "It's not my fault the television needs work!"

"That's not what I'm talking about, and you know it!"

He bounded up out of the chair, nearly knocking her over. "I'm going to bed."

"Oh, no, you don't!" She spun around as he pushed by her, kicking through a mound of popcorn on the floor. She snagged his shirtsleeve. "Not until we've talked this through."

He jerked his arm away but stood his ground, his back to her. "There's nothing to talk about."

"Yes, there is. I'm in love with you, and I think you have feelings for—"

He cut her off with a chopping motion of his hand. "Don't even go there! Any feelings I have for you are strictly carnal!"

Caroline drew herself up tightly. "I don't believe that."

"What you believe isn't my concern."

Sighing, she tried another argument. "Jesse, you can't live the rest of your life alone."

He turned on her then. "I'm not alone!"

"Yes, you are, and you know it. All these years since Kay died and not even your parents know what you've been feeling. If that's not alone, I don't know what is."

He looked as though she'd hit him. "You don't know anything about it."

"You've been beating yourself up all these years because you didn't feel for her what you do feel for me," she said doggedly.

He shouted at her. "Don't you dare tell me what I'm feeling!"

"Then you tell me!" she shouted back.

"Right now I could strangle you with my bare hands," he gritted out.

Caroline sighed. She wasn't the least frightened of him, and what had to be said had to be said. "Jesse, I've been thinking about it a lot, and you said it yourself. You didn't love Kay like a woman. That doesn't mean you feel the same way about me or that you will."

"Damn it, Caroline, I don't feel any way about you except frustrated! You're driving me crazy! Why can't you just let it alone?"

Caroline took a moment to gather her thoughts and square her shoulders so he would know that what she was going to say was not a knee-jerk reaction to his repudiation. "I won't leave it alone, Jesse," she finally said, "because I don't want to waste the next ten years of my life wishing I'd done or said something more to make you understand. I won't live with the kind of regret that has eaten you alive, Jesse Wagner. I know what kind of man I want and what kind of life I want."

"And how would you know that?" he retorted smartly. "You have no experience at—"

"I have plenty of experience, I'll have you know!"

"Oh, please. At your age?"

"Yes, at my age!"

Suddenly he was right in her face, his nose practically bumping hers. "And just how many men have you known, pray tell?"

"Enough!"

"How many?"

"Dozens!"

He reeled backward, arms flailing before settling once more at his waist. "Well, you sure had me fooled."

She was puzzled by the color draining from his face, by the way he rubbed a hand over his eyes as if trying to get his bearings in a room gone topsy-turvy. She threw out her arms. "I've never made any secret of what my life's been like! It's been a parade of men, one after the other, every kind of male imaginable."

"I don't want to hear any more of this," he muttered, backing away.

"How do you think I felt?" she demanded, pacing him. "Every time I turned around she was dragging some pool shark or short-order cook home with her. There was a new one every week, some of them so low on the evolutionary track that I thought once or twice she'd found the missing link!"

He came to a stop, his hands grasping her elbows and bringing her to a stop with him. "She?"

Caroline nodded, warming to the subject now. She'd never spoken of it before; it had seemed disloyal to her mother, but it had always been there, the sheer stupidity of her mother's life-style. Caroline shook her head, thinking about it. "She didn't want to be tied down. I never could figure it out. I mean, what she saw in some of them just escaped me. Not the physical, mind you. She always went for the lookers. It didn't matter what kind of jerk he was, if he looked the part, he could hang around—for a time. But God forbid he should get serious! One really kind word, one really thoughtful gesture, and he was history. Then here she'd come with another, gushing and laughing and hanging all over him—till the next one. Well, not me! No way!"

Jesse put a hand over his mouth, and she realized he was laughing. Frowning, she poked him in the ribs with a forefinger. "Stop it. It isn't funny."

"You're right," he said, sobering. "I'm sorry. I'm not laughing at you."

"What then?"

He shook his head, sobering. "Doesn't matter. I just... Well, I'm glad you feel that way, that you don't want to repeat your mother's mistakes, but you just set your sights on the wrong man this time, honey. That's all."

"I have not," she insisted, folding her arms.

"Caroline, you need a man who'll treasure you and give you a family."

"You can do that!"

"No, I can't. The treasuring part aside, I'm too old to think about starting a family now."

"That's absurd! I know women having first babies at your age!"

He made an exasperated sound. "Caroline, I'm just not a good risk."

"Baloney. You're no risk at all. You're exactly what I want, exactly who I want, and you need me, Jesse. I know you do."

He put both hands in his hair and pulled. "Why don't you just conk me over the head with a mallet? It would be less painful."

"Don't give me any ideas," she muttered.

Throwing up his hands, he turned away again. "I'm not having this conversation with you."

"Just give me a chance, Jesse!"

He rounded on her, whipping out an arm to point at her. "I'm not giving you anything!"

Caroline sighed. "Not even a good-night kiss?"

He jumped back in alarm. "Especially not a good-night kiss!"

"Coward!"

He roared, literally, but then he marched forward, grasped her by the upper arms, yanked her forward, and planted a kiss right in the center of her forehead. "There! Good night!"

Caroline made a face. He spun around and headed for the hall. "You call that a kiss?" she yelled.

"Good night, Caroline!"

"What about all this popcorn? Aren't you going to help me clean up the popcorn?"

"Good night, Caroline!" he bellowed, pounding up the stairs.

She screeched and kicked at a little pile of fluffy white kernels. The television was hissing again. She threw a pillow at it, then pushed her hair out of her face. She had to do something. She didn't know what yet, but something, anything. And she would. As soon as she thought of it.

He did his best to stay away from her. One night he even drove into town for dinner and a movie, alone. It was a stupid move. He let Caroline think that he was meeting someone, even though everyone he'd phoned said the roads were too bad to be out and about. He put the snow chains on the truck and drove in, anyway, ignoring the guilt that gnawed at him because he'd left her out at the ranch on her own. Then, after an indifferent meal, he got to the movie theater only to find it closed due to the inclement weather. He didn't know what was inclement about it. Winters were always cold and snowy in Colorado, just more so this year. In fact, so much so that he had to virtually creep back to the ranch to keep from driving off the road in the thick, swirling snowfall. Once he got there Caroline's obvious relief at having him home safe doubled the guilt he was already feeling.

After that, he stayed home. With the TV in the shop, it was somehow easier to concentrate on solitary pursuits like reading and paperwork, but then there wasn't much sense in doing paperwork by pen when a perfectly good computer sat boxed in the corner of the office. He'd already made one attempt at translating the computereze in the manual and had decided to leave it until he could attend a class. Later, out of sheer boredom, he figured he might as well give it another try and spent two full evenings reading and rereading what was obviously someone's idea of a bad joke before tossing the book aside and striking out on his own. Several hours of trial and error finally resulted in a functioning system, but try as he might he couldn't seem to get the software loaded. He was turning the air blue with his opinion of computer nerds who couldn't communicate in plain English when the office door opened and Caroline came inside to lean against the corner of the desk.

"Need some help?"

He snorted at that. "Yeah, I need a computer genius. Know one?"

She shrugged. "Might. But maybe I can help."

"Yeah, right," he snapped sarcastically. "You're a good little housekeeper, Blondie, but this is the latest setup and it needs—"

She'd walked over to the desk while he was talking and bent to take a look at the screen. He jerked back out of her way, avoiding physical contact at all costs. She tapped a fingernail against her chin, then said, "You've opened the wrong driver." Quickly she began working the mouse and typing on the keyboard. "Let's just get out of this, and double click this and..." She checked the disk in the A drive, reinserted it and typed in a command at the prompt. The drive began to whir, and a graph appeared in a small box, numbers clicking by at incredible speed. It only took Jesse a moment to realize that it was loading.

Damn. Was there nothing this youngster couldn't do? He took a good look at her from the back, the sleek torso tapering to an unbelievably narrow waist, the taut roundness of hips and buttocks, the slender length of legs that could wrap around a man with such agile grace. All right, so she wasn't exactly a child. Hell, she was a fetching, electrifying bundle of woman. He swiveled the chair so he wouldn't have to look at her, but the state of semiarousal that he'd been living in lately had already blossomed into painful fullness.

Caroline was replacing the disk and answering prompts again. The little graph popped up once more and went to flicking numbers. He tried to focus on that. After a moment the second disk was loaded and the prompt requested a third. As she reached for it, he rolled his chair forward once more and elbowed her aside. "Show me what you're doing here."

She sat down on the corner of the desk, propped her feet against the edge of his chair and leaned forward. In terse, simple terms, she explained the process and then went on to fully explain the various icons of the basic software already installed by the manufacturer. Suddenly it was beginning to make a warped kind of sense.

"How'd you learn all this?" he asked, impressed despite himself.

"I went to college, remember? You don't get through high school these days without a few basic computer courses, and you don't get through your first week of college without enough literacy to figure out the Internet and whatnot. Shoot, half the assignments these days have to be filed via E-mail."

He shook his head, sighing. "I went to college, too, and I typed up my papers on a word processor, but that was a far cry from this."

"True. It's called progress."

He looked her square in the eye. "Just goes to show how things change over the years."

She laughed. "With computers things change moment to moment, and you know it. Now, do you want to learn how to set up your accounts or not?"

He wanted to tell her that he could take it from there without her help, but they both knew that was a crock. He sucked in a deep breath. "Okay, whiz kid, lay it on me."

She folded her arms, glaring down at him with blatant censure. "I'm going to ignore that so-obvious ploy, because I'm more mature than you want to give me credit for."

A grin quirked at his mouth. "Touché. Now let's get some work done...if you don't mind."

"I don't mind," she told him, the silkiness of her voice lifting the hair on the back of his neck, but the next moment she got down to business.

The following hours passed with amazing speed and equanimity. At one point he realized that he was actually enjoying himself, and he had to hand it to her: she knew her stuff, particularly when it came to accounting. He only got about half of what she was telling him, but he still felt that he was getting enough of it to eventually figure it all out. It was actually pretty exciting, and it was only when he couldn't stifle the yawns anymore that he realized how late the hour had grown.

"I gotta get some sleep," he said, stretching.

Caroline nodded and pushed back the chair he had carried around the desk for her sometime earlier. "We can finish setting up the accounts and start updating them tomorrow, if you want."

"We'll see." It had been a surprisingly comfortable, easy evening, but he wasn't willing to push his luck. "I might just take some time to read all these manuals again. Maybe I'll actually understand some of them now."

She shrugged and got up. "Whatever you want. I spoke to your mother today, by the way."

He was surprised by that—and a little hurt. "Oh? She called specifically to talk to you?"

"That's right. Girl-talk stuff. She wanted to know if I thought she could get away with wearing olive green."

He couldn't help smiling at that. He'd never known his mother to express such concern over her appearance. "What'd you tell her?"

"I told her deep olive, not drab olive."

"Ah."

Caroline gathered her long, silky hair into one hand and pulled it across her shoulder. "She, um, didn't exactly say it, but I gather that your father is not being completely cooperative."

Jesse rubbed the back of his neck. "Yeah, he's complained to me a time or two about this counseling stuff."

"I don't know what his problem is," Caroline said. "All the doctors want to do is make sure that he knows what they're dealing with."

"I guess he just doesn't like being told what to do and think."

Caroline rolled her eyes. "Is that what you think it's all about?"

Jesse rocked forward onto the balls of his feet. "No. But that seems to be what he thinks it's all about."

"Well, I don't understand it," Caroline said. "If you ask me, he just doesn't want to face the severity of your mother's problem."

"Of course he doesn't. He loves her, and he hates the idea that she's in constant pain."

"But ignoring the problem is not going to make it go away."

"I don't think you can say he's ignoring the problem. He's in Denver, isn't he?"

"Yes, but is he doing what he should be doing there?"

Jesse threw up his hands. "I don't know, Caroline! I'm not sure it's really any of my business. I know it's none of yours."

Caroline caught her breath, obviously injured. "I'm sorry. You're right. But I can't help worrying about them."

Jesse groaned and rubbed the heels of his hands against his eye sockets. "I know, I know. I'm just tired, okay?"

She bit her lip, but she nodded. Still, she looked awfully small standing there with one arm wrapped almost protectively around her middle as if she needed a hug. He ruthlessly stifled the impulse to supply it.

"Listen, thanks. You've been a great help here tonight, and you didn't have to be. I appreciate it. Now get some rest, okay?"

She nodded again, straightening a little. "I'll be glad to help update the accounts if you want."

"We'll see. Can't work you all the time."

"Oh, I don't mind," she said. "I'm just glad I've found a way to use what I've learned without having to depend on it to earn a living. It's one thing to sit here with you talking over all this stuff and another to do nothing else but enter numbers and tally columns all day long."

He chuckled at that. "Yeah, I know what you mean. I'd never be able to keep myself fed with any kind of full-time office job. I wouldn't even want to try."

"Well, thankfully you don't have to," Caroline said. "Neither of us does."

"But then that means that we both have real jobs to do tomorrow."

"True."

"Good night, Caroline. Thanks again."

He saw the look in her eye, the one that said she craved a parting kiss from him, but he kept himself in check, and she finally went on her way. He couldn't help congratulating himself. Maybe he was getting a handle on this thing, after all.

Chapter Twelve

She couldn't possibly do it, but she had to. Somehow. He was the most stubborn man in the world, and he had found a way to hold her at arm's length indefinitely, unless she pushed. But it had to be a big push. Jesse Wagner was a lot of man, and he'd convinced himself that he was saving her from a fate worse than death by denying his feelings for her. Those feelings were there. Somehow she knew it. Now she had to help them break through ten years of convincing himself that he was incapable of them. She would do it. She had to do it.

It meant careful planning and timing—and courage, a great deal of courage. She took a leaf from her mother's book in that regard. Once she'd decided on a plan, she only had to talk herself into it. For that reason she stripped down to her panties and stood before the cloudy cheval mirror in the corner of her room, taking stock. She started at the bottom. Her feet were average in size, slender with high arches. She kept the cuticles pushed back on her toenails and the ends neatly trimmed, but they were just feet. No, that wasn't right. They were beautiful feet, sexy feet. That's what Irene had always told herself when she was painting her toenails.

Caroline smiled at the memory. Her feet were exact duplicates of her mother's. They would drive Jesse wild even without bright red enamel. She moved on to her calves. She had good legs. She'd been told so countless times. Even Irene had envied her legs. Irene herself tended to be a tad heavy in the thighs, and she'd always said it was unfair that Caroline had such good ones when she was unwilling to use them. Usually she said that while performing laborious leg lifts on the floor. A little heaviness about the thighs hadn't slowed Irene any, though. Caroline remembered her mother standing before the mirror in a tight, black leather miniskirt.

"You are a confection, Caroline. Jesse is going to eat you up. He won't be able to help himself."

She went on to her lower body. She'd always been most dissatisfied with this portion of herself. How could her hipbones jut out even slightly and her belly still round up like that? Irene had said that the hipbones meant she would be a good bearer of children and that men often preferred a slightly rounded belly on a slender woman. She was living proof, she would say. So, this was all right, too.

"He'll take one look and know you should be having his babies," Caroline promised herself.

Her waist was narrow and her midriff firm, and if her breasts weren't as ample as her mother's, they would improve after she'd had her first child. She wished all the fullness wasn't underneath, though. They plumped up nicely in a push-up bra, but Jesse wasn't going to make love to her in her bra. If it happened, he would have to be attracted to their natural shape. She wondered if her mother had been right about the disadvantages of sleeping on her stomach, not that it mattered. She'd never been able to break the habit. Ah, well, she had what she had and that was all there was to it. She squared her shoulders and lifted her chin, sucking in her belly and thrusting forward her breasts. At least her skin was good. Irene always said that bare skin was a woman's best asset, and the more the better. Caroline could only hope that she was right.

Turning, she scooped her hair over one shoulder and swept her gaze downward over her back and bottom. Irene had always thought her own rear end was good, and Caroline had seen enough men patting and squeezing it to believe that Irene was right. So she could only conclude that her bottom was good enough. She was not quite as plump there as her mother, but surely that was best since she was not quite as top-heavy as Irene, either. She put a hand on her hip and shifted her weight, pleased that nothing jiggled that shouldn't. Still, it was the front that counted most. She turned back to look herself over one more time. She wouldn't be chosen as this month's centerfold, but she didn't think anyone would throw rocks at her, either. If she worked this right, Jesse wouldn't be throwing, he'd be grabbing.

"You can do it, Caroline," she told herself. "If bare skin is what it takes, then it's bare skin he's going to get."

She dressed again and went downstairs to start lunch. It was past the normal time for it, but that was all part of her design. She had to set the stage just right. It had to look like an accident. Otherwise he'd hide behind his outrage and she would lose her chance.

She was throwing together thick sandwiches and opening cans of soup when the men came in. Tiger was first into the kitchen. He lifted both brows when he saw the mess on the counters and the bare table. Handsome, who was right behind him, let out a long, low whistle, but it was Jesse to whom Caroline addressed herself.

"I let the time get away from me," she said apologetically. "I was posting accounts this morning, and I just forgot to watch the clock."

"You were posting accounts this morning?" he echoed.

She winced. "I know. It was stupid, this being Wednesday. I have the bathrooms to do, and now I've gotten a late start." She slung a sandwich on a plate at the table. Handsome pulled out a chair and sat down. "Dinner may be late because of it," she went on.

Tiger watched Handsome attack the sandwich and said, "Heck, Miss Caroline, don't you worry about my dinner. I can pick up something on the way home tonight."

"I have a date," Handsome announced around a mouthful of bread and meat.

Caroline dispensed a smile. "That's thoughtful of you, Tiger. I'll make it up to you. One day real soon I'll bake you that coconut cake you like so much."

Tiger beamed. "Heck, I'd skip dinner once a week for that."

Caroline laughed, dumped a sandwich on a plate and shoved it at him. "No need for that." She glanced at Jesse. "I'll make yours now and get the soup on."

"No rush," he said, sitting down at the head of the table. "Listen, I can clean my own bathroom, if you want. It's not like I haven't cleaned it before."

"I'll get to it," she said briskly, slathering mustard on lightly toasted bread.

"I don't mind," he insisted.

She turned her face away to hide the quirk of a smile. "We'll see."

Actually, he would see. Everything. She could only pray that it would be enough.

He knocked off at four-thirty sharp. It was almost too cold to work the horses, anyway, and the clouds were banking over the mountains for another snow. Had it ever snowed so much in a single season before? If so, he couldn't remember it. The front walk was banked chest deep. In the mountains whole buildings were covered to the roofline. Crews were out clearing roads day and night, and the police were routinely checking the higher residences. Some days simply weren't fit for man or beast, but he trudged out as far as the barn, anyway, keeping himself busy and away from Caroline. Judging by the buildup of clouds, tomorrow promised to be just such a day. Maybe he'd stay in and work on the accounts. Yeah, right. He could imagine how that would end up: Caroline on his lap again, soft and warm and oh, so willing. Just the thought of it kept him warm all the way to the house.

With an effort of will that was becoming more and more difficult, he pushed away thoughts of touching Caroline, stepped up into the back hall and divested himself of his outerwear. By the time everything was properly stowed, he was well aware that his dinner would indeed be late, for the silence and complete absence of savory aroma told him clearly that the meal had not yet even been started. Ah, well. Maybe he could speed things along. He checked the kitchen just to be sure, found it as expected, helped himself to a banana from the bowl of fruit in the center of the table and moved lightly down the hall as he peeled it and bit off the end.

He climbed the stairs, devouring the remaining banana in three bites. He carried the peel into his room and dropped it into the empty wastebasket behind the door, then began unbuttoning his cuffs and rolling them back as he moved past the bed with its saddle-blanket spread and the mission-style cupboard that he used as a dresser. He paused near the open door to his bathroom, hearing a trickle of water. Either he'd left the water running in the sink or Caroline was in there cleaning. If it was Caroline, he'd tell her to leave it and go ahead with dinner. He could finish up himself. He stepped into the doorway. The first thing he saw was the pile of neatly folded clothing on the counter near the sink, but the significance of that didn't have time to register, for movement near the shower immediately snagged his attention. He turned his head. And froze.

His heart stopped. His jaw dropped. His lungs seized. His eyes widened to take in the sight before him.

Caroline kneeled on the tile floor, where she had been scrubbing the bottom of the shower with one hand while holding back her hair with the other. Naked.

Her head turned, and she saw him, but her expression didn't register. He couldn't take it in; all that pale, creamy skin got in the way. While he gaped and ogled and forgot to breathe, she slowly stood, tossing away the scrub brush with a muted clatter. With a minimum of movement, she rinsed her hand and twisted off the water, and all the while her gaze never left his face. She pushed her hair back and sucked in her belly, her arms hanging limply at her sides. He shook his head. Just the idea that she had to suck in any portion of that lush, svelte figure was beyond absurd. She was perfect, wildly perfect.

His gaze moved over her greedily, from her angel's face and long sweep of pale hair to the elegant column of her throat and the dainty vee of her collarbones where they met high in the center of her chest and downward. Her breasts were round and firm, slightly fuller underneath, the nipples peaking in saucy points tilted slightly upward, inviting a man's hands and mouth. Her rib cage was tiny, her waist amazingly narrow. The pucker of her navel pressed gently inward, and her belly rounded sweetly between the delicate protrusions of her hipbones, tapering to a small triangle of fine ash-blond hair only slightly darker than that on her head. He closed his eyes then, imagining those long, slender legs wrapping around him as he plumbed the female depths held in secret beneath that silky triangle.

He felt rather than heard her move toward him, and his eyes opened despite his best efforts to stay with the fantasy, though why he wanted to became a mystery the moment he looked at her again. She was utterly female, as delicate as a piece of porcelain, and his for the taking. He'd never been more aware of that than now. When she reached uncertainly for the towel folded neatly over the ring bolted to the end of the cabinet, he stopped her instinctively, his big, rough hand closing over her slender wrist, and then she was in his arms, standing literally on his booted toes, her body pressed against him, light as feathers, all cool skin and smoldering heat at the same time.

Her mouth met his. Her arms twined around his neck.

"Jesse," she said between slow, hungry kisses. "Jesse, Jesse, Jesse..."

The sound of his whispered name brushed across his nerve endings, scorching and cooling, singing and chanting, telling him relentlessly that he would be a fool to pass this by, whatever the consequences. Giving in was the most selfish thing he'd ever done, but he did it without argument or thought. Locking both arms around her, he lifted her against him and backed through the doorway, quieting her with his mouth. It wasn't a conscious decision but an inevitability that he couldn't even think about, not with her mouth parting beneath his lips and her tongue rubbing against his, not with her hands tugging at his shirttail as he carried her to the bed. He set her on her feet and grabbed the hem himself, yanking it off over his head. By the time the outer one was gone, she had the other hiked up under his arms. He made short work of it and threw back the bedcovers with one arm, reaching for her with the other. She came into the curve of his arm as if she belonged there, and he swung her down onto the bed even as she grappled with his belt.

When he began to straighten, she made a sound of protest, wrapped both arms around his neck and hung on. Bending over her, he struggled blindly with his boots and tossed them aside to clunk heavily against the floor. Suddenly she released him and went to work on his belt again. He managed to get one sock off before she dispensed with the belt. Then she encountered the buttons of his fly and growled impatiently as she struggled with the first. He laughed, absurdly happy, and slipped the metal buttons free with deft, practiced flicks of one hand while she lifted her mouth to his and demanded with her kiss that he hurry. To quiet and placate her, he used his free hand to cup her breast. It was his first inkling of just how sensual this woman was.

She rose up, literally, not at all mollified but instead frantically insistent. He shoved down his pants and both layers of underwear and kicked until he was free of them. After a weak attempt at that last sock, he left the damned thing and climbed into bed with her. She pulled him down on top of her, her legs together, her arms locked about his shoulders. Answering her eagerness with his own, he pushed her head into the pillow with the force of his kiss. His pillow. His bed. His woman. He couldn't deny that, didn't want to. Even knowing that it shouldn't be so, that he would later regret what they did here tonight, he couldn't abandon this unexpected joy.

She felt like heaven beneath him, surprisingly soft and yet firm, less slight than she had in his arms. In contrast, he felt like a great hulking brute, so afraid he would hurt her, bruise her, disappoint her. He reached through the veil of her silky hair and kneaded her heated flesh. The feel of that sleek, creamy skin created a need to taste it. Sliding his mouth from hers, he kissed her cheek and the curve of her jaw. The vulnerability of her throat beckoned him, and he curled his body in order to reach it. She arched, thrusting her breasts against his chest, and suddenly that was where he needed to be. Sliding downward, he filled first his hands and then his mouth with her breasts. That was when she spread her legs for him, restlessly scissoring them until he planted himself heavily between them and pinned her with the weight of his upper body.

She clutched his head as he suckled her and lightly scraped her hard little nipple with his teeth. Heaving and writhing beneath him, she told him eloquently of the depth of her need, and he was happy to satisfy the sharp edge of that need immediately. Holding her at the waist with both hands, he slid downward again, dropping his legs off the side of the bed and trailing wet kisses over that sweet belly until he came to the juncture of her thighs. She sucked in her breath in shock when he kissed her there, but her body instantly relaxed, totally accepting of everything he would give it. He slid his hands beneath her knees and lifted them, leaving her feet flat upon the bed. With his hands he pressed her thighs wide apart.

He had never seen anything so beautiful as this woman, never wanted anything so much as he wanted to give her this pleasure. He lowered his head, and with the first flick of his tongue, she came up off the bed. With the next, she clamped both hands into his hair and pressed him against her. She was like riding a wild bronc, bucking and rotating, uncertain what she wanted but reaching for it with everything she had in her. He made sure she got it, his own flesh leaping and throbbing as she cried out, arching her back and pulling her heels tight against her buttocks. He used his teeth, shaking with the need to be gentle, to give and not yet take, until she screamed. Only then did he surge upward, his hand sliding between her legs as he gave her a taste of herself with his lips and tongue.

She curled her fingers around the blades of his shoulders, digging in her nails, driving her own tongue into his mouth. He pinched and plucked, driving her mad and happy to do it. When he sensed that the moment was on her again, he pulled back so he could watch her face as he slowly pushed first one finger and then two up inside her. Panting, she wrapped arms and legs around him, her eyes mere slits, body heaving. When the first wave shook her, she clamped down on it.

"No!" she gasped. "Not again, not without you!"

"Yes," he said, just for the pleasure of saying it, of knowing

that he could make her come again and again, no matter her
protests. He smoothed her hair away from her face with one hand,
his upper body weight balanced on that elbow, while with the
other hand he plumbed her deepest secrets and made her body
sing unknown songs until she convulsed beneath him. He stroked
her through it, watching the muscles of her face go rigid and
slacken in the same instant. Her nipples grew into small, round
peaks atop the swollen softness of her breasts. Jaws clamped,
nostrils flaring, she moaned through her teeth, her lips peeling
back. She looked as though she could take bites of him, great,
hefty chunks. Tears came to his eyes simply because he had never
seen a sight more wonderful than this woman in the throes of a
climax that he had given her.

As the crest receded, he let himself concentrate on the feel of
her, the sleek, smooth skin, taut muscles and rounded softness
pressed to his own body, the wet pull of her woman's core on
his fingers. He felt ready to burst now. Just the thought of pushing
himself into that tight, wet heat was almost more than he could
bear. He laid his forehead against hers, fighting back the surges
of his own body, until she began to move beneath him once more,
rhythmically at first and then with growing urgency. Only then
did he take his hand away. Blindly she pulled at him, her hands
moving restlessly over his back and shoulders. For her the des-
tination was not enough, she needed, demanded, the journey itself,
every step of it, every inch. He was so very glad, so deeply,
desperately grateful. Positioning himself, he smoothed the hair
from her face.

"Look at me."

She slowly opened eyes heavy-lidded and knowing, her arms
sliding about his neck, legs coiling around his hips and thighs.
Her gaze lifted to his and locked there, her body undulating beneath him. A smile spread across her rosy mouth. "I love you,"
she whispered, each word piercing his heart so sharply that he
gasped. He laid his head against her breast, humbled beyond
words, and it was then that he heard the footsteps on the carpeted
landing. She heard it, too. Her head turned in that direction even
as his lifted, but before either of them could react further, the
door to his bedroom opened and his father stuck his head inside.

"Jesse? Son, are you—"

Caroline made a sound low in her throa[t]
that ripped Jesse to pieces, and in that insta[nt]
father must: the grown, supposedly responsi[ble]
to know better and the pretty, starry-eyed little
twined naked together in his bed. In that instant,
that his regret was not what mattered, had never be[en]
tered, that Caroline's shame was nothing, could be no[t]
pared to his. In that instant he became aware of hims[elf]
should have been all along, and he knew without thought o[r]
tion that he was no fit lover for this beautiful young woman s[tar]
ing him with her emotion and her need: he was big and clums[y]
he needed a shower and a shave; he was ten years too old; he
was uncertain of so much, regretted so much, understood so little.
In that instant he knew the depth of his feelings for this woman
and the depth of his fear for her.

A heartbeat, perhaps two—if anyone's heart had been beating
still—and Haney retreated, closing the door with a thump. Caroline made that awful sound again and covered her face with her hands. Jesse said the vilest, filthiest word he knew. He said it again as his feet hit the floor and again as he shook out his jeans and yanked them on. She sat up in the bed, the sheet clutched to her chest.

"Jesse—"

"Get dressed." He found his other sock and wrestled it on while standing on one leg. "I'll go down and talk to him."

"No!"

He snatched up his undershirt and started for the door, pulling it down over his head. She came up on her knees and lunged at him. "It's all right," he said with more ease than he'd thought possible. "I'll explain everything."

"You don't understand!" she cried, clutching fistfuls of his shirt. "It's my fault."

He pried one hand free. "No, no. He'll understand. It's all right."

"I planned it, Jesse! I wanted you to make love to me...so I planned it."

He stared down at her disbelievingly. "Planned it?"

de, Jesse!'' she cried, shak-
mes splatter on my clothes
. I wear a heavy apron over
I made sure you found me
et go of his shirt and sank
, and I'm so sorry.''

g but marvel. To think that
ch! It was almost more than
ow, and that was only to be
h his big, rough hands and
her against his chest. He

hair reverently, and then he put her
, wiped the tears from her eyes with his fingertips
left her there alone in his bed.

His legs seemed to weigh a thousand pounds apiece as he skirted the stairwell and went to his parents' room. The door was open, the room dark and empty. He went back to the stairs and rounded the newel post, descending to the hallway. He moved along it as though moving through deep sludge and finally came to the living room. His father was sitting in his favorite chair, his big body molded to it like lumpy upholstery. He stared straight ahead as Jesse came into the room, walked around the couch and sat down on its end. Jesse tried for a long time to think of something intelligent to say and finally came up with, ''Dad, I'm sorry you had to see that.''

Haney waved a hand lethargically. ''My fault. I wasn't thinking,'' he said. ''I haven't been.''

Jesse swallowed. ''You should know that nothing happened. I mean, not everything happened. It would've, but it didn't.'' He sighed. ''And now it won't.''

Haney lifted both hands to push them through his hair. ''You're both adults,'' he said in a voice like raked gravel. He turned an oddly uncertain look on Jesse. ''Sarah says that Caroline's in love with you. She's always wanted you to fall in love again. We thought for a while with that Nancy woman…''

Shock knocked Jesse back. ''You knew about Nancy?'' He couldn't keep the incredulity from his voice.

"Your mother wanted to meet her, but I told her to leave it alone. When you didn't bring her around...well, that was that."

"You knew about Nancy." He couldn't get over it.

Haney gave him a look. "It's a small town, Jesse, but that's not the point."

Jesse rubbed his hands over his face. They knew about Nancy, had known, perhaps, all along. He closed his eyes, shrinking where he sat. He could only pray he'd disappear completely. His father was speaking, and he had to shake his head to clear it enough to listen.

"So the question is, I suppose, how do you feel about her?"

Jesse gulped. "Caroline?" Of course Caroline. He licked his lips. "I definitely have feelings for Caroline. Let's just say that they're not quite the same as hers for me, not what she thinks hers are for me, anyway."

Haney lifted both hands in a gesture of helplessness. "I don't know what that means, but I don't want you to hurt her, Jesse."

"You think I do?"

Haney shook his head. "I don't want you getting your mother's hopes up, either."

"I understand."

"And I don't want you carrying on with Caroline in front of her, either. It's not respectful. What you do in private is your business, of course."

Jesse scoffed at that. "Since when?"

"Your mother says you should be on your own," Haney went on as if Jesse hadn't even spoken. "She says we've all been in a rut, and that ever'body's suffered for it."

"Where is Sarah?" Caroline asked from the doorway.

Haney jerked and turned his head away. Jesse looked at her in surprise. Heavens, he hadn't even thought of his own mother! Now that he did, however, he knew darned well that she wasn't sitting out in the cold car. He looked to his father. "Dad?"

Haney cleared his throat. "I left her in Denver."

Caroline walked into the room with all the dignity of a queen, her hands clasped tightly before her. "Is she all right?"

Haney bowed his head. "Depends on what you mean by all right."

Caroline came to stand in the space between Haney's chair and the end of the sofa. "Is she well physically?"

Haney nodded. "I think so, well as she can be."

Caroline breathed a sigh of relief. "I'm glad for my own sake that she isn't here right now."

Haney said nothing to that. Jesse closed his eyes and propped his forehead against the heels of his hands, his elbows on his knees. He felt as if he'd been pulled through a thrashing machine backward. He wished she had stayed upstairs, but with Caroline all his wishes were just so much nonsense.

"Haney," she said softly, "I doubt Jesse told you, so I will. What you saw up there, it was entirely my fault."

"No, it wasn't." The least he could do was take his fair share of the blame.

"Yes, it was. I planned the whole thing. I made it happen."

"Nothing happened," Jesse pointed out.

"You know what I mean," she snapped.

Jesse just couldn't bear any more. He got up slowly, laboriously. "It didn't happen," he said evenly. "It isn't going to."

He might as well have challenged her with a red cape. She put her hands to her hips and glared at him. "Yes, it will, Jesse Wagner. I love you, and if you think I'm giving up on you now, you've got another think coming!"

Emotionally he was very near the edge, and so he ran. He ran out of there like a scared hare. "I'm going to town. Don't wait dinner on me. In fact, don't expect me at all."

"You'll be back!" she called after him. "And when you get here, I'll be waiting. Do you hear me, Jesse? I'll be waiting!"

He stomped into an old pair of boots in the hallway and threw on his coat. He rammed a hat on his head and patted down his pockets, relieved almost to the point of collapse to find that he still had his wallet and his keys. He was in the truck and headed to town before he had enough presence of mind to even wonder what had sent his father home without his mother. Whatever it was, he could do nothing about it. He couldn't manage his own life right now, let alone anyone else's. In fact, he was very much afraid that no matter what he did, it would be the wrong thing for someone, for him or for Caroline or someone else, everyone, maybe. He had to sort it all out somehow, make some decisions and stick to them. Somehow.

"Well, that was effective," Caroline muttered cryptically, dropping down onto the sofa space so recently vacated by Jesse. "As if shouting actually accomplished anything."

"Tell me about it," Haney mumbled, and Caroline bullied her mind into a direction where it might do some good.

Sighing, she regarded him frankly. "Actually, maybe we ought to turn that around. Maybe you ought to tell me why you're here instead of Denver."

Haney made a face. "I messed up everything, didn't I?"

Caroline slumped into the corner of the couch. "No. Certainly not for Jesse and me, if that's what you're thinking. I shouldn't have done what I did. Jesse has to want me for all the same reasons I want him if it's going to work out at all. I should have realized that and saved us all a lot of embarrassment." She sucked in a deep breath, having said all she intended to on the subject. "Now, do you want to tell me about Sarah?"

Haney frowned. "It's not Sarah," he finally said. "It's me. I just don't know what to do about it."

"Haney, I know you love Sarah," Caroline prodded gently.

"'Course I do," he retorted roughly. "Sometimes too much, maybe."

Caroline thought that over and shook her head, saying confidently, "That's not possible. But maybe if you could tell me why you think it is, I could help."

He sat staring into space for a long time, but Caroline sensed that he was working up to what he wanted to say. At long last he leaned forward and rubbed his hands over his face. "I'm losing her. And I'm not ready. I won't ever be ready. When you're young, like you and Jesse, you think you got all the time in the world to be together, then one day you wake up and all your tomorrows are gone. At first, time seems to stretch out into infinity, and then suddenly you can see the end of it, and it's coming closer all the time, faster and faster. And no matter how hard you try, you just can't get ready for it."

Caroline felt a little exasperated, so she chose her words diplomatically. "Haney, arthritis is debilitating and painful, but it's not fatal."

"No," he said softly, flicking a speck of lint off his knee, "but life is, and arthritis is one of those things that comes at the end of it."

Now she really wanted to shake him, but she held on to her composure. "That just isn't so. A long time ago when people died a lot younger than they do now, it might have been, but not anymore. Besides, lots of young people get certain forms of arthritis."

"Oh, that's what they tell you," Haney scoffed, "but the truth is we're coming to the end."

She bit down on a flash of temper, but the words tumbled out, anyway. "For Pete's sake, Haney! No one is ever guaranteed a tomorrow. All any of us have, young and old alike, is right *now,* this day, this hour, this moment!"

"You can say that," he grumbled stubbornly, "because you're young and—"

Caroline completely lost her patience then. She launched to her feet. "That's a crock, Haney Wagner, and you know it! I have no more guarantee of a future than you do, than anyone does! Don't you understand that Kay thought she and Jesse had all the time they'd ever need? Don't you imagine that Champ's mother believed she'd have time to make up for all her mistakes? Sarah has arthritis, Haney! Yes, it's impacted her life and yours, too, but there are treatments. It can even go into remission, but if not, you can both learn to cope, to enjoy your lives again! That's what Sarah's trying to do, to bring the joy back into your lives, but she needs your help, and you can't give it to her if you insist on sticking your head in the sand! Stop worrying about what you can't change and start working on what you can! Because now is all there is for any of us. And you're wasting it by sitting here with your head in your hands while she's in Denver fighting to get your lives back!"

Haney sat gaping at her throughout her tirade and for several seconds afterward. It was during those final seconds that she began to regret her hasty tongue, so much so that she put a hand over her mouth to prevent any more thoughtless words from escaping. Haney, however, finally got his mouth closed, only to have it turn up in a reluctant grin. "You don't cut much slack, do you? No wonder you got that boy of mine running."

Completely deflated now, Caroline flopped back down on the couch. "You're right. I don't know what I'm talking about. I'm sorry."

"That's not what I meant at all," he said with a rough chuckle. He spread his hands. "You just don't mince words, and I guess maybe that's what I needed."

"You don't have to try to make me feel better," Caroline muttered, "especially not after everything that's happened today."

He waved that away. "No, I mean it. Those counselors, I guess they've been pretty much saying the same thing but polite, you know."

Caroline grimaced. "Haney, I didn't mean to be rude, really I didn't."

"You weren't rude," Haney told her. "You just laid it out there on the line, and you're right about everything you said. It's just—" He shook his head. "I walked out on her in the middle of one of those counseling sessions. I couldn't sit there any longer being lectured about this 'stage' of my life and 'classic male denial,' whatever that is. I just want her to get over it. I want..." He sighed and pinched the bridge of his nose. "What I want is to be thirty-five again, showing my boys their way around this place and counting the minutes until I can get their mama alone. I want to start from the beginning and do it all again exactly the same way."

Tears came to Caroline's eyes. "Haney, that's the sweetest thing I've heard a man say, but you know it's not possible to go back."

He nodded and rubbed his eyes with the heels of his hands. "I know, I know. All we've got is the here and now—if I haven't totally ruined everything."

Caroline smiled encouragingly. "Haney, you just get yourself back to Denver and tell Sarah what you've told me, and everything will be fine. And this time I do know what I'm talking about."

He lifted a hand to the back of his neck, saying tentatively, "I reckon she's forgiven me worse."

Caroline shrugged. "She loves you."

Haney smiled. "Yeah. Used to be, we'd fight sometimes just so we could make up."

"Then just look at this as a perfect opportunity for making up."

He chuckled. "Good idea. First I'll call her, then tomorrow bright and early I'll head back."

Caroline sat back and smiled. "Well, now that that's settled, how about some dinner?"

He slapped his firm middle. "Great! Suddenly, I'm starved."

She got up. "You call Sarah while I get things started."

He got up, too, and she headed for the kitchen, but suddenly he stopped her. "Caroline!"

She turned back warily. Now would come the lecture she'd been dreading since the moment Haney had opened that bedroom door. "Yeah?"

"Thanks," he said gently, surprising her. "And don't worry about Jesse. We Wagner men are slow, but we're not stupid. I'm betting he'll come around."

She heaved a sigh of relief. "I hope you're right. I have to believe you are."

"Jesse'll work it out, you'll see." He lifted a brow, adding, "He's got a mighty high incentive, if you ask me."

Blushing, she nodded hopefully and hurried toward the kitchen. Well, it wasn't exactly the outcome for this day that she'd expected, but it could have been worse. After all, not a single rock had been thrown by anyone. In fact, had Haney not interrupted, Jesse would be making love to her now, but it was probably best that it hadn't happened, after all, not that way and not at this time. If they were going to have any kind of future, she and Jesse had to come together in honesty and love. The question was, would it happen? She could only pray and hope, like Haney, that her tomorrow would come.

Chapter Thirteen

He didn't come home that night. He didn't come home the next morning, so he wasn't there to see his father off. He didn't come home for dinner, either, which seemed to give Handsome ideas again, so much so that Tiger dragged him out of the house almost before he finished his dinner. Caroline heard them arguing as they trudged toward their respective vehicles.

"She's Jesse's girl," Tiger said.

"Well, he sure doesn't act like it!" Handsome retorted.

"She's still Jesse's girl," Tiger insisted, and Caroline had to agree. No matter what, she was Jesse's girl. She wasn't even sure she could stop being Jesse's girl if she wanted to. So she locked the house up tight and settled down to wait for him in front of the now-repaired television, a book on her lap.

Some time after ten, she got up and went upstairs to bed, but after tossing and turning for nearly an hour, she gave up and went back downstairs in her flannel pajamas to sit in front of the television again and wonder what, exactly, was supposed to be entertaining about late-night programming. Eventually fatigue and sheer boredom did the trick, and the next thing she knew, something jerked her awake.

She sat up on the couch, blinking in the heavy darkness and wondering what was wrong, and then it hit her. The television. Someone had turned it off. Jesse. She pushed her hair back and looked around the room. After a bit, her eyes adjusted and she caught the outline of a figure sitting in Haney's chair. She cleared her throat and tried to keep the edge off her voice.

"So, have a good day?"

He said nothing for a moment, and then he sighed heavily. "No."

"Good. Serves you right. Me, neither, so I guess that makes us even."

"I had to think," he said.

Nodding, she folded her legs beneath her and settled down for a talk. "Okay. Would it have killed you to call, though?"

"No. But getting so drunk I couldn't call almost did. I woke up about four this afternoon with my third—and final—hangover ever. But then I vowed that the last time, too."

Caroline smiled into the dark. "And how long did that vow last?"

"Oh, going on ten years, I reckon."

She laughed. "Well, maybe this one will have some real sticking power."

"It ought to," he said drily. "I thought someone had split my skull down the middle with a dull ax when I woke up in that motel room this afternoon."

Caroline tried to keep the question behind her teeth, but she couldn't help it. She had to know. "Did you wake up alone?"

A heartbeat later he said, "Yeah, and I went to bed alone, too."

She was glad that the darkness hid her face just then because she couldn't have kept the relief from showing if her life had depended on it. "I shouldn't have asked that," she managed shakily.

"No, you shouldn't have." She heard a rustle of movement as he slid forward to the edge of his seat and then his voice, muffled by the hands he held to his face. "God, Caroline, don't you know that you're the only woman I want?"

She didn't know who got up first, and she didn't care, not even when she smacked her shin on the edge of the coffee table. It stopped hurting the moment his arms came around her.

"I know it's not right," he was saying, "but I want you so much."

She hushed him with fingers pressed against his lips, then replaced them with her mouth, exulting in the eagerness of his response. Everything about him was so dear, the hard strength of his body, the earthy, male smell of him, the roughness of his callused hands, the scratch and pull of his two-day growth of beard, even the deep catch in his breath when she pressed her upper body more fully against him. Her own breath caught when he cupped her bottom in his big hands and thrust the proof of his maleness against her, his kiss suddenly more aggressive than her own.

She wrapped her arms around his neck and welcomed his tongue into her mouth. It was not enough. Coiling one leg around him, she opened herself to the thrust and grind of his pelvis. The pressure alone made her head swim, and yet it was still not enough, not nearly enough. Apparently it wasn't enough for him, either, because he slid one hand over her hip and down to the thigh of the leg upon which she balanced herself, lifting it and coaxing it around him as he took her weight into his arms. A sound of need rippled up from deep in his chest, echoing into her mouth. He turned, bumped his way around the coffee table and dropped both of them down onto the couch into a sitting position. She moved so that she knelt astraddle his lap, her hands framing his face as she kissed him. He shoved his hands up under the top of her pajamas, cupping and squeezing. The pleasure of that simple touch was astonishing, and she arched against his palms, rocking her pelvis against him. Moaning, he jerked his hands away and turned his head, breaking the kiss.

"I can't do this," he said raggedly. "I shouldn't do this, no matter how much I want to."

Caroline matched her forehead and the tip of her nose to his. "We both know I want this, Jesse, and we both know how I feel about you. So the only question I have right now is, do you love me?"

He caught handfuls of her hair in his fists and pulled her head back so that he could look into her eyes. "Yes. But—"

She stopped him from saying more by laying her cheek against his mouth. "That's all that matters to me, Jesse."

He covered her ears with his hands and turned her head, determined. "Caroline, I can't promise you—"

"It doesn't matter now. Just don't stop. Make love to me, Jesse."

He groaned. "Caroline, sweetheart, I—"

"I won't lie to you, Jesse," she said quickly. "I want you to be the only man ever to make love to me, but if you can't promise to be the only one, then please be the first. Don't let some other man be my first, not when I love you so much, when I know I'll always love you."

"Caroline. Ah, God, I want to believe I can give you everything you'll ever need, be everything you'll ever want, but I can't risk it."

"Then don't," she said, unbuttoning her pajama top, "just be what I need and what I want now. We'll let tomorrow take care of itself, but tonight... Love me tonight, Jesse. Love me."

With a sigh of defeat and mingled anticipation, he capitulated. His trembling hands brushed open the front of her shirt. She shrugged it off her shoulders, letting it slide down her arms and fall away. He moaned and filled his hands. She caught her breath as his warm palms molded her pale flesh. Her head fell back, and a molten need surged between her legs. He seemed to know and thrust his hips upward accordingly, grinding against her in a movement that partly assuaged and partly inflamed her need.

"Hurry, Jesse," she panted, answering his thrusts with her own.

Quickly he twisted and lowered her onto her back, pulling away long enough to throw off his clothes. She lifted her arms for him, but his hands came down on her waist, clutched the elastic band of her pajama bottoms and peeled them down and off, tossing them over the end of the couch. She spread her legs for him, and he came down between them on one knee, his hands sliding beneath her hips and lifting her.

"This could hurt," he said when he was positioned to enter her.

"I don't care." She wrapped her legs around him and opened her arms. He leaned forward and kissed her, slowly sinking into her core. She tightened her embrace as he came down on top of her, desperate to have him buried deeply inside her. At one point she felt a small pinch of discomfort, but it was completely overshadowed by the heat and fullness stretching her to completion. Finally he stopped and broke the kiss, his muscles rigid as he nuzzled her cheek.

"I'll try to go slow," he whispered roughly, "but I'm not really sure I can."

"Don't," she answered breathlessly, pulsing against him. "Jesse, I need—"

"I know," he said, thrusting deeply.

An arrow of light drove straight to her head. She cried out, arching beneath him and holding him tight. He moved again and again, the ecstasy blinding her with light from within. She clutched and clawed at him, finally finding her rhythm and rising up to meet him, thrust for thrust. When she reached the zenith he was buried deeply inside her, but then suddenly he was pulling out.

"No!" she cried out, surging upward and clamping her hands down on his hips, legs locked around him.

With a strangled moan he drove into her again, shuddering and jerking his head back. A moment later he collapsed atop her, heart hammering, lungs pumping. "Sweet heaven!" he gasped against the curve of her neck. Caroline tried to hold on to him, but her body had turned to butter, a languid peacefulness settling over her. Her arms and legs slid away, the weight of his body pressing her into the sofa cushions.

"Oh, Jesse," she whispered, and felt the curve of his smile against her throat. After a moment he levered himself up onto one elbow, and for the first time she realized how truly small and uncomfortable that couch was for two people, especially when one of them was so big and heavy.

"No pain, I take it."

Laughter bubbled up out of her throat. "No pain, just wonderful pleasure."

"Yes," he said, kissing her.

To her surprise she felt desire quicken again. Her body contracted, and his leaped in response. "Oh, my," she purred, wrapping her arms around his neck.

He chuckled deep in his throat. "Something tells me we've just begun this night."

"I hope so."

He rose up on his knees then, pulling her up with him. "But not here."

"Upstairs," she agreed.

He got to his feet, then suddenly froze. "Where's my father?"

Caroline smiled as she stood and leaned against him. "In Denver with your mother where he belongs."

Jesse relaxed. "Good," he said. Scooping her up into his arms, he headed for the hallway. She laid her head on his shoulder and rubbed her hands greedily over his bare skin, marveling at the warm strength that she felt beneath her fingertips. She wouldn't think of tomorrow, she told herself. After all, hadn't she told Haney only the day before that all any of us could lay claim to was now? She would take this moment and hope for more, pray for more, and somehow it would be all right. It had to be all right. He loved her, and if he loved her, what could be wrong?

When they reached the landing, she squirmed out of his arms and took control, pulling and prodding him into the closest room, which was, luckily, his own. They laughed and tussled like children, falling in a heap on the bed and wrestling with the covers until they were beneath them, cooled skin warming against cooled skin until passion flared hot and laughter became moans of pleasure and gasps of need, until the night dissolved into satiation and, finally, sleep.

Jesse watched the light lift and the shadows pale, Caroline snuggled against him in sleep. Never in his life had he experienced anything like the past night. Despite a pleasant exhaustion, he hadn't closed his eyes for a moment since the last time they'd made love and Caroline had slid reluctantly into much-needed sleep. He didn't want to miss a second of this. He knew that he would never know its like again, and he meant to eke every mote of joy from this time with her as her lover. He still marveled that she had chosen him.

Oh, he was attractive enough, but for a woman like her, attractive wouldn't normally cut it. With her looks, her talents, her style and her intelligence, she could have just about anyone, but she had picked him, a nearly thirty-eight-year-old hulk still living with his parents after a miserable, failed marriage that had ended in the unnecessary death of the last woman who had loved him. He was proud enough of who he was, a cowboy and a rancher, a horseman and a stockman, a businessman. He'd been as good a son and a brother as he could be. He thought he'd been a good uncle to Champ. He had friends who enjoyed his company and business associates who trusted him. The ranch hands treated him with respect and easy joviality. But this was different. For no good reason that he could see, Caroline had chosen him.

I want you to be the only man ever to make love to me, but if you can't be the only one, then please be the first.

The first man to make love to her.

It was overwhelming, incredible. It was enough. It had to be. And yet...

He'd long ago accepted the fact that he was a failure only in one area, as a husband, and that failure had barred him from trying his hand at another role, that of a father. He wondered if he'd crossed the line last night. God knew he hadn't done anything to prevent it, and he was confused by that now. It didn't fit with who and what he was. He was the responsible one—not that Rye had been irresponsible exactly, only wilder, younger, more emotional. Jesse had watched his brother make a name for himself on the rodeo circuit, where it was said that he'd performed in more bedrooms than arenas, and Jesse had often felt the need to caution Rye. Yet, last night he had lain here with this woman in his arms, made love to her over and over again and, after a merely token attempt, had done nothing whatsoever to protect her from impregnation, while a box of condoms was stored discreetly in the far corner of a shelf in his closet, close at hand.

How could he have done it? It was the single most irresponsible act of his life, and at this moment he felt nothing more than confusion and a certain wryness at his own lack of shame and outrage. As he lay there, putting off the moment when she would leave his bed forever, he allowed himself to imagine what it would be like if she were, indeed, pregnant. Smiling to himself, he tightened his arm about her slender waist and carefully weighed her breast in his hand, picturing her big with child, her stomach distended, breasts swollen. Perhaps the perfect oval of her face would round out a bit, her hips spread. He lightly stroked her long, pale tresses, wondering if pregnancy would tax her so that it lost some of its shine and silkiness. In all likelihood, he would never know. In all the time he and Kay had been together, she had never conceived and they had never done anything to prevent it, having intended from the beginning to grow a family. He was not likely now to become a father after a single night.

Just for a moment, disappointment assailed him. He thought with some bitterness of Rye, who would soon have a second child to love, but then he turned off that feeling and concentrated instead on the woman in his arms. For the first time, he wished he were the younger brother instead of the elder. If he could only be twenty-eight again, he would allow himself less self-knowledge. He would take a chance, risk it all, even knowing that she would be the one taking the greater risk. He would be selfish, unruly, swept away by the emotions he was feeling. It probably wouldn't work out. This acute love and staggering desire would undoubtedly fade, perhaps not as quickly as before but almost assuredly.

Yes, the feelings would fade. One night she would smile at him with invitation in her eyes, and he would feel sick in the pit of his belly. He'd try not to show it, but she would soon see through the pretense, and her hurt and confusion would torture them both. He would do his best, but it wouldn't be good enough. Every day and every night she would wonder why he couldn't love her as he should and he would wonder how to fix it. Stay or go? Pretend or talk honestly?

No, he couldn't do it to her. Last night aside, he was the responsible Wagner brother. He would do what he should. Any pain they might feel now would be nothing to what they could feel if he let himself forget the facts of his life. He was who he was and what he always would be.

She stirred, moving against him languidly, and he smiled once more, knowing that he would never forget the way she twitched her nose and moaned softly as if greeting the day with equal parts welcome and trepidation. He knew the exact moment when she realized where and with whom she was. Smiling, she shifted and rolled against him, the warm scent of her skin and their love-making drifting over him.

"Mmm, good morning," she mumbled, snuggling beneath his chin, her cheek against his chest, one slender leg sliding between his. Desire flared, tugging almost painfully at his groin. He knew that if he gave in to it this time, he would never do what he must. He jerked away.

"Good morning, sleepyhead," he said lightly. "We'd better get up. I've got a busy day. We're haying the mountain fringe where the snow is deepest today, and we'll have to do it horse-back. That takes a lot of preparation, especially in the condition I'm in." As he spoke, he slipped away from her, sitting up on the side of the bed with his feet on the floor, the covers across his lap.

She pushed her hair out of her eyes, looking deliciously rum-pled and thoroughly loved. The delicate skin of her chin, neck and cheek had been lightly abraded by his beard. He knew he ought to feel bad about that, but he couldn't quite manage it. Those were his marks on her. Last night and just now she was his and his alone. He wouldn't think about later, about some other man claiming her one day.

"Are you okay?" she asked softly.

"A little sore is all. You?"

She sat up and drew her knees to her chest beneath the cover. "I'm wonderful," she said dreamily, wrapping her arms around her legs.

He couldn't help smiling. At least he'd improved in some areas. "Good. I'm glad. Think you could rustle me up a bite of break-fast?"

She grinned. "Well, I have this little problem?"

"Yeah?"

She lay back, stretching luxuriously. "I don't seem to have any clothing."

Laughing, he got up and went to the closet, snagging a pair of jeans for himself and a shirt for her. He tugged on the jeans where he stood, his back to her, and found to his chagrin that this would not be an easy day in the saddle. Resisting the urge to stay and watch her get into it, he tossed her the shirt and moved on into the bathroom. Memory flashed a picture before his mind's eye: Caroline, naked and incredibly tempting, intentionally so. He leaned his hands against the sink and tried to catch his breath. In that moment when he'd first seen her, he'd known that what happened last night was inevitable. Later he'd told his father, himself and her that he wouldn't let it happen, but he'd known, deep down, that it would. Once. He'd given himself one night with her. And now it was over.

He managed to shave, brush his teeth and comb his hair without ever looking himself in the eye. While he was doing so, she put on his shirt and left his room, presumably to dress and start his breakfast. He dressed with care, layering his clothes for warmth and comfort. It would be a long, difficult day, but that was just as well. Perhaps he wouldn't have time to think, to remember. First, though, he had to get through breakfast. He had to say his piece, stick to his guns, and get out with enough sense intact to go about his business. He was very much afraid he wouldn't make it, afraid she'd look at him with those hurt, worshipful eyes, and he'd cave like the rickety character he was. He steeled himself with a mental picture of Kay after she had stepped into that puddle of electricity. A moment later he reluctantly went down to face the music.

She was humming to herself while she fried his eggs, wearing nothing but his shirt and a pair of once-fuzzy house slippers. The urge to go to her, to slip his arm around her waist and squeeze, to kiss the soft flesh of her neck, was almost overwhelming. He pulled out the chair at the end of the table and sat down. She tossed him a smile and slipped a plate of bacon and toast from the warming oven with one hand, while scooping up the eggs with the other. She tilted the spatula over the plate and the eggs slid into place. Delivering the plate with a flourish, she turned away to pour him a cup of coffee, then turned to lean a hip against the counter, watching him with a sparkle in her eyes, her long, bare legs crossed at the ankle.

He gulped coffee and began cutting up his eggs with fork and knife. They were cooked to perfection, the whites firm and solid, the yellows warm and liquid. He couldn't bear the thought of putting them in his mouth. Carefully, resignedly, he balanced the fork and knife on the rim of the plate and reached for his coffee cup again, motioning her over to the table.

"Sit down. We need to talk."

His tone put her on notice. Her smile faded somewhat, but she gamely pulled out a chair and perched. "You can't tell me you regret what happened last night."

He shook his head, his gaze on his plate. "No, I can't."

"But it was too much too soon," she said gently.

Relief flooded through him. She had just given him a small escape, a way perhaps to briefly put off the inevitable. "Something like that."

"I knew that's what you were thinking," she said, rubbing a fingertip across the tabletop, "so I have a proposition for you."

A proposition? He was almost afraid to ask, but he couldn't help smiling at the possibilities. "And what would that be?"

"We'll back up, start over, go at a normal speed."

"And what would that mean?"

"A date."

He laughed. He couldn't help it. He'd just spent the most intimately, erotically satisfying night of his life with this woman, and now she was asking him out on a date. Talk about getting the cart before the horse! Still, a so-called date was a heck of a lot safer for her than another night in his bed. In the meantime, he'd find some way to make her understand that they could have no future together—for her sake. "Okay," he said. "What'd you have in mind?"

She shrugged. "I don't know. I'm feeling a touch of cabin fever, though, so I definitely want to get out of here."

"Maybe there's a movie in town you want to see."

She shook her head. "Something a little more...interactive, I think. How about dancing?"

He lifted an eyebrow at that. "I doubt you'd care much for my brand of dancing."

She stared at him. "Are you kidding? A little Texas two-step, a couple of line dances, I can handle anything you want to throw at me, Wagner."

He chuckled at that. "In that case, I know a place we can go, but I'm warning you, I'm barely acceptable as a dancer."

"We'll see," she said, getting up. "Tomorrow's Saturday, so say about 9 p.m.?"

"All right."

She grinned at him. "Now that that's settled, eat your breakfast while I pack you a hearty lunch. I assume you won't be coming in for it as usual."

"You assume correctly," he said, picking up his knife and fork again. "Don't forget Tiger and Handsome."

"As if I would."

He grinned as he forked up eggs. She was nothing if not efficient, that woman. The eggs were a little cold and congealed now, but he hardly noticed, his appetite returning in force. By the time he had shoveled down his breakfast and sucked up a second cup of coffee, she had packed a crate full of hot soups, coffee, thick sandwiches and steaming chocolate pudding. Dinner would be beans with ham hock, honey corn bread and a green salad, she informed him. He kissed her goodbye before he even stopped to think and strode out into a cold, snowy day armed with hearty food and a heartier smile. Life was good, better than it had been in some long while, and if it was to be temporary, all the more reason to enjoy it while he could. He had the rest of his life to pull cold comfort from doing the right thing. For now, for a little space in time, he would be cautiously happy and shamelessly thankful.

Caroline listened to the door close behind him and sagged against the counter in relief. That had been close, terribly so. She wasn't surprised that he was having second thoughts. He had done so from the beginning, but she had almost let her disappointment wreck it. Thank God she had found sense enough to back off and regroup. She had hoped that last night would be all he required to put his doubts to rest, but she knew that he doubted himself, not her, and last night had been merely the first step in teaching him how wrong he was to pronounce himself a failure at marriage when he had so obviously married the wrong woman. He needed a chance to get used to the idea of being one half of a couple, this time with the right woman.

He would never think of her as a sister. She had made dead certain of that. Now all she had to do was convince him that he could think of her as a wife and a lover. Might as well discover life on Saturn while she was at it. But she wouldn't quit. He had to understand that, eventually. She wouldn't quit, and she wouldn't let him quit. Ever. So tonight she'd keep her distance, and tomorrow they'd dance, and after that she'd take every step as if her very life depended on it, because it did. When she came right down to it, it did.

He had made a mistake, no doubt about it. Correction. He had made another mistake. This date thing wasn't a reprieve, it was torture, pure and simple. He'd had some vague idea about showing her how ill-suited they were, and instead he found himself part of an official couple. The most shocking aspect of it was that everyone else seemed so accepting of them! He wondered if he really publicly came off like the sort of selfish lowlife who went after the just-barely-beyond-jailbait set. He knew without doubt by the way some of them were looking at Caroline that a few of that ilk were numbered among his own friends, and it didn't do his blood pressure any good to see it. Not that he could blame them for looking.

She wore tight black jeans, chained half boots and a narrow belt studded with silver conchos around an impossibly narrow waist. A black leather, fringed vest over a simple little white T-shirt that looked like it belonged on a third-grader and a red-and-white bandanna, rolled and tied like a headband to hold back her hair, completed her outfit. She looked good enough to eat. That narrow band of pale, taut skin between the hem of her T-shirt and the waistband of her jeans was driving him crazy. Every time his fingertips grazed that skinny patch of bare skin desire shot through him like a bolt of lightning. Blond lightning.

That's just what she felt like in his arms. He couldn't help thinking about having her naked beneath him. He couldn't bear watching her dance with someone else.

His feet ached, he'd danced so much this night. His jaw felt frozen in a permanent clinch because he'd smiled through gritted teeth so often. Through it all, though, he managed to maintain the fiction of a happy-go-lucky night out in the midst of a fierce winter. If one more moron pounded him on the back as if in congratulations, however, he wouldn't be held responsible for his actions. He desperately wanted a second beer, but as he was driving, he wouldn't indulge. Caroline, to her credit, had been nursing her third for hours now. He half hoped that when she was finished with it, she would want to go—and he half dreaded the possibility. If being here surrounded by grinning idiots was agony, being alone in the house with her was sheer hell. He'd lain awake the entire past night, talking himself out of slipping up the stairs to her room, praying she wouldn't slip down them to his.

The door at the end of the bar opened, and Jesse turned that way instinctively, groaning when Handsome stepped through with a pretty brunette on his arm, Tiger at his back. Caroline followed his line of sight. Chuckling, she said, "Be nice. You're the one who told them where we were going."

"Yeah, but I didn't expect them to trail us."

"You said yourself that this was the best club in the area."

He grumbled imprecations beneath his breath, watching through slitted eyes as the unwelcome trio made a beeline across the room toward their table. Handsome was the first to reach them, dragging his brunette by the arm.

"Hey, Boss, Caroline. How's the band tonight?"

"Pretty good," Caroline said. "Their steel guitar got snowed in, but I can't say its loss is noticeable. They're on a break now."

"I noticed." Without waiting for an invitation, Handsome pulled out a chair and waved his date down into it, then turned one around for himself. Tiger snagged an extra from a nearby table and sat down between Jesse and the brunette, who turned out to be Helena. "Helena, this here is my boss, Jess Wagner, and his gal, Caroline," Handsome said. Jesse gritted his teeth and nodded a greeting.

Caroline lifted a hand across the table, and Helena curled red-tipped fingers around it, giving it a limp shake. Jesse gave the other woman a cursory once-over. Her makeup was too heavy. Her hair had one of those ultratrendy cuts that made it look like a bunch of limp feathers. Her jeans and cut-out blouse were unremarkable. He wasn't impressed by the glimpse of red boots that he'd caught as she'd moved across the floor toward them. She was pretty enough, he supposed, with her big brown eyes, but not up to Handsome's usual standards, in his book, anyway, certainly not up to Caroline's.

The band wandered back to the stage, tuned up and launched into a popular C&W tune.

"That's our cue," Handsome said. Popping up, he spun his date out onto the floor. Tiger looked between Jesse and Caroline, then awkwardly climbed to his feet. "Want to dance, Caroline?"

She shook her head and leaned into Jesse. "No, thanks, Tiger. I'm about danced out."

Tiger looked at Jesse in surprise. "Oh. You, too, huh, Boss?"

"Me, too," Jesse said, mentally ordering his arm to stay balanced across the top of Caroline's chair. It ignored him and dropped down to loosely encircle her, his fingertips coming to rest over that little strip of bare skin at her waist. She draped her forearm across his thighs and laid her head back against his shoulder.

"Well," Tiger said, looking around the room for likely prospects. He spotted one and moved off in her direction.

Not a word was said at the table until the dance ended and Tiger moved back to his chair, his partner claimed by another cowboy. Handsome and Helena stayed on the floor. The music started up again, and Tiger tapped his toe in time to it. He turned once more to Caroline. "Want to take a turn now?"

Caroline smiled. "Actually," she said, "Jesse has exhausted me." She leaned forward and confided conspiratorially. "Don't ever let him tell you that he isn't a good dancer."

Tiger grinned and nodded. "I figured."

Caroline leaned back again, sighing. "To tell you the truth, I'm about ready to call it a night."

Jesse leaped to his feet, practically yanking her chair out from under her. "See you Monday morning, Tiger. Enjoy the weekend. Tell Handsome and the bru—uh, Helena so long for us. 'Bye."

Caroline chortled as he propelled her through the maze of tables and out the door, trailing their coats. He paused in the cold night air long enough to throw her coat on her back and shrug into his own. "What's so funny?" he groused.

She turned a perfectly innocent face up to him. "Nothing. I just had a good time, that's all."

He muttered the requisite reply. A good time. Yeah, right up there with having your fingernails yanked and your skin groomed with a wire bristle brush. He handed her up into the truck and trudged around to the driver's side, buckling himself in with sharp, brusque movements. Thank God it was over. Sort of. Now all he had to do was figure out how to make it to his bed alone and actually sleep there. If she pressed the issue... He gulped, remembering the feel of her bare skin beneath his fingertips. Lord help him.

She hummed all the way home, her pale hair flowing over her shoulders and arms. Once there, she let herself out of the truck before he could get around to help her, then marched off up the walk through a dusting of fresh snow as if she had enough energy left to hike around the world. Jesse followed her into the house with growing trepidation. Shouldn't she be more tired? Surely she didn't have the energy to... No, he wouldn't even think about it.

He took off his coat and hung it on the peg, then hung his hat next to it. She had already shed her coat and put it on a hanger next to one of his mother's garments in the tiny closet for that purpose. Now she turned and strolled down the hall toward him. He steeled himself. She slid her arms around his waist and looked up at him. "I had a wonderful time, Jesse. Thank you," she whispered huskily.

He cleared his throat, his hands hovering dangerously around her shoulders. "My pleasure," he lied—only somehow it was true, despite everything.

She lifted up on her toes and kissed him lightly on the mouth. "Good night," she whispered, lowering herself again and turning away.

He felt as though his boots had been welded to the floor as he watched her sweep around the corner. His heart seemed permanently lodged in his throat. He listened as her footsteps softly receded, then he slumped against the wall and moaned.

Sweet heaven! What was he going to do? He wasn't sure how long he could hold out. If his parents didn't come home soon, he couldn't be certain what he'd do. He had to make some space for himself. He needed breathing room. He would just have to take the bull by the horns tomorrow morning and put it to her bluntly. No more dates. No more nights of passion.

No more nothing.

He had to have some breathing space.

He had to.

Chapter Fourteen

She took it surprisingly well.

"I understand. You've been alone a long time. You need some space."

"It's not you," he hurried to assure her, pushing away his breakfast.

She smiled serenely. "I know."

He frowned, wondering why he wasn't more relieved. "As long as we're clear."

"Perfectly. By the way, your mother called a few minutes ago."

He felt his spirits lift somewhat. Surely they were on their way home. "What'd she have to say?"

Caroline refilled his coffee cup and carried the pot back to the burner. "They're going to Phoenix."

Both his cup and his jaw nearly hit the tabletop. "What?"

She turned back smoothly, an unconcerned smile on her pretty face. "I said, they're going to Phoenix."

"When?" He didn't mean to raise his voice and had to gulp down a swearword before it escaped.

"Today, of course," Caroline said lightly, as if he hadn't just roared at her. "They have to fly from Denver anyway, so they arranged to go today. Sarah's feeling much better, by the way. Haney, too, apparently. I venture to say our worries are over, there."

Jesse could only think that rescue had been snatched away at the last moment. He licked his lips, trying to think. "H-how long?"

"How long will they be gone, do you mean?" Caroline asked and shrugged. "They didn't say. Couple of weeks, I imagine. But don't worry. I have everything under control."

That, of course, was exactly what he feared most. He pushed away his cup and got heavily to his feet. His only hope was to work himself into a stupor and pray that she had the decency and the sense to keep her distance. If he could have seen the smile she aimed at his back as he went out, he'd have quaked in his boots.

His lunch was waiting in the warming oven. Jesse helped himself and ate in unaccustomed silence, expecting her to put in an appearance at any moment. She had to be in the house because her old car was still parked in the drive, but she didn't show before he finished the meal. Having exhausted his supply of Sunday chores, he took himself into the living room and settled down to watch a football game on television. Every once in a while he heard her moving around upstairs. Apparently she ran a bath, took a long soak and went back to her room. He tried not to think about her lolling naked in a tub of warm bubbles, her long hair bundled up on top of her head, then he realized that someone had scored, and he didn't even know which team had the ball.

Disgusted, he changed the channel. Later, he changed it back again. The game ended without him being able to recall a single play. She came downstairs and went into the kitchen. He stared at a television news program and listened to the muted sounds of his dinner being put together. After an hour or so, she came to the doorway and announced cheerily that dinner was ready.

Pretending an intense interest in a commercial, he mumbled that he'd be there in just a minute. The commercial ended. He aimed the remote control and flicked off the television on his way to the kitchen.

"Smells good," he exclaimed, stepping a heartbeat later into an empty kitchen. He couldn't quite believe she was gone already. After a second glance around the room, he turned back to the hallway, intending to call out to her, but he caught himself at the last instant. He'd asked for space, after all, and she was giving it to him. That in itself was cause for celebration. Wasn't it? Yes, of course it was. So why didn't he feel the relief that he should?

Thoroughly confused, he pulled out the chair and sat down at the table. A moment later it occurred to him to pick up his fork and actually eat. He couldn't have said afterward what he'd put in his mouth, but eventually his plate was clean, and suddenly the evening stretched before him, empty, lonely and uninteresting.

Caroline forked a baby carrot into her mouth and turned the page, chewing. It had taken some intense doing, but she was, for the moment, completely absorbed in the Western she was reading. Slade, his six-gun spinning away from his hand, crouched in the corner of the old shed and waited, blood leaking from the flesh wound in his shoulder. Her bedroom door creaked open, revealing...

Jesse!

She turned the book facedown and sat up on the bed, her dinner plate held aloft in one hand. "Hi. Everything okay?"

He shrugged and leaned against the door frame. "Just wondered what was going on with you."

She folded her legs, balanced the plate atop them and popped a broccoli floret into her mouth, chewing thoughtfully. "Well, Slade's trapped in a line shack by the rustlers, but Annie's on her way, having finally figured out that her no-good half brother is stealing her blind and blaming it on Slade, who's an ex-con, but that was a setup, too, though I don't know how they're going to prove it yet." She waved around a chunk of pan-grilled chicken breast on the end of her fork. "I figure it has to do with the territorial governor." She ate the chicken, nodding to herself.

Jesse gaped at her. "What on earth are you talking about?"

She gestured with a slice of roasted potato at the book on her bed. *"Blood on the Saddle.* It's your book."

"Oh." He laughed. "In that case, you're partially right about the territorial governor."

"Hmm. That must mean it's that oily little clerk."

"Bingo."

"But how do they prove it?"

"You don't really want me to spoil it for you, do you?"

She sat up straight suddenly. "Old Charlie, the forger Slade met in prison. He'll prove the confession was a fake."

Jesse nodded. "And get his own sentence commuted so he's paroled into Slade's care."

"And after Slade marries Annie, the three of them run the ranch at a profit, Slade, Annie and Old Charlie together."

"Now you know the whole story," Jesse said.

She sighed. "No point reading the rest now."

His mouth wiggled suspiciously. "Well, there's a good movie on television in about a half hour. Why don't you come on down and watch it?"

"What's it called?"

"Blood on the Saddle."

She made her eyes big and round. "No way!"

He laughed. "You're right. I made it up. Tonight's movie is another old Western you've probably seen at least a dozen times."

"Can't miss that!" she exclaimed. "I'll hurry." She popped more broccoli into her mouth.

"No rush. I've already washed up the dinner dishes."

She sat up straighter and smiled at him. "Thanks. You didn't have to do that."

"No problem. Didn't have anything else to do."

She smiled and speared another steamed carrot. "I'll just finish this, take care of my own dishes and meet you in front of the TV."

"Deal." He turned to go, then paused. "Oh, dinner was great, by the way."

"Thanks."

"Welcome," he said, already descending the stairs.

Caroline smiled to herself as she gobbled the rest of her now cold dinner. Jesse was not the loner he pretended to be, and when he needed company, she intended to be there until he realized that right next to him was where she belonged. It would be difficult—a wrong step could send him running fast in the opposite direction—but she could be patient and step easy for just as long as it took.

The movie had started by the time she snuggled into the corner of the couch with an afghan his mother had crocheted, but since they both knew the plot already, he had no reason to rush her. He had been careful to seat himself in the recliner, knowing that taking a place next to her on the couch would be asking for trouble, especially given his inability to concentrate on the television. He just couldn't seem to keep his gaze off her. He enjoyed watching her enjoy the movie more than the movie itself. When she laughed her whole face lit up, and when the hero kissed the heroine, Jesse thought Caroline blinked away a tear, though he didn't dare look closely enough to be sure.

When the movie was over, they sat through the evening news long enough to hear the weather report. For once they could expect clear skies and sunshine, with the temperature inching up above freezing. Caroline stated her intention to do some much-needed personal shopping, and then there was nothing to do but go to bed. They rose at the same instant. Jesse shut off the television. Caroline got the sofa lamp on their way out of the room. He switched on the overhead light in the hallway, then shut it off again as they reached the stairwell. The light on the landing above cast shadows over the stair steps as they climbed them, side by side. Then they were turning around the newel posts, he going one way, she going the other.

''Good night,'' she said, strolling alongside the banister, her fingertips trailing lightly over its polished top.

Jesse stood in front of his door and watched her slowly make her way toward the second stairwell, feeling absurdly as if he'd left something important unfinished.

She paused with one foot resting on the bottom step that led up to her room and trilled her fingers at him.

He was striding toward her before he even knew he was going to do it.

She met him halfway, skipping across the floor on her tiptoes, hers arms opening. He wrapped his arms around her waist and pulled her against him; her own came down around his neck. His mouth found hers and negotiated for fit. An instant later, he decided a second night with her wouldn't necessarily be a bad thing. He might even get some sleep afterward. His big empty bed would shrink to fit with her in it. Tomorrow would fade from thought; he could dwell in the moment, know that rare instant of peace before he had to worry again about screwing up her life. He could be selfish one more time, and then he would be responsible. Except...

He began to realize that she was pulling away. He was shocked, uncertain. And then he was just standing at arm's length, blinking at her. She was smiling, her eyes sparkling like diamonds. ''Good night, Jesse,'' she whispered, slipping away.

He watched her climb the stairs until she disappeared into the well, then impulsively he went after her, only to stop short. He couldn't go up there again. He couldn't take her to bed again. He couldn't even touch her again. It wouldn't be fair. She was aiming for—and deserved—a wedding ring, which he simply could not give her. Desultorily he headed for his own room, his footsteps dragging as he envisioned sliding between those cold sheets all alone. *Better to face it now than later,* he told himself. The only problem was, he just didn't believe it.

His mother called from Phoenix the next morning, and this time he was there to take the call. He hadn't slept well and was moving slow. Tiger had already been to the house to see what was holding him up, and Caroline had left his breakfast on the table to go out and warm up her old car. He sat at the table and picked at his food while listening to his mother chatter happily about the warm weather and sunshine there in Phoenix. He was surprised to hear that his father had actually gone out to play golf with friends. Sarah was planning to attend a luncheon and fashion show. They were both feeling great and having a wonderful time. How were

Caroline and the boys? Was he dressing warmly when he went out?

He hung up feeling that she had barely listened to his answers, but at least he knew approximately when to expect his wandering parents home. They expected to fly into Denver on Saturday and head back home by car on Monday. He only had a week to get through on his own with Caroline.

As if summoned, Caroline walked into the room then, tugging off her gloves. "Well, so much for my shopping trip."

"Problems?"

She made a face. "The car won't start again."

"Well, I knew it was something more than the battery," he said.

She nodded. "I know. You warned me, but it's just not worth putting any money into." She sighed. "And it's such a beautiful day to be out, too. Oh, well. Guess I'll just have to be careful not to work up a sweat."

"Why's that?"

She wrinkled her nose. "I'm out of deodorant, among other things."

Well, he couldn't let the woman try to get along without the necessities of life, now could he? He got up from the table and carried his plate to the sink. "You can take the truck if you want."

She bit her lip. "I don't know, Jesse. It's so much bigger than my car, and Tiger says the roads are slick with all the ice and snow melting."

He'd known it would come down to this, of course. So much for keeping his distance. "I'll take you in, then. The boys can exercise the horses for me. Anything else can wait."

She beamed at him. "You don't know how much I appreciate this, Jesse."

"I'll give Tiger some instructions and meet you out front in ten minutes."

"Great."

It was a pleasant morning. Mindful of the male aversion to shopping, she sought to keep the activity to a minimum, choosing a discount store where she could most likely find everything she needed. To her surprise, Jesse picked up a shopping basket and offered to take half her list. She jotted down the less personal items on a separate slip of paper and handed it over. He hunted her down in the sundries section not twenty minutes later and presented his selections for her approval. She couldn't fault a single choice. Unfortunately, she wasn't having as much luck finding a certain item on her list. He read it aloud over her shoulder.

"Facial cleanser." He swept a hand sideways. "There's a whole row of them."

"I know. Just not the one I use."

"And what, specifically, do you use?"

She named a certain mentholated cream. He rolled his eyes. "They still make that stuff? My mother used that when I was a kid."

She shrugged. "It works, and it's inexpensive."

His gaze flitted over her face. "It must have something going for it," he said softly. "Your skin's flawless."

She grinned. "Hardly, but thanks for the compliment."

He looked away. "So, what're you going to do?"

"Guess I'll have to try something else." She reached for a popular brand, only to have her hand caught and pushed away by his.

"Can't argue with success," he said. "I'll take you by a pharmacy downtown where they're bound to have it."

"You don't have to go to that trouble."

"No trouble."

"Well, if you're sure..."

He brushed aside further discussion. "What else is on your list?"

She consulted her scribbles even though it wasn't necessary. "Shampoo."

"You use something that smells like strawberries, don't you?"

She looked up in surprise, a now familiar warmth stealing over her. So he'd noticed that, had he? Trying to calm the sudden ricochet of her heart, she nodded. "Sometimes."

He walked around the end of the aisle and came back moments later with a bottle of expensive herbal extract.

"I usually go for the store brand," she told him.

"I like this kind," he said. Flipping open the top, he waved the bottle beneath her nose. The aroma of strawberries practically made her mouth water. She uttered not a word of protest when he recapped the bottle and dropped it into her cart.

Forty minutes later—half of that time spent standing in line at the checkout—Jesse loaded her purchases behind the seat of the truck, then handed her up into the passenger seat. They drove downtown. Caroline loved the old historic district with its blend of turn-of-the-century hotels, unique art galleries and modern businesses. The pharmacy was wedged between an air-conditioning repair shop and a jewelry store on a side street. Jesse circled the block three times before finding a parking space, even though Caroline offered to hop out, run inside, make the purchase and wait on the sidewalk for him to return for her.

"I'm ready for a cup of coffee," he said. "They keep a pot simmering behind the soda counter."

"They have a soda counter?"

"The best," he confirmed, letting himself out of the truck. He came around to open her door and literally escorted her across the sidewalk and into the store.

She found her face cleanser within moments and seconds later was parked on a stool at the counter in front of a root beer float piled high with whipped cream. "You don't know what you're missing," she told Jesse as he sipped his coffee.

"I know the coffee's good."

"The float's better," she said, spooning up a generous mouthful and carrying it to his lips. When he opened his mouth to refuse, she poked it inside. He grabbed a napkin and wiped his chin, but he was eyeing her float with new interest.

"Dang, that goes surprisingly good with coffee."

Laughing, she ordered a cup of coffee for herself and a second spoon and straw for him. They demolished the float in no time, and it did go surprisingly well with coffee. Spirits were high when they climbed back into the truck for the drive home. Caroline closed her eyes, savoring the moment, before saying, "Thanks, Jesse. You made the shopping a lot more pleasant than usual."

He shrugged. "You're easy. You don't turn over every item on the shelves."

She shook her head. "That lends itself to impulse buying. I go with a list, I buy what's on it, and I go home again."

He grinned. "Save the impulses for root beer floats with coffee."

"Exactly."

They laughed together, then drove on in silence. She turned over and over the past few days in her mind, judging the progress they'd made, weighing her next step, her next words. She knew what she wanted to say and do, but she also knew she had to go very, very carefully. Unfortunately, she couldn't find a careful way to manage it. Finally, as the truck turned into the drive in front of the house, she just let it out.

"Jesse, I need to ask you something."

He sent her a leery look, brought the truck to a stop in its usual place, killed the engine and turned to face her, one arm draped along the back of the seat. "Okay. I think."

She took a deep breath, released her safety belt and plunged in. "You don't think of me as a sister, do you?"

He blinked at her. "What?"

"Never mind. I know you don't. You couldn't possibly, not after... I mean, considering the way you—we... That is—"

"No! I don't think of you as a sister," he interrupted tersely. "Why would you even ask a question like that?"

"Well, it was something Kara said to me—and what you said about the unsatisfying aspect of your marriage. The sex, I mean."

"That's it! Conversation finished." He jerked the key from the ignition and reached for the door handle.

"No, wait!" She launched across the cab and grabbed his hand. He went perfectly still. She was sprawled across his lap, her hands clasped around his wrist. Suddenly every nerve ending in her body was screaming for him. Slowly she released her hold and lifted herself off his thighs, but she couldn't quite pull completely away. From the center of the seat she leaned close and engaged his eyes with her own. "What Kara said, it was about Rye's first marriage, and it got me to thinking."

He made a face and, as if against his better judgment, said grudgingly, "And what did Kara say?"

Caroline licked her lips, noting with a thrill of satisfaction that his gaze went immediately there. She swallowed, feeling a little breathless. "What Kara told me led me to believe that Rye's first marriage was similar to yours in some ways."

His gaze lifted once more to her eyes. "Such as?"

"Well, he apparently said that sex with Di'wana was a disappointment, that it was like making love to his sister."

Jesse frowned. "She told you that?"

Caroline nodded. "Rye mistook his feelings for Di'wana. She was his best friend's cousin, and she latched on to him as a way out of the Chako traditional life-style. I figure he was, in a way, too much the gentleman to disappoint her. He thought that what he felt for her would be enough, but it wasn't, and you said the same thing about Kay. You've even said how much more experienced he was when he married Di'wana than you were when you married Kay. So if he could make that mistake, you surely could."

Jesse seemed to think that over, but then he shook his head. "I'm not my brother."

"No, you're not, but you're a Wagner, after all. I figure you grew up knowing that Kay had a crush on you, and you did love her in a way. Plus, you wanted to be married. She wanted you. There was no one else to lay claim to your heart. It was a natural mistake for the kind of young man you must have been."

"Even if that were so," he said softly, "it was a mistake that got her killed."

"It did not!" Caroline drew one leg up onto the seat beneath her, leaning closer. "Her death was an accident, nothing more. If not for that fallen electrical wire, the two of you would have separated. You'd have gotten a calm, friendly divorce. She'd have found the man of her dreams, and eventually you'd have found me. Because I'm right for you, Jesse, and in your heart you must know that, just as I do."

He closed his eyes then, his face contorting as if in pain. "I might believe that,'' he said. ''I might even wish it. But you're just so young, Caroline.''

She smacked him then, right in the center of his chest with the flat of her hand, not hard enough to hurt but hard enough to pop his eyes open. ''I can't believe you said that! Not after everything that's gone on between us!''

He pushed her hand away, and somehow their fingers got entangled so that they were tussling back and forth. ''Caroline!''

''I'm no more too young than you're too old, Jesse Wagner!''

''But, honey, I am for you!''

''You're not!'' she exclaimed, shoving against him with both hands so hard that suddenly she was toppling forward. He caught her in his arms, cradling her against him, and all at once everything seemed to freeze, his mouth just inches from hers, her hands on his shoulders, her body angled across his. He groaned deep in his throat just before his hand cupped the back of her head and pressed her face upward. She met his mouth hungrily, fighting only to get closer now. It was like setting a match to tinder.

Suddenly the cab of that pickup truck went up in flames. In the conflagration, his hat got knocked off. Then her elbow, connected with the horn in the center of the steering wheel, and suddenly she was plastered against the dash, Jesse scrambling for the door handle again. He bailed out of the cab, hitting the ground at a run, chest heaving.

''No!'' he barked, pointing a finger at her. ''You promised me space!''

''All right!'' she exclaimed, holding up both hands in surrender while crawling backward across the seat on her knees. ''I was caught off guard, too!''

She plopped down onto her bottom. He shoved his hands through his hair. ''Damn!'' he said, stomping a chunk of ice thrown up by the truck tires. ''I don't know how this happens!''

''Oh, yes, you do,'' she grumbled. ''You're just too stubborn to admit that you can't keep your hands off me!''

''As if you were constantly fighting me off!'' he accused.

''Why would I want to do that? I'm wild for you!''

''Well, you shouldn't be!''

''Says you!''

"That's right!" He slammed the door then and stomped around to her side, crunching and sliding on the icy, wet snow. He yanked her door open and practically yanked her through it. "You are dangerous!" he said.

"Only when I want to be!" she retorted.

He screamed and beat both fists against his head. "Why me?"

"Because I love you!" she shouted back.

"I love you, too!" he roared. "That's not the point!"

"Yes, it is!"

Suddenly all the fight seemed to go out of him. He stood with shoulders slumped, hands hanging limply at his sides. "Maybe it is," he said miserably. "But if it is, it just means that I have to do what is best for you."

"You're what's best for me, Jesse," she said gently, imploringly.

He stared at her with naked longing in his eyes. "I wish I could believe that," he whispered. "Oh, how I wish I could believe that." Then he turned and trudged slowly toward the barn, his bared head glistening copper in the sunshine. Caroline watched him go, wondering if she'd blown her last chance or if she'd somehow managed to force him one step closer to the truth. She could only pray for the latter. She watched him until he disappeared inside the barn, a small, lonely figure.

Finally, gathering up her purchases and his hat, she went into the house and closed the door.

Chapter Fifteen

He didn't know what to do. He was fighting a losing war, and he knew it. About the only thing he could think of was to take his goodies and go home, but he was home, and Caroline wasn't about to quit the field. She was, thankfully, willing to call a truce.

When he finally got back to the house that evening, having skipped lunch, he found his dinner on the dining room table and Caroline seated there. "You're right," she said without preamble. "I did promise to back off, and I will. I mean, I have."

He frowned, but he knew that if she slunk off to her room he'd just wonder and worry and finally climb those stairs to see for himself that she was all right, and that would give her hope that he shouldn't allow her to have. He pulled out his chair and sat down. "We're going to pretend today...and last night...and last week never happened. Understood?"

She lifted a shoulder in capitulation. "I can if you can."

"Then it's settled." He picked up his fork and looked over the table. Tender meat loaf flaked with tomatoes and peppers. Yellow squash, battered and fried. Fluffy creamed potatoes. Mustard greens in jalapeño sauce. He knew a peace offering when he saw one. "Looks great," he told her softly, hearing the boys come in the back door. "Thanks."

She smiled wanly. "Just my way of saying I'm sorry."

"Not necessary."

"Still—"

Whatever else she might have said got lost as Handsome and Tiger clumped into the room. Jesse told himself that it was just as well, and as she didn't address the matter later, he was content to let it rest. It was the only contentment he was to know, however. For though she cut him just the slack he needed during that next week, his days were consumed with wondering what she was doing, while his evenings became agonies of awareness.

The little things drove him crazy: the way she hummed while she prepared his meals, an unguarded smile with those stars dancing in her eyes, a pat on the shoulder in passing, a quiet admonition to dress warmly as winter had returned with a vengeance. He was on the verge of insanity, praying at odd moments that she wouldn't bend over to pick up something she'd dropped or stretch when she yawned or sigh in that satisfied way before she dropped off to sleep in front of the TV. His dreams were so erotic that he fought sleep himself and bumped around the house in the mornings in a stupor until she pushed his first cup of coffee into his hands. Even then it was all he could do to keep from tossing the coffee over his shoulder and reaching for her. Then, at long last, his parents came home. And his world as he knew it came to an end.

He glared at his mother over the dinner table. "What do you mean you're moving to Phoenix?"

Sarah calmly buttered her biscuit. "Just during the winters, dear. Your father and I will still spend our summers here."

"But what about *me?*" Jesse demanded.

Sarah cocked her head. "What about you? It's not as if you're being abandoned. You're an adult, after all. You have everything you need." She glanced over her shoulder at Caroline when she said it, and it was just the last straw for Jesse, the very last straw.

"You don't know what you're talking about!"

"You know your mother better than that," Haney scolded from

his place. "She knows exactly what she's talking about. The new treatments can do a lot, but these winters are just going to aggravate her arthritis. By spending the winters in Arizona, we can keep her very nearly pain free and actually enjoy life for a change."

"We're entitled to enjoy ourselves," Sarah put in. "Your father's ready for semiretirement. We both agree that we need to be concentrating on our marriage again."

At that, Haney reached across the table and covered his wife's hand with his. Jesse noted with amazement—and not a little chagrin—the unspoken message that they telegraphed with their eyes. It was a wonder that the tablecloth didn't ignite! Holy cow! At their age! He laid this all at Caroline's feet. Before she came, his parents were just two old married people who occasionally grumbled about being in a rut, and now they were acting like newlyweds! And his life was turned upside down and dumped like a heap of trash! It was time to take a stand.

Jesse pushed his chair back from the table and stood up. "You don't leave me any choice," he said to the room at large, embarrassingly aware that his voice was strangled and tremulous. He cleared his throat, then fixed his attention on Caroline and said, "You're fired."

The stunned look on her face quickly gave way to anger. "Oh, no, you don't!"

"Jesse, you can't do that!" his mother exclaimed.

"It's done," he said, striding for the door as a choking sadness welled up in him.

"You can't just send me packing, Jesse Wagner!" Caroline shouted at him. "I won't go! You can stop paying me! You can put me out in the street, but that won't end it!"

"It's over!" he said, quitting the room in a rush.

"Jesse, you're behaving like a fool!" his father growled after him.

Caroline followed him out into the hall. "This is the coward's way out, Jesse!"

"As if I cared about that!" he muttered, realizing suddenly that he was headed in the wrong direction. If he went up those stairs, she'd just follow him there, too. He reversed course and pushed past her.

"I love you, and I know that you love me!" she cried. "We belong together!"

His heart felt as if a fist had reached inside his chest and squeezed it to the bursting point. The pain was blinding, but he stumbled into the back hallway and grabbed for his coat. She was right there with him. "Let me go." The small hands that clutched at him seemed to brand him everywhere they touched.

"You can't do this, Jesse! You're supposed to marry me!"

He drew safely out of her reach and made a last-ditch effort. "Too young!" he gasped, fumbling for the doorknob. He left her shrieking inarticulately in the hallway, the sound equal parts anger, frustration and pain.

The cold stung his nose and ears. He'd left his hat behind, but that didn't explain the icy wetness on his face or the fog that clouded his vision as he slipped and slid toward the barn. It didn't explain the aching emptiness that seemed to be consuming him from within, or the black loneliness that settled over him like a cloud. Most of all, it didn't explain the panic that seized him, the awful certainty that his sacrifice would be for naught, and somehow the one pride of his life, his willingness to shoulder responsibility, suddenly seemed a cold, inadequate comfort.

"I cannot believe he said that!" Caroline smacked the countertop with her palm and spun back toward the center of the kitchen. "I can't believe we're still talking about my age!"

"Well, of course, you're not fired, dear," Sarah said comfortingly from the doorway.

"No, of course, you're not," Haney grated, looking over his wife's shoulder. "That boy's no idiot. He'll come around. Why, you're every bit as good a cook as my wife, and you got this place running like a top."

"That's hardly the point, Haney," Sarah said.

"But it is the point!" Caroline exclaimed. "Part of it, anyway. Haven't I proved that I'm mature enough to run his home, help out with the business, feed the hands, be a mother to his children?"

"Well, of course, you have," Sarah replied placatingly.

"No question about it," Haney agreed.

"I am not some teenager!" Caroline pointed out. "I'm not a child, even if he does want to treat me like an infant!"

"It's that hard Wagner head of his," Sarah commiserated. "You know what Kara had to go through with Rye." She leaned her head back and smiled at her husband, then. "They're worth it, though, these Wagner men." Haney chuckled and winked, giving her a slight squeeze with his hands at her waist. Sarah flushed head to toe.

Caroline missed it all. She was seeing and hearing someone else, Kara way back in December, discussing this very problem. Kara had suggested one tack, but Caroline had chosen another at the time. Well, she was backtracking.

Seems to me nothing ages a woman like dressing too young.

"I'll do it if I have to resort to diapers!" she muttered, missing the confused look that passed between Sarah Wagner and her husband. Suddenly she focused on Sarah. "I have to go shopping first thing tomorrow."

Sarah looked surprised, but she merely nodded. "Whatever you say, dear."

"I'll need to borrow your car."

"That's fine."

"I could be all day. There will be alterations."

"I can do lunch," Sarah said, "and if you're not back by dinnertime, Haney can help me there."

"We'll go out to eat," Haney said dismissively. "If Jesse doesn't want to come, he can just do without. Might do him some good to study on what he'd be missing if we did let him fire her."

"Oh, I'm fired, all right," Caroline stated determinedly. "In fact, I quit. If he wants to keep me around after this, he can just darn well marry me, and you remember I said so!" With that she swept out of the room. She had phone calls and plans to make. She only hoped that man appreciated all the trouble she was going to for him. It might be simpler just to reshape his head, but she loved that head, and despite everything, she wanted him just as he was. And he wanted her. Whatever it took, she wasn't going to let him do this to them. They belonged together, and by golly, they would be together, one way or another.

"It has to be in the freezer in the barn," Sarah said firmly.

Jesse sighed in exasperation. "Mother, I told you. I cleaned out that freezer myself when I made the switch. There is no roast in there!"

"Well, it's not in this freezer," Sarah stated flatly. "I know we have it because it's on tomorrow's menu, and you know how meticulous Caroline is."

"Leave Caroline out of this."

"Why should I? It's your fault she quit, you know."

"She didn't quit. I fired her."

"No, you didn't. We didn't let you fire her, but I don't blame her for quitting after you tried."

Jesse clamped down on the angry words that wanted to escape his mouth. If he let them out, his father would just come in and scold him like he was ten years old again, and they'd wind up shouting at each other again, and he'd feel like a heel and escape early to bed again, only to twist and turn and drive himself insane again with memories of— No. No, no, no. He wouldn't go there. He wouldn't. Even if he had to go out to the barn in the cold, dark night to look for a roast that wasn't there. Not that it would help. God knew he was sunk. Nothing he could ever do would get that woman out of his brain. No matter what he said or did, he couldn't escape the bald fact that he loved her, craved her like air.

"Where's the flashlight?" he asked, beaten.

Sarah opened a door over the washing machine and took down a long, battered metal tube that looked like a scruffy yellow baseball bat. That old thing took six batteries and weighed a ton, but the newer models always seemed to fizzle out, and they'd be right back to the old standby. Right now Jesse wondered if he even had the strength to carry the thing. Missing meals and sleep were taking a toll. When his mother slapped it into his palm and his arm didn't come off, he supposed that was a good sign.

"Dress warmly now," his mother admonished, practically shoving him out into the kitchen, across it, and into the hall.

"Take your time. I mean, I'm going on up, so when you get the roast back to the house just put it in the refrigerator to thaw overnight."

"Fine. Except it's not going to be there," he grumbled, putting on his coat.

"You never know," she said, buttoning the top button for him and folding up his collar. "Sometimes we find things when we least expect them."

"Whatever."

He shoved on his hat, flicked on the flashlight and stepped out into the night. He was so tired that his knees felt weak, but he aimed the beam and followed it down the hill. When he got to the barn, he was shocked to find that he'd left the lock off. Damn, he was lucky he didn't make a habit of that. Someone, anyone, could waltz in here and steal him blind. Equipment, horses, feed, it was all there for the taking. Well, at least this trip wouldn't be for nothing, after all. He let himself into the deep, dark cavern of the equipment shed and reached for the overhead light, then thought better of it and aimed his flashlight toward the stable corridor. He didn't much feel like operating in a harsh overhead light. In truth, he could walk this way blindfolded and in his sleep, but in his state he saw no point in taking stupid chances.

The familiar, warm, loamy aroma of horses and rich feed enveloped him as he stepped onto the cement walkway between the stalls. His horses shifted and whickered softly in recognition. He stopped to pat a rump here and there and mumble a few comforting words of affection. At the end of the row of stalls, he turned into the stairwell and aimed his flashlight upward. The freezer sat at the top of those stairs. It seemed like miles to him at that moment, and he knew darn well that blasted roast wasn't even there. Briefly he considered just going back to the house and telling his mother that he wanted sandwiches for dinner tomorrow, but the truth was he couldn't care less. All he really wanted was Caroline. Doggedly he lifted his foot to the bottom step, and after that it was just a matter of putting one foot in front of the other, up, up and up, until he reached the top.

He gained the landing and reached for the handle of the freezer door. It was then that he heard movement behind and to the side of him. Wheeling around, he swung the arc of the flashlight across the dark loft—and encountered a blanket suspended by ropes perpendicular to the floor.

"What the—"

Suddenly a body hurtled out from behind the blanket, turning a cartwheel.

"Gimme a *J!* Gimme an *E!* Gimme a *S-S-E!* What does it spell? Stubborn!"

Jesse staggered back at the first sound of her voice and hit the light switch at the top of the stairs. The sight before him boggled the imagination. She leaped into the air, kicking her heels back and throwing out her arms. When she came down on the balls of her feet again, she tumbled into another cartwheel, nearly knocking into the mixing table in the process. His jaw seemed to be hanging somewhere around his knees.

"Caroline?"

She bounced on her toes and flipped up the back of her little pleated skirt. "I forgot the pom-poms!" she said breathlessly, gyrating through the motion of a cheer, the twin ponytails on the sides of her head bobbing and flopping. "Still, the sweater says it all, doesn't it?" She stopped and threw back her shoulders, giving him an eye-popping view of the school emblem emblazoned across her chest. The red-and-white sweater fit her like a second skin, the generous mounds of her breasts distorting the shape of the big alphabet letter sewn onto the fabric. He took it all in, the white knee socks and red shoes, red pleated miniskirt, red-and-white sweater, the twin ponytails branching off from a part down the middle of her head.

"You're dressed like a cheerleader?" he bawled in disbelief.

She rocked from side to side on the balls of her feet as if contemplating another daredevil stunt. "Isn't this how you see me, Jesse? Some teenager with a crush on the captain of the football team? Well, I dated the captain of the football team, for your information, and he was just another immature lunk trying to get his hands inside my blouse! After I slapped him and told him to lose my phone number, he dated my friend Janie. This is her uniform, by the way."

"I hope it fits her better than you!" he snapped.

"Oh? I don't look like you think I should?"

She looked absurd, squeezed into that ridiculous getup, and it occurred to him suddenly that that was exactly her intention. Well, if she wanted to play... For the first time in days he relished the thought. Folding his arms he said, "This is the most childish stunt you've ever pulled."

"Childish!" she huffed. "I may be young, but I am *not* childish!"

"I've had just about enough of this!"

"Good! Because I reached my limit yesterday!"

"You don't know the first thing about limits!"

"Oh, don't I?" she scoffed, walking toward him. "I don't believe in placing limits on love, Jesse. You've placed yourself off-limits to a normal, happy life with a family of your own, but I won't let that stop me, because I know what I know. You're afraid to try to make a life with me, Jesse, because you love me, and that scares the daylights out of you! I know what you're thinking. What if something bad happens again?"

He massaged his temples and nodded, admitting to himself that she was exactly right, but then he smiled as she painted the most absurd of pictures for him.

"What if I cut myself peeling potatoes and blood poisoning sets in and I die a slow, painful death right before your very eyes? What if I trip on the stairs or just fall out of bed some night and break my neck?"

He put his hands to his hips and shook his head over that. Falling out of bed? Not his bed, he decided. If he ever got her back there again he'd keep her firmly anchored to the sheets.

"What if I get arthritis in thirty years," she went on as she stood before him, "or, God forbid, cancer? What then?"

He knew what then, but she was on a roll and didn't even seem to hear him trying to capitulate. "Caroline, you're—"

"I'll tell you what then, Jesse!" she said. "We fight for every minute we have left and we thank God for everything we've built together—providing, of course, that you step up to the mark, admit you're wrong, and do what you know you should!"

"You're right," he tried again. "I know—"

"You have to understand that I'm not a child, Jesse! I'm a woman who knows exactly what she wants!"

"I do, Caroline. I—"

"And I know what you want, even if you won't admit it! So admit it, Jesse, because it's absurd to say I'm too young!"

"Well?" she demanded.

He had to bite the inside of his cheek to keep from laughing. She had made her point. No child could make his head whirl like she did. No child could make him want to lay hands on her like she did. Which was exactly what he was going to do.

"Well," he said with mock severity, "you asked for it." He grabbed her by the hand and headed across the room to the pile of feed bags at the other end.

"What are you doing?"

He parked himself on a stack of feed sacks. "I'm about to spank your butt!"

"In your dreams!"

He yanked her facedown over his lap and flipped up her skirt. "The next time you think about turning some man's life upside down, remember this!" he said, raising his hand.

"I never would!" she protested, bucking. "Jesse, you know you're the only man I'd ever go after!"

And that was exactly why he couldn't smack that perfectly luscious bottom, especially not with those bikinis not quite covering it. Groaning, he dropped both hands to those firm, plump mounds and squeezed. Caroline gasped and froze. He moved his hands to her side and pushed her off his lap. She scrambled up onto her knees next to him.

"Jesse?" she queried breathlessly.

He drilled her with his eyes. "Strip," he demanded. "Down to the skin."

She stared at him a long, heart-stopping moment. Then she whooped and leaped to her feet, tearing at hair bows and shoe buckles in a frenzy. Her hair slid down around her shoulders, and the straps of her shoes flopped wildly. Laughing, he collapsed back onto his elbows. One of the bags on the end of the pile behind him slid off onto the floor and split, but he ignored it.

Time enough to clean up spilled feed tomorrow. Time enough for everything. "Slow down before you hurt yourself."

She yanked off one shoe and tossed it at him. "If anybody gets hurt here, Wagner, it'll be you. I'm young and resilient!"

He lifted both eyebrows. "Is that a challenge of some sort?"

"If the boot fits," she answered saucily, throwing the other shoe at him.

It bounced off his shoulder. Eyes narrowed, he shoved up to his feet. Raising one foot at a time, he tugged off his boots and socks, leaving them where they fell. Then he lifted a hand, indicating that it was her turn. She puckered her lips against a grin, wrenched free buttons, pulled down her skirt and peeled her sweater up and off. Hands on her hips, she inclined her head. He threw off his coat and stripped away his shirt and undershirt, the latter pulling wrong side out as he tugged his hands from the sleeves.

Caroline shoved down her petticoats and kicked them aside, standing before him in panties and bra. Hands shaking and mouth dry now, he unbuttoned his jeans and pushed them off his hips and down his legs, along with his long johns. Stepping out of them, he lifted his gaze to her svelte, shapely body, his heart slamming inside his chest as she reached behind her to unclasp her bra.

The straps slid down her arms and off over her fingertips. He didn't notice, she so completely captivated him. True, he knew what to expect, but somehow the reality overwhelmed every memory he had of her. And he knew now that it always would— that memory, however dear, would never be enough.

She shivered and crossed her arms. Abruptly, he became aware of the coolness. It was always warmer here above the stables than anywhere else in the barn, but standing essentially naked was asking for a chill. Quickly striding across the floor in his briefs, he yanked the corners of the blanket free of the rope knots and carried it back to the neat stacks of feed bags. Shoving and pulling, he slid the bags around until he'd created a nest for the two of them. Spreading the blanket over it, he straightened and shucked his briefs before lifting a hand in invitation. She skimmed the pink panties down her legs and stepped out of them as she walked toward him, her hand floating up and into his. Smiling, he lifted her fingers to his lips.

"Once," he said softly, "a jolt of electricity turned my life upside down." Her gaze softened, head tilting so that her long, pale hair flowed over one shoulder. "Then a bolt of blond lightning set it right again," he whispered. "It just took me a while to acclimate." He smiled. "I don't think my head will ever stop spinning, but that's all right as long as you're here to anchor me."

"I love you so much, Jesse," she said tremulously.

He shook his head, amazed all over again. "I know. It makes no sense to me, but there it is."

She laughed, dashing away tears with her knuckles. "You're going to marry me, Jesse," she said. "Aren't you?"

He chuckled softly, cupping her face with his hands. "I don't know what else to do with you."

She slid her arms around him, stepping close and laying her head upon his shoulder, her face tucked into the curve of his neck. Skin against skin, she whispered, "We'll be together the rest of our lives."

He wrapped his arms tighter. "I can't promise you the rest of your life, Caroline, but I can promise you the rest of mine."

"That's all anyone can promise, Jesse," she said, lifting her head, "so it'll do for starters."

He laughed. "Well, if there's more and anyone can get it, you can!"

"There's more," she said, grinning devilishly as she shoved him down onto the makeshift bed and straddled him.

"Do tell," he teased, smoothing back her luxurious hair with both hands.

She shook her head, pale strands sliding free. "This requires demonstration."

He strained upward to kiss the corner of her mouth. "I ought to warn you, I'm a slow learner."

"Ah, well," she said with mock resignation, "we have years and years to get it right."

He caught his breath as she sank down atop him, her body sliding against his, blinding light and sensuous power sheathed in silky skin and softly rounded, feminine muscle. "We already have it right,'' he said huskily. ''I think I've known it for a long time, but I was afraid. Losing Kay was hard enough, but losing you...''

''So you tried to push me away,'' she said softly.

He swallowed the lump in his throat with a bark of laughter. ''I tried to hold you off!'' She smacked him on the shoulder with her fist. ''I was never very good at it!'' he went on. Then he sobered. ''It's a funny thing about love. You can't make it right when it's wrong and you can't make it wrong when it's right, no matter how hard you try.''

Levering herself up onto her elbows, she threaded her fingers into the hair at his temples and gazed down into his eyes, her love shining brightly. ''Make babies with me, Jesse.''

Smiling, he rolled her beneath him, pressing the rigid evidence of his willingness against her. ''We may already have,'' he said softly. ''We didn't use any birth control before, you know.''

''All the more reason for a quick wedding,'' she replied, grinning.

''True,'' he agreed, adding blandly, ''and besides, you're not getting any younger.''

For a moment she looked stunned, but then she put her head back and laughed until they were both shaking. Amusement gradually gave way to gasps of passion as their bodies melded and settled into complementary positions. Drawing up her knees and hugging his flanks, she looked up into his eyes.

''When did you decide?''

''About us?''

She nodded.

''Last night, I suppose, or maybe today. I don't know as you can call it a decision, really, more a realization.''

''That we belong together,'' she said.

A slow smile curved his lips. ''That whether I pushed you away or you cut a major artery slicing veggies, losing you is losing you—and I can't do it.''

She wrapped her legs around him, whispering, ''I knew you were the one.''

''The only one,'' he vowed.

Reaching back, he flipped the blanket over them, and it was soon toasty warm there in that moaning, gently writhing cocoon.

Epilogue

Jesse struggled up the walk under a giggling, wiggling 125 pounds of woman, purposefully kicking up minishowers of snow with the rounded toes of his shiny black boots.

"Oof! Unngh! Arrgh!" His breath puffed out in smoky white clouds.

She pushed back his black hat with the satin ribbon band and rapped her knuckles on his forehead. "Cut it out, you! I know for a fact I'm light as a feather today." She leaned back in his arms, throwing the hand that grasped her bouquet high over her head and kicking up one slender leg encased in a filmy white silk stocking. Her short, white, gossamer veil floated on the air. "My feet have hardly touched the floor all day."

He laughed, then pretended to cough and wither, knees wobbling, shoulders sagging. "I know, honey. It's just that at my age all this excitement saps my strength."

She smacked him on the shoulder with the flowers, which were tied simply with a white ribbon. "In that case, I guess we'll just have to put off the wedding night until you build up your energy."

He straightened up, sighing. "Oh, all right." Then he wiggled his eyebrows in an exaggerated leer. "But that's saying nothing about the wedding afternoon."

Caroline put back her head and laughed. The sound tinkled like bells on the clear, cold air. In two quick strides, Jesse carried her up the steps to the porch, where he swung her down and set her on her feet. She teetered on her high satin-covered heels, then leaned into the loop of his arms, her cheek pressed against his shoulder. Jesse braced himself against the porch post and just stood for a moment, staring at the frosty peaks of the mountains against the clear blue sky.

His wedding day. Even standing here in cowboy black, his best silver-on-gray vest buttoned over a formal white shirt complete with starched collar and black string tie, his bride in his arms, he could hardly believe it. He looked down at the top of her head, her pale hair covered by fluffy layers of sheer white attached to a simple cloth-covered headband. She straightened and pulled away from him, her hand slipping down the sleeves of his black suit coat. He smiled, looking at her.

She had chosen a simple, elegant, street-length dress with a slim skirt. The strapless bodice was overlaid with sheer white fabric that hugged her slender arms and shoulders like skin, closing in a narrow satin ribbon at the base of her throat. Her long pale hair had been wound into a simple knot on the back of her head. He had never seen anything or anyone more beautiful. The narrow platinum band on her ring finger matched the one on his own hand, an oddly humbling reminder of the certainty of their love. He'd offered her diamonds, but his practical Caroline had refused, saying that she'd rather have babies, that she already had everything else she could possibly want, meaning a home, family. Him. He marveled again that she had found him.

Found him, hell. She'd come after him with the same determination of Hannibal crossing the mountains. And he was unspeakably grateful.

She smiled, even as she shivered in the cold, clear air. He would warm her. She would be glowing with warmth before the rest of the family caught up with them. They had sneaked away from their own wedding luncheon, craving some time to themselves before the family descended again, demanding cake and champagne and teasing them about honeymooning at home. It seemed pointless to go somewhere far away just to spend all their time in bed trying to satisfy this ravening beast that was the passion between them, especially when everyone else would be going away tomorrow morning, his parents to Arizona, his brother and family back to New Mexico. He'd have her all to himself again, but this time... Ah, this time...

Suddenly energized, he dipped and scooped her up again, whirling her around in a circle while they both laughed and her veils flew. Then he headed for the door. She switched her bouquet to the hand she'd slid around his neck and reached for the knob.

''Welcome home, Mrs. Wagner,'' he told her as he carried her across the threshold. She was kissing him as he kicked the door closed again.

In that single, spare moment when thought was still possible, it occurred to him that his life had finally—finally—begun, and he knew that it would be long and full and loving. And probably wild, confusing, frustrating. God knew she'd run him ragged from the beginning! But he was up to the chase. Oh, yes. He was born for it. For her. For Caroline. Maybe he'd spent the better part of the last four decades just waiting for her, but if so, it was worth it. More than worth it.

Welcome home, Mr. Wagner, he told himself as the world dissolved and he plunged headlong into happiness. Not bad for an older man. Not bad at all.

* * * * *

And Baby Makes Three

FIRST TRIMESTER

by

SHERRYL WOODS

Three ornery Adams men are about to be roped
into fatherhood...and they don't suspect a thing!

And Baby Makes Three

APRIL 1999
The phenomenal series
from Sherryl Woods has readers
clamoring for more! And in this special collection,
we discover the stories that started it all....

Luke, Jordan and Cody are tough ranchers set in
their bachelor ways until three beautiful women
beguile them into forsaking their single lives for
instant families. Will each be a match made in
heaven...or the delivery room?

Available at your favorite retail outlet.

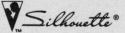

Silhouette®

PSBR499

If you enjoyed what you just read,
then we've got an offer you can't resist!

Take 2 bestselling love stories FREE!
Plus get a FREE surprise gift!

Clip this page and mail it to Silhouette Reader Service™

IN U.S.A.	IN CANADA
3010 Walden Ave.	P.O. Box 609
P.O. Box 1867	Fort Erie, Ontario
Buffalo, N.Y. 14240-1867	L2A 5X3

YES! Please send me 2 free Silhouette Special Edition® novels and my free surprise gift. Then send me 6 brand-new novels every month, which I will receive months before they're available in stores. In the U.S.A., bill me at the bargain price of $3.57 plus 25¢ delivery per book and applicable sales tax, if any*. In Canada, bill me at the bargain price of $3.96 plus 25¢ delivery per book and applicable taxes**. That's the complete price and a savings of over 10% off the cover prices—what a great deal! I understand that accepting the 2 free books and gift places me under no obligation ever to buy any books. I can always return a shipment and cancel at any time. Even if I never buy another book from Silhouette, the 2 free books and gift are mine to keep forever. So why not take us up on our invitation. You'll be glad you did!

235 SEN CNFD
335 SEN CNFE

Name _____ (PLEASE PRINT) _____

Address _____ Apt.# _____

City _____ State/Prov. _____ Zip/Postal Code _____

* Terms and prices subject to change without notice. Sales tax applicable in N.Y.
** Canadian residents will be charged applicable provincial taxes and GST.
   All orders subject to approval. Offer limited to one per household.
   ® are registered trademarks of Harlequin Enterprises Limited.

SPED99   ©1998 Harlequin Enterprises Limited

Coming from *New York Times*
bestselling author

JENNIFER BLAKE

Down in Louisiana, a man'll do whatever it takes…

Luke Benedict figures he's the only one in
Turn-Coupe, Louisiana who can save novelist
April Halstead from someone intent on
revenge. *If* he could get April to cooperate.

But that's not about to stop Luke. He'd never
turn his back on a friend—especially one whose
life is in danger. And if he's got to kidnap a
woman who despises him to keep her safe, he
will. 'Cause down in Louisiana, *this* man will do
whatever it takes….

LUKE

On sale mid-February 1999 wherever
paperbacks are sold!

MIRA®

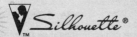

Silhouette®

SPECIAL EDITION®

COMING NEXT MONTH

#1237 A FATHER FOR HER BABY—Celeste Hamilton
That's My Baby!
When Jarrett McMullen saw Ashley Grant again, the sweet beauty he'd once loved and let go was pregnant—and alone. And though the amnesiac mother-to-be couldn't remember her past, Jarrett was determined to claim a place in her future—as the father of her child....

#1238 WRANGLER—Myrna Temte
Hearts of Wyoming
Horse wrangler Lori Jones knew she'd better steer clear of Sunshine Gap's ruggedly appealing deputy sheriff, Zack McBride, who was close to discovering her darkest secret. But then the sexy lawman took her boy under his wing—and made a lasting impression on Lori's wary heart!

#1239 BUCHANAN'S BRIDE—Pamela Toth
Buckles & Broncos
He was lost and alone...but not for long. As luck would have it, feisty cowgirl Leah Randall rescued the stranded stranger, tenderly took him in and gave him all her love. But would their blossoming romance survive the revelation that this dynamic man was a long-lost relation of her sworn enemy?

#1240 FINALLY HIS BRIDE—Christine Flynn
The Whitaker Brides
After nearly a decade, Trevor Whitaker still left Erin Gray breathless. Their bittersweet reunion brought back memories of unfulfilled passion— and broken promises. But her ardor for this devastatingly handsome man was intoxicating. Would Erin's fantasy of being a Whitaker bride finally come true?

#1241 A WEDDING FOR MAGGIE—Allison Leigh
Men of the Double-C Ranch
When Daniel Clay returned to the Double-C ranch, the tormented cowboy knew he was unworthy of his beloved Maggie. But when their night of love left Maggie pregnant, Daniel stubbornly insisted on a convenient union. But then a headstrong Maggie made a marriage demand of her own....

#1242 NOT JUST ANOTHER COWBOY—Carol Finch
Alexa Tipton had her fill of charming rodeo men. So the serious-minded single mom was beside herself when she became irresistibly attracted to the fun-loving Chance Butler. The sexy superstar cowboy began to melt her steely resistance, but could she trust their happiness would last?